Lonesome Lies Before Us

also by Don Lee

Lonesome Lies Before Us

a novel

Don Lee

 W. W. Norton & Company

Independent Publishers Since 1923

New York | London

This is a work of fiction. Names, characters, places, and incidents are the products of the author's imagination or are used fictitiously. Any resemblance to actual events, locales, or persons, living or dead, is entirely coincidental.

Permission to quote from the song "Picture Cards" by Blaze Foley was kindly granted by Texas Ghost Writers Music.

For information about permission to reproduce selections from this book, write to Permissions, W. W. Norton & Company, Inc., 500 Fifth Avenue, New York, NY 10110

For information about special discounts for bulk purchases, please contact W. W. Norton Special Sales at specialsales@wwnorton.com or 800-233-4830

Manufacturing by Quad Graphics, Fairfield
Book design by Fearn Cutler de Vicq
Production manager: Anna Oler

Library of Congress Cataloging-in-Publication Data

Names: Lee, Don, 1959– author.
Title: Lonesome lies before us : a novel / Don Lee.
Description: First edition. | New York : W. W. Norton & Company, [2017]
Identifiers: LCCN 2017009442 | ISBN 9780393608816 (hardcover)
Subjects: | GSAFD: Love stories.
Classification: LCC PS3562.E339 L66 2017 | DDC 813/.54—dc23
LC record available at https://lccn.loc.gov/2017009442

W. W. Norton & Company, Inc.
500 Fifth Avenue, New York, N.Y. 10110
www.wwnorton.com

W. W. Norton & Company Ltd.
15 Carlisle Street, London W1D 3BS

1 2 3 4 5 6 7 8 9 0

for Jane Delury

Lonesome Lies Before Us

In his teens, Yadin Park had considered himself ugly—a judgment that was overly harsh, yet, at the time, not entirely unfounded.

To begin with, he had been big. Not obese, exactly, but chunky, ungainly, tall, a couple of slugs over six feet. Since a child, he had yearned to be smaller, less conspicuous, inhabit less specter, but his body always betrayed him. He swelled his shirts. His neck distended. He was pigeon-toed, and his pants buffed where his thighs corraded. His feet were clowns. Then there was his head, which to him felt elephantine. His hair was black and matted in wiry waves and seemed vaguely pubic in origin. His face, he believed, bordered on barbarity, with its hocked jaw, thin, chapped

9

lips, and knob of a nose. Most tragic had been his skin, pocked and gullied with acne, rippling hieroglyphs of teen-age sorrow.

Thankfully, as he entered manhood, his appearance mellowed. His body subtly wedged, fat shifting to muscle, and his skin cleared. More than once, women told him he was sexy. Yet Yadin could never purge the image of himself as someone who was grotesque, and, haunted by a host of other wounds, he remained cripplingly shy.

Little wonder, then, that starting out as a singer-songwriter, he was offered publishing but not recording contracts. People loved his songs, they loved his voice, yet he was a dreadful performer, forever petrified onstage. Early on, he did shows with the lights down low, facing the drummer, his back to the audience throughout. Then for a while he employed squinty light installations, akin to eighties Lite-Brites, blinding, glowing yellow pegs that, as he sang, slowly changed arrays, projected onto a screen from behind so that he was silhouetted in the black-dark of the bar or club or auditorium, apprehension pooling as the crowd waited for the stage lights to come up at some point during the set, which he never allowed. Bowing to complaints, he discarded the backlights and grew a beard and wore baseball caps, snug down, and large sunglasses, and annealed himself with various and voluminous anesthetics—pharmaceutical, herbal, hallucinogenic, and fermented. In the end, this did not, as anyone could have predicted, go well.

He released four albums in his twenties and thirties through a small indie label. Each one sold less and less. He never produced a crossover hit, never scratched the Billboard 200. His music was in the nebulous, uncomfortable classification of alt-country, not quite folk or rock or down-home country. In other words, not at all radio-friendly. Save for a few critics in *No Depression* and *American Songwriter* who extolled his songs—beautiful, mournful, anguished, devastatingly sad, they raved—the media ignored him. At best, he was an underground cult favorite, virtually anonymous. The small indie label became a subsidiary of a major label, the major label merged with an even bigger label, the subsidiary was folded, and the new mega-label dropped him.

Now it was 2011 and he was forty-six, eking out a living as a carpet installer in Rosarita Bay, a town on the California coast that had seen its own vicissitudes, briefly blooming into a hip tourist haven, then—with the recession—falling back to seed. He worked for Matsuda Wall to Wall, a small operation with just the owner, Joe Matsuda, and two other employees besides Yadin. They did commercial, residential, marine—whatever they could get—but lately most of their projects were on derelict houses that had been foreclosed and were now, with the glints of economic recovery, being quickly rehabbed and flipped.

This morning they were working on a ranch house in the Spanish Flats neighborhood east of Highway 1. The developer wanted them in and out in one day, and he'd opted for a low-pile olefin. He didn't care that the carpet wouldn't last, wasn't very stain-resistant, would flatten and indent and wear out. It was cheap, but would look good enough when the house was shown. He had wanted to stinge out even further with four-pound rebond padding, but Joe convinced him to spend a bit more for the six-pound to defer wrinkling and buckling. It was a crap job, but Joe took pride in his work.

When they ripped up the old carpet, though, they discovered that the subflooring was in bad shape. Much of the plywood was mildewed and rotted and warped, there were gaps and holes, nails protruding and bent. They needed at least another day to do the job properly. Joe called the developer, who refused more time for repairs.

"What a prick," Joe said to them.

They did the best they could, Yadin starting on the living and dining rooms with Rodrigo, Joe on the bedrooms with Esteban. They scraped, whacked, scrubbed, swept, and vacuumed. They snipped new tackless strips to size and nailed them down, rolled out and trimmed the padding, stapled the edges with hammer tackers.

Outside, they pulled out the spindles of new carpet from the two blue company vans, whose sides advertised MATSUDA WALL TO WALL. JUST CARPET! and, in smaller letters, 100% CUSTOMER SATISFACTION GUARANTEED and NO MONEY DOWN. They rolled out the carpet in the driveway, measured, notched the corners, rerolled, and chalk-lined the backs before cutting them. They carried the sections of carpet inside and unfurled and knifed them and started gluing them together with handheld irons. They didn't break for lunch until midafternoon, when they had dry-fitted most of the house.

They sat on the tails of the two vans, which were parked on the street with the rear ends facing each other, the doors open. Piles of old carpet were humped on the front lawn. It was gray and chilly, typical May weather for Rosarita Bay.

Joe finished a salami and cream cheese on toasted sourdough, and as he fished into a Ziploc for a second sandwich, he glanced at Yadin's stainless-steel bento box.

"What the fuck is that shit?"

Yadin pointed with his spoon. "Lentil salad. Quinoa salad. Red cabbage salad."

"Any of it have any taste?"

"Not much." He had been on this diet for six years now—not out of vanity, but for medical reasons—and the restrictions were rather extreme. No salt, no MSG, no caffeine, sodas, or chocolate. No processed foods. No milk or wheat or corn or eggs or peanuts. No cigarettes or alcohol or drugs of any kind, prescription or recreational. None of his clothes fit anymore. He had lost forty pounds in all, and for the first time in his life, he looked almost svelte. In mirrors, he was unidentifiable to himself.

"Rodrigo," Joe said, "you got another tuna? Trade?"

"Not a chance, man."

"Esteban? What you got there?"

"Nothing for you, boss."

Yadin snuffed a laugh. He listened to the crinkling of tinfoil, the rustling of plastic wrap. Wind waffled through the trees. Birds chirred. He relished the sounds. He knew that someday soon, their clarity would be denied to him forever.

"You motherfuckers are cold," Joe said. "Cold. I ought to fire you all."

Joe was sixty-five, a tree stump—short and thick and strong—but after forty years of laying carpet, he had been slowing down of late. Stooped, grunting with pain when he had to get up and down. With all the kneeling and bending, back problems were not unusual for those in the trade. Neither were carpal tunnel, arthritis, thoracic outlet syndrome, and an ailment called carpet layer's knee—prepatellar bursitis—from pounding the kickers.

Ironically, Yadin had gotten his CFI certification because he had thought carpet installation would be easier on his body, not to mention steadier work that paid better. Even when he had been signed as a recording artist, he'd always had to take on odd jobs between album releases. He'd pumped gas, mopped floors, plowed snow, washed dishes, worked the line at a pet food factory. Mostly, though, he had been a day laborer on landscaping and demolition crews.

He didn't know now which type of work had contributed most to his present medical condition, an inner-ear disorder called Ménière's disease that was slowly robbing him of his hearing. The leaf blowers and lawn mowers? The reciprocating saws and sledgehammers and crowbars? They didn't wear lead-safe coveralls or masks back then. They didn't use ear protection, either. In fact, Yadin often blasted music from a Walkman over the din. Stupid. All that cumulative exposure to noise, dust, asbestos, mold, insulation, the myriad toxic chemicals he'd breathed in, gutting houses and killing weeds—he had never imagined the effect they would have. Carpet was not markedly better, with all the VOCs in glue, fibers, things like chlordane that were sprayed into carpets for fleas. Along with kneepads, he wore a ventilator mask and acoustic earmuffs now. He was the only one on the crew who did.

They went back inside the house and started kicking out and stretching the carpet into place. Every now and then, Yadin hummed into his mask. The night before, a thread of a melody had begun noodling inside his head, and today, as the notes fattened and congealed, he'd go somewhere private and take out his cellphone—an old flip model—and call his home landline and leave messages on his ancient answering machine, singing the melody. It would have been simpler to use a portable recorder, but he preferred this method, was superstitious about it. Later on in the afternoon, a few words and phrases burbled up, and he tore off pieces of brown masking paper and scribbled the lyrics down with a Sharpie and stuffed them into his pockets. This was how he'd always written music. After a long fallow period—lasting almost a decade, in fact—he had regained his old fecundity in the past month, and now songs were sprouting out of him unabated. A chord progression, a melody, a chorus or a verse, a title would emerge, and he could work out the rest of the song in a day or two, often mere hours.

They finished carpeting the ranch house a little after seven. Yadin rode back to the office with Joe, staring at the twilit road before them, listening to the groan of the van engine, the rear struts squeaking whenever they crossed an intersection and dipped into a concrete valley gutter.

"It's looking more and more like I'm going to have to let someone go," Joe told him.

Yadin numbed. Of the crew, he had been with Wall to Wall the shortest time.

"Not you," Joe said. "Don't be an idiot. You're practically family."

Yadin had been dating Joe's older daughter, Jeanette, for over two years now, yet there was a tenuousness about their relationship that never let Yadin feel secure about it. "You heard something about the city council vote?" Yadin asked.

"Nothing beyond the two proposals."

"What disposals?" Yadin asked.

"Proposals, proposals," Joe said louder, impatient. "It's not looking good."

After a succession of budget cuts, furloughs, and layoffs, Rosarita Bay had begun contracting out its municipal services: public works, inspections, recreation. In two weeks, on June 3, the city council would be voting on whether to outsource the library and the police department as well, which would have a direct impact on Wall to Wall. They had won a bid to recarpet the police station later that summer, a major contract that might soon be null and void, with no money down.

An hour south of San Francisco, Rosarita Bay was encircled by foothills and farmland. To the north was a picturesque harbor, to the south a marsh preserve, and to the west the Pacific Ocean, roiling in endless horizon. The Main Street lined with gas streetlamps and shops with shiplap siding, and the town held a well-attended pumpkin festival every October. It should have been a popular seaside town for day trips and weekend retreats. It should have been a burgeoning bedroom community.

Yet, for most of its history, Rosarita Bay had remained a backwater. There were only two roads in and out of town, Highway 1 on the coast and Highway 71 through the San Vicente Mountains; the weather was dismal most of the year—a microclimate of fog and wind and rain; and the town had long been known as a developer's graveyard, saddled with some of the most stringent zoning regulations in the country.

The latter began to change a decade ago, when a new generation of residents elected themselves to the city council. Gated communities of fancy homes sprang up, strip malls emerged on Highway 1. Chic restaurants and art galleries and coffeehouses opened on Main Street, and, after thirty years of opposition, a massive luxury hotel and golf course were constructed along prime oceanfront. The population grew from ten to twelve thousand, and it seemed that Rosarita Bay was on the verge of becoming the next Carmel or Taos or Aspen.

Now, there was talk of Rosarita Bay filing for bankruptcy, even formally dissolving the town and becoming an unincorporated part of San Vicente County. It wasn't just the lingering recession that was hurting them. The owner of a parcel of scrub grass had filed a lawsuit against Rosarita Bay because the sewage department had botched a storm drain project, inadvertently turning the plot into wetlands that could no longer be developed. A federal judge had ruled for the plaintiff, and the town had had to issue bonds to cover the $25 million settlement.

It had become a sad place in which to live, businesses closing, people having to relocate. Yadin constantly feared he'd become another casualty. He was vested here. He had Jeanette. He had a house—the first piece of property he had ever owned. He didn't want to leave.

"I thought you had a string of jobs lined up for us this summer," Yadin said to Joe.

"Not enough to make up for that contract," Joe told him. "I should've never specialized in just carpets. Everyone wants fucking hardwood now. Carpet is dead."

Yadin had inherited his house four years ago, in 2007, from a grandmother he'd met just twice as a kid, the last of any relatives he knew of. He was living in Portage, Michigan, at the time, another in a series of random, anonymous Midwestern towns where the rents were cheap but in which he never remained long. He readily drove cross-country to Rosarita Bay to take possession of the house on Las Encinas Road, which he had never visited.

It wasn't much to look at from the outside, just a ramshackle cottage. From the inside, it was even shabbier. The rooms had once been stuffed with his grandmother's furnishings and bric-a-brac, but everything was gone now, the house purged, save for the orange and green shag carpeting. What little furniture Yadin had were street finds or foraged from Craigslist and thrift stores. There was a café pedestal table with a mismatched ladderback chair in the dining area. A scabby upholstered armchair and an ottoman, also mismatched, in the living room. An old Sony Trinitron TV on a plastic milk crate. The master bedroom was even sparser, just a twin bed and a bureau, although half of one wall was covered, from floor to ceiling, with neatly stacked cardboard boxes.

Home from work, Yadin passed through the kitchen, where his answering machine sat on the counter, the red light blinking, announcing the messages to himself singing the melody. He was tempted to attend to them right away, but resisted the urge. He wanted the new song to germinate a little. In his bedroom, he took off his flannel shirt and construction boots and emptied out the pockets of his gray work pants onto the bureau: keys, wallet, cellphone, some change. He pulled out the day's scraps of paper, flattened them, and stacked them in a pile. The bureau's top drawer was filled with similar crumples, patterned in inky scrawls, alongside a jumble of microcassettes.

He took a shower and changed, then returned to the kitchen and opened the refrigerator. Several plastic tubs were tucked inside; otherwise, there was not much in there except bottles of mineral water. The cupboards and drawers were equally bare. The laminate counter had a thirty-inch cutout where the stove should have been; he had intended to replace the stove at some point until he realized that, with his diet, he never cooked anything anymore.

For dinner, he pulled out the same stuff he'd had for lunch: lentil salad, quinoa salad, red cabbage salad. These were new recipes, and he had made large batches of them the previous night to store in the tubs. He would be eating them the rest of the week. Sitting down at his café table with the salads, he wished it were one of his evenings with Jeanette.

They rarely saw each other more than twice a week—at church, at her house, sometimes at Joe's house, but never at Yadin's house. She hadn't entered the cottage in two years, in fact, ever since he had had to declare bankruptcy and liquidate most of his possessions. Looking around the gloomy interior, he could hardly blame her. Yet he didn't fully understand why, after all this time, she kept herself so distant from him. The house wasn't the reason, he knew. She seldom even called or texted him during the week, saying she was too tired from work, too overwhelmed with things she had to do for the church. He wanted to spend more time with her, talk to her more, feel closer to her, be with her. But she remained remote.

After washing his plate, bento box, and utensils, Yadin turned on the television and tuned in to the second half of the San Francisco Giants game. The closed captioning scrolled across the screen, the sound muted—a permanent setting. The audio control buttons on the set had been squashed and inoperable when he'd found it. He had an old transistor radio for the simulcast, but it never quite synced with the TV broadcast, always off by half a second or so. Still, baseball wasn't the same without the sounds.

Watching the game in his armchair, Yadin fingered a rosary. It was made of black cherry and had a two-and-a-half-inch crucifix. He had ordered it online last month and hadn't memorized all the prayers yet, but pushing the beads between his left thumb and the callused tip of his fat index finger—nail bitten to the quick—soothed him.

At the bottom of the seventh inning, he began humming to himself. He couldn't wait any longer. He wanted to work on the new song. He turned off the transistor radio and walked over to the answering machine on the kitchen counter. He'd accidentally broken the cover off the machine long ago, exposing the two microcassettes inside, but it was still in good working order. He pressed the play button, skipped ahead several messages, and increased the volume. Leaning in with his left ear, he listened to himself singing the melody, hoping it'd pan out as the final track of his new album, which would be his first in nine years. He had been working on the record every night for the last three weeks, since the end of April. He'd told no one about the project thus far, not even Jeanette.

He had thought he was done with music, retired, and had said as much to Jeanette. His hearing was failing, and he knew he had no chance of making a comeback as a recording artist. He was too old, and alt-country singer-songwriters like him, already on the periphery, had been hurled into the abyss. The industry had changed. Everything had fallen apart. The only way musicians could succeed in the business today was by touring, and he had never been good on tour, and it would be impossible for him to tour now.

Yet something had happened to him this spring. He had gone on a spiritual journey of sorts. It had begun during Lent with reading the poetry of Gerard Manley Hopkins and, after a detour, had ended unexpectedly with his writing music again. A few songs here and there. He didn't think anything would come of it, so he'd kept quiet about it. But as the songs accumulated, he thought he might be able to produce one more album, one last album, which he could perhaps self-release, floating it out into the world, without fanfare, as a swan song. Once he began toying with the idea, he was anxious the work wouldn't be any good or he wouldn't be capable of finishing an entire LP, so he'd stayed mum. Now, with the album nearly complete, he was facing another, more practical problem: finding the cash to release it. He knew that Jeanette—Joe as well—would be upset learning he was making music again, squandering away what little money he had saved to rebuy musical equipment, so he'd delayed telling them. If he couldn't figure out a way to put out the album, he would likely never tell them.

In his bedroom, he gathered the paper scraps from this afternoon, then went across the hall into the second bedroom, the only part of the house that was not drywalled. The walls here, oddly—maybe it had once been an office or a den—were wood-paneled, but not with the usual knotty pine veneer. This was real wood, western red cedar, eight-inch clear tongue-and-groove. A while back, Yadin had torn up the shag, looking to create higher-frequency reflections, and had uncovered wide maple plank, which he had left untreated. Together, the cedar and maple produced a wondrous acoustical alchemy—bright and warm. His only other alteration had been to nail a piece of bent plywood over the window, stuffing the cavity behind it with fiberglass, to muffle street noise and act as a curved deflector. Otherwise, he hadn't had to do anything else to turn the room into the perfect home recording studio.

He sat in a straight-backed chair at his worktable—a salvaged door, cantilevered from the wall with industrial shelving brackets—on top of which were an old TASCAM four-track cassette recorder, a Grace preamp, and two studio monitors. Microphones and stands and amps surrounded the table. Lying on the floor were effects units and cables. On the walls, from pegs, hung several guitars, both acoustic and electric. A snare drum kit was in one corner, a keyboard in another.

He read through the paper scraps and copied lines into a spiral-bound notebook. He took down one of his guitars and strummed some chords.

This guitar, a 2008 Martin D-21 Special—it was okay, nothing really special. He had gotten it off eBay for relatively cheap. It had a solid tone with good bass and crisp treble registers, but the mid-range was a little thin. It just

didn't compare with his vintage 1957 D-21, which had
had Brazilian rosewood on the back and sides. That guitar had been sweet and clear, meaty, with a sublime sustain
and just enough overtones so everything came out rich and
lively. With all guitars, but especially Martins, the more you
played them, the better they sounded. He used to leave his
old D-21 in front of a stereo speaker, the bass full on, and
pump music (black metal was the most effective) at it all day
while at work, vibrating the guitar's spruce top to mature it,
make it really resonate. He had loved that D-21. He'd had
it for over fifteen years. Even with a crack along the pick-
guard, it had been worth well over six thousand dollars. In
the sixties, when the Brazilian government put an embargo
on timber shipments, Martin had switched to East Indian
rosewood, so older Martins were prized. But a few years
ago, desperate for cash, he'd had to let the guitar go for a
quarter of its value.

He had begun playing guitar at thirteen, on an Eko
Ranger VI dreadnought that his father had left behind, along
with a cache of LPs—mostly canyon rock, bluegrass, and
outlaw country albums. Yadin had been into punk at the
time, and had found his father's taste in music corny, the way
he'd become mawkish listening to records, muttering, "Goddamn," occasionally even weeping.

He had been a Goodrich tire sales rep for the Midwest
region, and was continually being transferred. Three or four
times a year, he had moved the family along Interstate 80—
Iowa, Illinois, Indiana, Ohio—sometimes hauling Yadin,

his younger brother, Davey, and their mother east, sometimes west. With all the relocations and their father gone
so much, there were predictable problems, Yadin and Davey
missing him, their mother lonely and resentful. The infre-
quent times he was home, there were fights, accusations of
cheating. The boys, a year apart, sequestered themselves in
their own world. They rode BMX bikes and flew kites and
built model airplanes. They chased frogs and dug for worms.
They tied makeshift flies and pretended they were fishing
in Montana; they skateboarded inside drainage pipes and
pretended they were surfing in Hawaii. Mostly, they played
baseball together. Yadin had a good arm, Davey a beautiful
swing, and every day during the summer, they fungoed balls
into the dying light of dusk.

But when they were living in Elyria, Ohio, and his brother
was ten, Davey began to feel listless. He looked ashen and
sickly and couldn't bring himself to go outside anymore. He
was diagnosed with aplastic anemia. In Cleveland, doctors
performed biopsies on Yadin to determine whether he could
be a bone marrow donor for Davey, but his tissue wasn't
compatible, and Davey died less than four months later.
The next year, Yadin's father took off on a road trip and
never returned. After another year, Yadin and his mother
embarked on their own itinerancy, mainly in the Mid-
Atlantic and South, as she pursued a training program and
then jobs as a phlebotomy technician, a vocation spurred by
all the times she had witnessed lab techs botching Davey's
blood draws, not finding a vein and having to jab him over

and over. She vowed that would never happen to another kid—not on her watch.

Left on his own most evenings, Yadin began picking through his father's LPs. The Stanley Brothers' Mercury recordings, Bill Monroe, Vern Williams, Red Cravens. Then Mickey Newbury, Emmylou Harris, Chris Hillman, Clarence White, Linda Ronstadt, John Prine, Lightnin' Hopkins, and Doc Watson. The musicians who most interested him, however, the two who destroyed him, were Townes Van Zandt and Gram Parsons. Listening to "Waiting 'Round to Die" the first time, Yadin was immobilized by Van Zandt's nasally, high lonesome voice, curdled with so much hurt. The same went for Parsons's "Hot Burrito #1," his aching warble, pleading for help.

All these songs about longing, regret, and betrayal, about broken hearts and belated apologies, about drinking, cheating, and leaving, about the lonely road and cheap motels and drifters, dreamers, outcasts, and the forlorn—they changed Yadin in ways he could not express yet could feel. After listening to them, his brain seemed to process things differently, the light now tinted and heavy. The songs were depressing and desolate, but they somehow gave him solace. He felt adrift in a world he didn't understand, a world that did not, in turn, understand him, and the songs validated those feelings. There were musicians—grown-ups—who felt this way, too, and they not only evoked the sorrow and bewilderment and loneliness inside him, they reveled in it, they even kind of celebrated it. They made those emotions grander, more mysterious, as if there were a deeper truth and purpose to them. He wanted to know how these songwriters did it—make pain into something beautiful. He wanted to do it himself. He began practicing the guitar and singing and writing his own songs to the exclusion of all else. He never finished high school.

In his studio, he played an intro on his guitar, accenting chords with hammer-ons and pull-offs and some walkups and walkdowns, then sang:

> *Lonesome lies before us*
> *Whatever place we're in*
> *We search this world for memories*
> *Unfinished, that never end*
>
> *Distance always owns us*
> *And what it was to be free*
> *The distance always showed us*
> *Our own frayed reverie*
>
> *I'm not ashamed that I miss you*
> *I've got my same old sins*
> *I look for you in all the spaces*
> *I always wished we'd been*

People were often confounded by Yadin's singing voice, considering how soft-spoken and taciturn he was in conversation. It was a high baritone, big, commanding, splintered with husk and yearning. To unsuspecting listeners, it was a voice that belonged to a natural frontman, a heartbreaker, someone who ferried hidden vulnerabilities that drew women, even when they knew he wouldn't stay. It was a voice that belonged to someone better-looking.

He scratched a few more words into his notebook, and began to sing again.

Jeanette Matsuda stood on the periphery of the huddled housekeepers. It was eight a.m., and two dozen of them were crammed into a basement hallway next to the laundry room, gathered for what was called the forum. Every morning, at every Centurion hotel worldwide, all employees reported for the forum—a fifteen-minute meeting in each department. Ostensibly the point of the meetings was to announce operational matters, but they also served as pep talks to reinforce the Centurion's core values, with discussions on ways to improve service.

The housekeepers at the Rosarita Bay Centurion Resort & Spa were usually a voluble crew, but this morning, when Mary Wilkerson, the director of housekeeping, asked if anyone had an issue to discuss, no one volunteered.

Nervously Jeanette lifted onto her toes and, peeking over the shoulder of a taller girl, surveyed the group. She rarely spoke at the forums, shy about contributing. She'd been on the job only a year, and felt she should defer to the floor supervisors and team leaders. Yet she was among the oldest employees there—thirty-nine—and she knew that if she ever hoped to be promoted, she should pipe up occasionally to show leadership potential.

"Anyone?" Mary said. "Come on, someone must have something, even if it seems trivial. Nothing's ever trivial here."

To Jeanette's surprise, Meghan, who was brand-new, barely out of high school, raised her hand.

"Oh, good," Mary said. "Yes, Meghan?"

"There's something that's been driving me crazy."

"Go ahead. What is it?"

"My shoes squeak."

The group snickered.

"No, no, this is a legitimate concern," Mary said. "It's something that would disturb our guests, so that makes it pertinent. Are they new shoes? Have you broken them in?"

"I've had them over two weeks," Meghan said. "I can't exchange or return them. They were on final sale."

"You have them on?" Mary asked, and when Meghan said yes, everyone peered down at her shoes, a cheap-looking pair of black oxfords. "Walk around," Mary told her.

The girls cleared a path for Meghan and hushed as she marched back and forth on the polished concrete floor. Her shoes indeed squeaked.

"Do they squeak when you're on carpet, too?" Mary asked. "Or just on hard surfaces?"

"All the time."

"Then it's not the outside sole," Clarisa, a floor supervisor, said. "It's the inside sole, rubbing against the bottom. Put baby powder underneath the insole."

Some girls concurred, swearing by Gold Bond. Others disagreed and suggested going wet, rather than dry, with saddle soap, olive oil, or hand lotion.

With everyone debating remedies so seriously, Jeanette got caught up in the discussion and, mustering her pluck, said, "This may sound bizarre, but Alberto VO5 might work."

"Really?" asked Emily, a team leader.

"You'd be surprised, the things you can do with VO5," Jeanette said.

"They still *make* Alberto VO5?" someone—Jeanette couldn't see who—asked, eliciting a round of chuckles, and immediately she regretted speaking.

Her father had slicked VO5 in his hair for many years. When she was a child, Joe had told her to smear a dab of it to eliminate the cheeping noise in her shoes, and had imparted a dozen other applications for the hair cream: making zippers glide easier, hiding scratches on wood, polishing stainless steel, cleaning grease or paint from your hands, breaking in a baseball glove. "This has more uses than WD-40," Joe had said. "I don't know why they don't advertise it. Talk about stretching your dollar."

Other girls chimed in with remedies for the squeaking—silicone spray, superglue—which prompted further debate.

"All right, all right, let's move on," Mary said. "We have a very busy day ahead, one hundred forty-two departures, one hundred fifty-five arrivals. We'll be sold out this weekend with the equity summit conference, and remember next weekend is Memorial Day, so we need to stay on top of things. Here are our VINPs."

She held up page-sized color photos—images culled from the Internet—of the Very Important Noble Persons: two CEOs and several hedge fund managers. "Memorize and address them by their names," Mary said. "Why do we go the extra mile with these personal touches?"

"It shows we care," they chorused.

"Yes. You are ambassadors of the Centurion brand. We also have one upcoming celebrity VINP. She won't be arriving until Wednesday, but since word might slip out, I thought I should tell you now. I want to remind you that there should be absolutely no gossip spreading outside the resort that she'll be here. Understood?"

With the other housekeepers, Jeanette nodded and waited for the name of the celebrity.

Mary brandished a photo of a pretty middle-aged woman with strawberry-blond hair. "Mallory Wicks," she said, leaking delight.

"Who?" a girl next to Jeanette whispered. Most of the other housekeepers did not recognize her, either.

"The actress," Jeanette whispered back.

Mallory Wicks, a former country singer, had starred in a prime-time soap opera called *City Empire* in the mid-nineties, and Jeanette recalled following the undulations of her career (sadly, more troughs than crests) in entertainment gossip magazines.

"Okay, some of you may not be old enough to remember her," Mary told them. "I always liked her because we have the same initials. I heard a rumor she's scouting for a possible film and might use the hotel as a location. Wouldn't that be thrilling?"

Jeanette wondered for a second if Yadin would know who Mallory Wicks was, and would be impressed that she'd be at the Centurion. But then she thought better of it. He didn't keep up with pop culture, and he disdained mainstream country. One of his favorite jokes was that if a commercial country song were played in reverse, the singer would reconcile with his adulterous wife, his runaway dog would return home, his overturned pickup truck would roll back onto its tires, and he'd get sober and released from prison.

She thought it sad that Yadin had never made any real money from his music career. There was no doubt he'd been very talented, even if his type of music didn't exactly appeal to her. (She listened to classic rock on the car radio, and that was the extent of her musical indulgences.) Yet in many ways, she was relieved he had quit trying to make music. She knew it must have been agonizing for him, the decision to give it up, and she admired him for his pragmatism.

"That's it for today," Mary said. "What's our motto?"

The housekeepers said loudly, "We are noblewomen and noblemen who take pride in serving noblewomen and noblemen!" This was, Jeanette and the other girls knew, an awkward poaching of the Ritz-Carlton's credo ("We are ladies and gentlemen serving ladies and gentlemen").

"Thank you," Mary said. "I hope you have a splendid and rewarding day."

The girls clapped and collected their room assignments. Jeanette's assignment sheets included several notations from Charisma, the Centurion Group's global database of guests' habits and preferences: A VINP, one of the hedge fund managers, was to get handmade truffles and Pellegrino on his welcome tray; a surgeon preferred to be addressed as "Doctor."

At the first of her assigned rooms, Jeanette knocked on the door, waited, and knocked again. Once she was reasonably sure there wouldn't be a reply, she inserted her keycard, cracked open the door, and called out, "Housekeeping," just to make certain. Hearing nothing, she wedged open the door and positioned her cart in front of the jamb.

For Jeanette, making the bed was still the hardest part of the job. After stripping the old linen, she laid out a flat bottom sheet (Centurion hotels never used fitted elastic) over the featherbed so each side draped evenly. She tugged on the sheet until it was smooth, and proceeded to fold crisp, precise hospital corners. Then she lifted the king-sized mattress, a custom-made Sealy Posturepedic Plush that was twelve inches thick and weighed one hundred fifty pounds.

Like her father, Jeanette was short and far from willowy, but she lacked his brawn. It demanded all her strength to heft up the mattress and suspend it long enough to tuck in all the corners and edges. Then she snapped out another flat sheet, yanked out the wrinkles, and constructed the foot pocket—a pleated envelope at the end of the bed so their guests' feet would not feel squished.

All the while, she thought about the forum. She worried that mentioning Alberto VO5 had made her appear out of touch, passé, *old*. She had no idea, actually, if VO5 was still being manufactured. Her father didn't use it anymore. He had lost a lot of hair over the years, and what remained, he kept cropped in a buzz cut, which Jeanette clipped for him every three weeks.

She inserted the goose-down duvet into its freshly laundered cover and prodded it over and over until she was able to produce a flat, absolutely unblemished surface. Then there were the six down pillows: two Euros, two kings, and two standards. She karate-chopped them into their cases and layered them in pairs against the headboard. In the middle, she added a small decorative pillow with the Centurion's trademark colors, burgundy with gold trim, the resort's emblem of a torch and a rising sun embroidered in the center. She hung a gold scarf over the base of the bed, and finally she was done.

Cleaning the bathroom was equally challenging, but for Jeanette, the bed felt more important. It was the first thing guests saw when they entered a room, and she wanted it to be exquisite, flawless. In this way, she was both perfect and ill-suited to be a housekeeper in a luxury hotel. She was unrelenting about the details, she would never let anything slide, she truly cared about the hotel's commitment to unparalleled customer service. On the other hand, she often found her-self behind schedule, trying to completely eradicate a stain or pluck up every single hair.

The normal workload was twelve rooms per eight-hour shift, an average of forty minutes apiece. The time required for individual rooms varied wildly, however. The COs (Checked Outs) were nominally the easiest, but it was unpre-dictable how guests would leave things. (Guests with children were the worst. Food ground into the carpet. Spills. Soiled diapers.) The OCCs (Occupieds), contrary to expectations, took longer. At other hotels, they might just make the beds with the same sheets for stay-overs, but not at the Centurion. There was no pretense about protecting the environment, no cards that promoted going green and reusing linens and tow-els. Everything, without exception, was changed every day.

The real problem, though, was with the OCC guests' possessions. The housekeepers were instructed to tidy up, put things in stacks at right angles, pick up clothes and fold them, hang them in the closet when appropriate. But it was sometimes hard to discern what should be moved, left undis-turbed, or discarded. It entailed judgment calls, and Jeanette hated judgment calls, the possibility of doing something wrong and having a guest complain.

In many ways, being a housekeeper at the Centurion Resort called for clairvoyance (or outright spying), trying to anticipate the "unexpressed desires and needs" of guests, as corporate phrased it. This meant observing and reporting that someone liked to sleep on, say, the left side of the bed, so the turndown attendant would know which side of the sheet and duvet to fold down in the evening and where to put the two squares of chocolate, water bottle and glass, slippers, and robe. It meant observing and reporting that someone had eaten all the cubes of melons but none of the pineapple on a fruit plate, so room service could be told to put extra melons with the next order.

The housekeepers' aprons were stitched with a pocket to hold a pad and a pencil to record their observations, which were then entered into the Charisma database. The housekeepers had a quota of generating at least two Charisma slips by the end of each shift—filling out more would accrue extra points for them in another database, the employee recognition system named Empower—but if a guest had an impromptu request, they were told to break away from whatever they were doing and take care of it right away.

If a guest inquired where the spa was located, they were to escort the person every step of the way to the spa, not just give directions or point. If a guest had a loose button and asked for a needle and thread, they were to take the garment promptly to the tailor downstairs in the laundry room. If a guest was stepping outside for a jog, they were to go to the fitness center and fetch a cold sports drink and one of the towels that had been moistened and refrigerated for cooldowns and have them waiting in the guest room. (And they were trained to say, during each encounter, "You are very welcome," never "No problem"; "It would be my pleasure," never "Okay"; "Please accept my apologies," never "Sorry";

"Good morning" or "Good afternoon" or "Good evening," never "Hi" or "Hey" or "How you doing?")

All of this took time—time that Jeanette did not have. Although the staff could indulge in a free lunch buffet every day in the employee cafeteria, she hardly ever took advantage of it; she would often realize when her shift ended that she had not eaten at all. Her usual assignment these days was ten rooms, two being suites, in which she could spend an hour and twenty minutes—leisurely-sounding, but the suites featured a large main room with a sofa and a dining table, a private terrace with a fire pit, a separate bedroom, and an additional half bath.

Every day, when Jeanette punched out at four-thirty, she was utterly drained, her body aching. She wasn't the only one. This afternoon in the locker room, women were slumped over in fatigue, rubbing their shoulders and calves, applying heat patches to their backs, swallowing ibuprofen, wrapping band-aids around fingertips and Ace bandages around ankles and knees.

Anna Goines, who had a locker near Jeanette's, was kneading her thigh and sniffling, sneezing.

Jeanette gave her a packet of Kleenex. "Coming down with something?"

"I hope not," Anna said. "I've already had two colds this spring."

Colds and the flu were a common occupational hazard. "Do you wear the gloves when you're cleaning?" Jeanette asked. A box of disposable blue gloves was issued to each cart.

Anna blew her nose. "Sometimes."

"Try to make a habit of it," Jeanette said. "Especially when you're doing bathrooms."

Anna was young. Twenty-one. Eighteen years younger than Jeanette. Like everyone else, Anna had attended two days of classroom orientation, after which she'd undergone three weeks of training, a team leader shadowing her every move, and then she had had to pass a ninety-day probationary period. But since then, she hadn't been doing very well, Jeanette knew. Little things, like getting caught cleaning a room with the TV turned on, chewing gum, talking on her cellphone in a stairwell, and violating the grooming standards, which were spelled out in explicit detail in the *Policies & Procedures* manual they had been given upon hire, a thick binder that delineated everything from the angle of throw pillows to the order in which magazines should be stacked to what kinds of makeup and fingernail polish were permitted.

They were each furnished with a brass-plated name tag and two burgundy uniforms with gold piping, yet they had to buy their own shoes (black, leather; no boots, sandals, thongs, open-toes, clogs, mules, moccasins, sneakers, or platforms) and panty hose (dark-tinted or neutral only), which tended to run from kneeling so much and got expensive to replace. Anna was pretty, with nice legs, which she enjoyed showing off. She had been docked for wearing heels exceeding two and a half inches and hosiery that was not only too sheer, but had seams running down the backs. She sported a banana clip in her hair one day and, on another, earrings larger than the size of a quarter.

Jeanette doubted Anna would last very long at the hotel. So when she saw Mary Wilkerson enter the locker room and head toward them, Jeanette assumed that Anna had committed another infraction of some sort and was about to be reprimanded. Instead, Mary said, "Jeanette, could you come to my office for a minute?"

"Uh-oh, the principal's calling you," Anna said. "What did you do?"

Jeanette asked herself the same thing. What could she have forgotten? Where could she have slipped up?

She went to Mary's small, cramped office and sat across the desk from her. A *STRIVE FOR FIVE!* sign was tacked to the opposite wall, directly above Mary's head. The signs were posted all over the lower service level of the hotel. The Centurion Group owned forty-seven properties worldwide, all known for their posh appointments and amenities, yet only a handful were rated with five stars. Most—like Rosarita Bay—were four stars. Now that the economy was rebounding, the highest priority for the Centurion Group was to start earning the coveted five stars from Mobil and the five diamonds from AAA for the majority of their hotels. To do so, corporate had been studying the Ritz-Carlton and Four Seasons' management principles and had begun emulating—in truth, stealing—them.

Mary was looking through Jeanette's personnel file. She was new to Rosarita Bay as the director—just two months.

This was the first time Jeanette had sat down with her for a one-on-one conversation, and it made her nervous, not knowing why she had been summoned. Was she about to be laid off or, inconceivably, fired? Could it have been the VO5 comment? She couldn't afford to lose this job.

For fourteen years, she had been the assistant records clerk at city hall. After being downsized out of the position two years ago, she had submitted dozens of applications for jobs in and around town, yet didn't receive a single interview, despite her qualifications: She was familiar with computers; she had taken business classes at San Vicente Community College; she could tout all sorts of additional administrative experience from being on the board and various committees for her church, although she knew most employers would not view that work as relevant. She had been unemployed for months. Finally she had succumbed to taking a job as a housekeeper at a motel in Pacifica, half an hour north on Highway 1. As a teenager, she had worked as a maid at a Days Inn one summer, and she had cleaned rooms at a B&B in town during high school and also upon graduation, after recovering from what used to be called a nervous breakdown.

Mary fanned out several pages of printouts on her desk. "I've been looking at your QCs," she told Jeanette. "Do you know what your QCs have been this year?"

Whenever they finished a room, they would dial *93 on the phone, and a floor supervisor would soon inspect their work, going through a lengthy quality-control checklist.

The highest possible score was one hundred; anything below ninety-three was unacceptable. The QCs were averaged monthly for each housekeeper and entered into the Empower database.

"They've been pretty good, I think," Jeanette said, despite knowing each of her scores. In her short time here, Mary had made it clear that humility was a trait she appreciated.

"I would call 'pretty good' an understatement. They've averaged 99.1 every month except for April, when you averaged 99.9. I've never seen QCs like this."

"No?"

"No. I am thoroughly impressed. You should be proud."

"I am," Jeanette said.

Mary laid down the QC printouts. "Are you? Are you really proud?"

"Yes."

"You don't think it's a comedown? It doesn't bother you, being a room attendant after all those years at city hall, having a college degree?"

"I only have an associate's," she said. "SVCC doesn't give out bachelor's." It was an enduring point of shame for Jeanette that she had never obtained a four-year degree.

"It doesn't bother you?" Mary asked.

"Not at all," Jeanette said, although of course it often did. The worst part was explaining to people what she now did for a living. When she said she worked at the Centurion, they would invariably ask in what capacity, and when she gave them her official title, "room attendant," they would look at her, sometimes puzzled, sometimes knowingly, until she admitted she was a housekeeper.

"I'm glad," Mary said. "I'm glad, because I can teach people how to do the job, but I can't teach them how to love it. You have to love what you're doing, or else you can't inspire others to give their best. That's the first step to being a good manager."

Hearing the word *manager*, Jeanette's attention swelled. She had been waiting for this possibility. Being allowed to clean suites had been considered a promotion of sorts, though one without a salary bump or a new title. From the start, she had longed to move up within the Centurion Group. She had hoped she could switch at some point to another area of the hotel's operations. She knew she wasn't young or attractive or perky enough for front of the house, for example in desk reception, but she thought something in reservations or accounts receivable would be perfect for her. She had been disappointed to learn that such transfers were not, in practice, very realistic, yet at this point any advancement was welcome.

"I think you have great potential here," Mary said. "I'm going to promote you to team leader as of June first, Wednesday after next, and then, you never know, maybe you could become a floor supervisor sometime in the future. Would that interest you?"

"Yes, it would. Very much," Jeanette said, and she was embarrassed to find herself near tears.

She changed clothes in the locker room and walked to the loading dock, where Anna and several other girls were waiting for the employee shuttle. The hotel had an underground garage, but there were barely enough slots to valet the guests' cars. Employees parked in an outdoor lot across Highway 1 and took a shuttle back and forth.

"Did you get into trouble with Mary?" Anna asked her. She had changed out of her uniform into a miniskirt and high heels and had applied makeup to her face. Earrings, in the shape of peacock feathers, tickled her shoulders, and a Chanel tote was slung over her shoulder—a knock-off, Jeanette knew, because the logo had interlocking O's instead of C's. She subscribed to several style and celebrity magazines—a frivolous expenditure, yet she loved flipping through them—and had recently read an article on how to spot counterfeits.

"She just wanted to go over an incoming guest's allergies," Jeanette said, electing not to brag about her promotion just yet.

"Did she say anything about the fitted sheets?" Anna asked.

A bill had been recently introduced in the state legislature. It would require hotels to replace flat bottom sheets with fitted elastic to reduce worker injuries.

"No."

"Corporate doesn't care about us at all," Anna said. "Like the panic buttons they're thinking of giving us."

"What about them?" Jeanette asked.

"They're a crock."

"I think it's pretty considerate of them," Jeanette said.

"They're not considering us," Anna said. "They're considering their liability. They just want to protect themselves in case something happens and one of us decides to sue."

"That's pretty cynical."

"It's true. Don't be naive," Anna said.

Jeanette wondered how Anna had made it through the vetting process, particularly since she had barely squeaked by herself. The Centurion looked for team players who were dedicated, respectful, and ethical. During interviews (four rounds total for housekeepers), they were asked about their personal habits, such as how often they washed their hands and if they ever threw trash out of car windows. Yet, more than cleanliness and honesty in their workers, the Centurion sought people who were cheerful and friendly, who smiled easily, none of which were Jeanette's natural inclinations.

Without quite realizing it, she had fallen into a persistent low-grade funk over the years, which became more pronounced when she was laid off and then was being rejected for job after job. Incessantly she would interrogate the choices and decisions she had made, and had convinced herself that she was a failure, a loser. She had crimped inward, fearful that if she exposed herself, she would be ridiculed or betrayed.

She was trying to resuscitate herself by following the counsel of her church's new minister, the Reverend Franklin Kuchenbecker. His presence, his compassion, his sermons— they were inspiring Jeanette to try, as he always exhorted, to be more positive, to bring gratitude and kindness into her heart, to actively seek out joy in her life and imbue it with beauty and light.

She was making this effort, in no small part, for Yadin. He was a sweet man. He was kind to her. Gentle. She trusted him. She felt safe with him. He would never cheat on her or lie to her. He got along with everyone in her family, particularly Joe, who had been the one to initially suggest that she date Yadin. Admittedly, he'd been much more of a reclamation project than Jeanette had ever imagined, his financial status revealed to be horrendous, but she had helped him through it. He was past all of that now—not exactly solvent, but stable.

Granted, there wasn't a lot of passion between them, and this was chiefly her fault, she knew. Both had been in love just once in their lives, while very young, and both had been heartbroken. Neither had ever married, nor had been in a relationship of any significant length. They might have been together more out of attrition than anything resembling ardor, but they cared for each other, they helped each other, they were companions. It was enough for Jeanette, and she had hoped it would be enough for Yadin, but lately she had begun to worry that it wasn't.

The employee shuttle arrived at the locking dock, and she and Anna boarded the bus. As the shuttle climbed the service road to ground level, Jeanette noticed how bright it was outside. Usually, this time of year, the marine layer would retreat only in the early afternoon, revealing blue sky for a few hours before the fog returned and swallowed them again in slaty gloom. She looked out to the ocean, the golf course, the majestic façade of porticos and Corinthian columns of the sprawling six-story hotel, which was perched atop steep sandstone bluffs. When she cleaned rooms, she never paid attention to the view anymore, but on occasion it struck her anew, the contours of light, the colors, the spectacle of the property—indeed of Rosarita Bay as a whole. She had lived here all her life, and sometimes she forgot how beautiful it was.

"Hey, what are you doing tonight?" Anna asked. "Anything?"

On the rare nights she wasn't seeing Yadin or didn't have church business, Jeanette always meant to do fun things, healthy things, productive things, cook a nutritious meal, go to the YMCA or for a walk, take up a new crafting project, read a book, but usually she was so tired and dehydrated and hungry, she would simply microwave something for dinner and watch TV, falling asleep before nine.

"No plans," she told Anna.

"You want to go to the Memory Den for a drink?"

"That dive?"

"It's kind of fun," Anna said. "Okay, how about the Brewing Company? What do you say?"

Jeanette turned to Anna. She was chewing a wad of gum, and her breath smelled wintergreen. Most of the other girls, unlike them, were married and had children. Jeanette could see that Anna was seeking a friend, and she was unexpectedly moved that she was reaching out to her. Perhaps, she thought, Anna was salvageable. Perhaps Jeanette, when she became a team leader in twelve days, could mentor her, shepherd a future for her at the Centurion. She could use a friend herself, she thought. Half of her former coworkers from city hall, after getting laid off, had moved out of town, and the other half never seemed to call her anymore. Yet she ended up saying to Anna, "Some other night? I'm pretty wiped," for what she really wanted to do that evening was review, one more time in depth, the *Policies & Procedures* manual.

3. Tell It to the Angels 4:09

Yadin and Jeanette stood with the three other members of the choir at the front of the sanctuary, flanked by the pianist, Siobhan, and the music director, Darnell. None of them wore robes for this morning's service, although Yadin had on his Sunday best—a white button-down shirt and khaki pants—and Jeanette was in an equally conservative blouse and skirt. Nearly everyone in the congregation, however, was dressed more casually, many in jeans, some even in T-shirts.

With the others in the choir, Yadin and Jeanette sang:

> *Wanderer, worshipper, lover of leaving*
> *It doesn't matter*

Ours is not a caravan of despair
Come, even if you have broken your vow
a thousand times
Come, yet again, come, come

Yadin never envied Darnell's job, having to find hymns like this one, based on a poem by Rumi, that weren't overtly religious. Darnell made most of his selections from a hymnal called *Singing the Living Tradition*, but sometimes he resorted to old pop tunes like "Lean on Me" and "All You Need Is Love."

Before coming here, Yadin had only been in churches for the occasional funeral or wedding. His mother had been a nonpracticing Jew, his father nothing, as far as Yadin ever knew. He grew up not thinking about religion at all, and this had continued throughout his adulthood, although as he was lurching through the worst of his afflictions, he had sometimes found himself praying. *Please, God, don't let me suffer anymore. Please, God, help me. Save me.*

When he had started working for Wall to Wall, he ran into Jeanette sporadically in the office, and Joe told his daughter, offhand, that Yadin had once been a singer of some sort. Thereafter, Jeanette kept asking him to join the choir at her church, which he resisted for months ("I'm not a believer," he would tell her. "You don't have to be," she would tell him, adding, "I'm a devout atheist," baffling him no end), until he realized that she might be using the invitation as a pretext to see him more. He decided to attend a service, reluctant as he was about encountering unfamiliar ecclesiastical rituals.

He needn't have worried. Unitarian Universalism was a liberal, progressive faith. It welcomed anyone, from Christians, Jews, Muslims, and Buddhists to agnostics, pantheists, pagans, and atheists. Although some congregations flirted with UU's Protestant roots, the First Unitarian Universalist Church of Rosarita Bay was staunchly humanist. It was as unreligious as a church could get. Often, an entire service could pass without the mention of God or any other deity.

Singing in the choir was another matter. It was distressing enough auditioning for Darnell. How would Yadin do in front of a weekly audience? He had never, in his entire life, performed sober in public. He wouldn't be able to wear sunglasses or a hat. He had shaved off his beard. There would be nowhere to hide, no avenue of escape. No amount of experience had ever diminished his fear of singing live, regardless of the circumstances.

But his nerves were allayed by the knowledge that these were not his songs they would be singing, and he would be among a group of amateurs, and the congregation would be small, twenty-five, thirty people at most, consisting largely of graying ex-hippies, tree huggers, and earth-mother flakes. They were a mellow, geriatric flock, hardly judgmental. The average age at the church was almost sixty.

He could relax in this environment, and it turned out that being in the choir gave him pleasure. Jeanette had a nice soprano, and the other members could more than hold their own. They worked well together. Yadin had forgotten, after being away from music for so long, what it was like to be part of a musical group.

He had joined his first garage band in eighth grade, then had belonged to a real band in Raleigh, North Carolina, where he had gone after dropping out of high school, then had had backing bands in studios and on the road. With those bands, he had found fraternity. He had been an oddball, a freak, but the musicians in those bands had all been freaks. In this choir, in this church, Yadin discovered a similar form of kinship. It provided him with comfort and safety, and taught him to be more social, less anxious, around people.

When they finished singing the hymn, their minister, Franklin, risking the appearance of bourgeois conformity by wearing a stole, stepped up to the pulpit—or, rather, a lectern. Their church was in a building that was formerly a day-care center. The sanctuary was a fluorescent-lit room with drop-ceiling tiles, and they had stackable chairs instead of pews.

"And now, if you're comfortable," Franklin said, "please remain standing for today's call and response."

They looked down at their programs.

"*We need*—" a child burst out.

Everyone laughed gently. It was Rebecca, Franklin's five-year-old daughter, in the front row. Franklin's wife, Caroline Storli, whispered to Rebecca, "Not yet, honey," and nodded to her husband.

Caroline was tall and very thin, with long black hair, and

was dressed in a gray sweater with a cowl neck and black slacks. A monochromatic, seemingly prim outfit. Yet when she bent down to speak to her daughter, Yadin caught a glimpse of her bra, and was a little taken aback to see that it was flame-red, lacy, and semitransparent.

"We need one another when we mourn and would be comforted," Franklin called.

"*We need one another when we are in trouble and afraid,*" they responded.

"We need one another when we are in despair, in temptation, and need to be recalled to our best selves again."

"*We need one another when we would accomplish some great purpose, and cannot do it alone.*"

"We need one another in the hour of success, when we look for someone to share our triumphs."

"*We need one another in the hour of defeat, when with encouragement we might endure, and stand again.*"

"We need one another when we come to die, and would have gentle hands prepare us for the journey."

"*All our lives we are in need, and others are in need of us.*"

"Please be seated," Franklin told them.

Yadin and Jeanette glanced at each other briefly, and smiled.

Theirs had been a slow courtship. Neither had dated for many years, and it took over six months before they saw each other outside of choir rehearsals and church activities. Finally Joe invited Yadin to his house for Thanksgiving with the family, and again for Christmas. On New Year's Eve, Jeanette had Yadin over to her bungalow, and they watched half of a British romantic comedy on DVD, switched to the Times Square festivities on television (tape-delayed three hours), and kissed for the first time at midnight. She was a little tipsy. She had opened a bottle of champagne and, since Yadin didn't drink, had finished almost all of it herself. She said, "I like you a lot, Yadin. Do you like me?"

"Yes," he told her. "I do."

"I think we could be good together—good for each other."

"I feel the same."

"But there's something you should know," she said. "I'm not a very sexual person. How do you feel about that?"

"What do you mean, not a sexual person?" he asked.

"I'm not frigid or a prude," she said. "I just don't have much of a sex drive these days. Would that bother you? I mean, of course it would. But how important is that to you in a relationship?"

"Not very much. It wouldn't be a big deal to me," he told her.

"Are you sure?"

"Jeanette, I'm not a kid anymore."

It would be another two months before they had sex, yet from that early morning on New Year's Day, two and a half years ago, it had been understood that they were a couple.

After church, they usually drove to San Vicente to pick up a week's worth of groceries and a tank of gas at Costco, occasionally stopping at Target or—reluctantly, given the poor treatment of its workers—Walmart when it didn't make sense to purchase items in Costco's bulk sizes.

Today, as on many Sundays, coming back up the hill toward Rosarita Bay after their shopping, they got trapped in traffic on Highway 71—possibly an accident, construction, a breakdown, anything on the winding road could cause gridlock. Jeanette was driving them in her 1999 Honda Civic. They had left Yadin's van, which was even older and in dubious shape, in the church parking lot.

"I put your meats with the frozen foods in the cooler," Yadin told her. "They should keep." He had forgotten to bring the blue ice from his van.

"This is ridiculous," Jeanette said, "having to drive all this way just to go to Costco's. Why can't there be a coastside Costco's?"

There was no big-box retail anywhere near Rosarita Bay. Shockingly, their lone supermarket, the Safeway, had been shuttered without warning last fall, supposedly because it was underperforming. The town now had just two small upscale markets on Main Street, New Harvest Organic and Cuchi's Country Store.

"The way things are going," Yadin said, "we might not even have New Harvest anymore."

"Why's that?"

"Adelina thinks they might have to close." Adelina, Rodrigo's wife, was a cashier at the store.

"I hate to say it, but it's not a mystery why, with their

prices," Jeanette told him. "Only tourists can afford those prices. I can't believe you used to do all your shopping there."

Early on, when Yadin had told Jeanette how much he was spending on organic groceries, she had been aghast, and then began taking him with her to Costco. Jeanette was, if anything, thrifty.

"You haven't heard anything more about the council vote, have you?" Yadin asked. "Your dad's not optimistic."

"Siobhan thinks it's a done deal." Siobhan Kelly, the church pianist, was a sergeant on the Rosarita Bay police force.

In last November's election, residents had struck down Measure K, which would have raised the local sales tax by half a cent. The following month, the council sent out requests for proposals to outsource Rosarita Bay's police services, and throughout the winter and spring there had been numerous study discussions, presentations, special meetings, and closed sessions, with San Vicente County's sheriff and the city of Pacifica emerging as the top contenders.

This morning at church, Siobhan had told Jeanette that the sheriff's office, which already had a substation near Rosarita Bay, had pledged to hire five of the eight current police officers as deputies.

"Would that include Siobhan?" Yadin asked Jeanette.

"She doesn't know."

"What about the library? It's still safe, right?"

Motions to contract out the library, or close it altogether, had appeared less urgent of late. The city had already cut the library's staff in half, and there was strong public support to stem further reductions.

"You'd know better than me," Jeanette said.

"How would I know?" Yadin asked.

"Caroline."

"We don't talk like that," he said. In point of fact, they hadn't talked much at all in the last month.

"Don't you?" she said.

"We've only ever talked about poetry."

"This poetry thing, I'll never understand," Jeanette said.

Caroline was Rosarita Bay's library manager. Yadin dropped by the flat-roofed, one-story brick building at least once a week to use their computers, initially seeking financial and legal information, then online classifieds, then new recipes. A sign on the front door offered FREE INTERNET, NOTARY, PHONE, COFFEE, RESTROOMS, SMILES, AND IDEAS. He saw Caroline off and on there, as well as every other Sunday at church, and in March and April, after he heard her give a lecture on Gerard Manley Hopkins, they began talking more, but not about anything personal.

They fetched Yadin's van from the church parking lot, then convened at Jeanette's house, where they did their laundry. Yadin didn't have a washer/dryer.

Jeanette rented a one-bedroom bungalow in Vasquez Canyon, in the hills above town. Originally the bungalow had been designed as a guesthouse on the two-acre property, which had a larger home for the owners, an elderly gay couple in San Francisco who rarely visited now. In exchange for being the property caretaker, Jeanette received reductions in her rent, a generous deal, since not much was required of her, other than scheduling the landscaper and seeing that the main house was maintained and occasionally cleaned (which she didn't have to do herself).

Their laundry took hours. Whereas Yadin was apt to throw everything into the drum willy-nilly, Jeanette was finicky about separating out colors and washing undergarments on delicate and hanging them to dry to give them longer life. In the meantime, they each did their bills, writing out checks and affixing stamps to envelopes, Jeanette double-checking Yadin's figures and forms, especially for his mortgage payments and his credit card. Ironically, the best way for Yadin to rebuild his credit rating was to make regular purchases on credit. He'd gotten a credit card from a bank that was, in exchange for usurious fees and rates, bankruptcy-friendly. His limit on the card was three hundred dollars, and he charged no more than thirty percent of the limit, ninety dollars, on it each month, and then paid his bill in full upon receipt.

Afterward, they made dinner. Yadin assembled another new recipe for a salad, a portion of which he served to Jeanette, who heated up a frozen lasagna for herself. They ate in the living room, then did the dishes and settled on Jeanette's double bed to watch *60 Minutes* and *The Amazing Race*. She received free satellite TV as part of her rent, but the hookup was only in her bedroom.

The bungalow was a mere six hundred fifty square feet,

and, as in Yadin's cottage, all of the furnishings were secondhand, and nothing matched. Yet there was a vast difference in their gestalts. Jeanette's house was light-filled and
cozy, the décor artsy and eclectic. Everything was vintage.
A worn velvet couch, a walnut stool, Moroccan poufs and
kilim pillows on the floor, gauze curtains on the windows.
There were linen doilies and silver bowls, vases and teapots,
flowers and plants, mushroom lamps and a chandelier. On
the walls—painted different shades, ranging from teal-blue
to deep orange—hung a sari, a dreamcatcher, tapestries,
watercolors of landscapes, Art Deco posters, and little col-
lages made from postcards, Polaroids, and small reproduc-
tions. Some were Depression-era images, others snapshots of
Jeanette and her family when she had been a child. The postcards featured landmarks in various European and Asian
cities that she had once dreamed of touring.

All of this could have been claustrophobic, yet each item
had been so lovingly selected, each piece so thoughtfully
arranged, that the overall effect was soothing, airy, inviting.
The house had the charm of a bohemian apartment in bygone
Paris or Greenwich Village (albeit without a speck of dust),
suffused with whimsy and personality. It was, unequivocally,
a home, one that Jeanette had shaped and curated continu-
ously during the nine years she had lived in the bungalow.
Yet, in many ways, it seemed to Yadin like someone else's
home—someone hipper, more adventurous, vivacious, someone who was a free-spirited, globe-trotting artist. It had
stumped him, seeing the bungalow for the first time that New

Year's Eve. He had thought, getting to know Jeanette better, he would eventually be able to reconcile the playfulness of the layout with its architect, but he had yet to do so.

As they watched TV on her bed, Jeanette picked at a bowl of microwave popcorn—a nightly indulgence, to go along with two goblets of red wine, although this evening she'd also had a gin and tonic to celebrate her promotion with him. Shifting positions on the bed, she winced and grunted—sounding exactly like her father.

"Back hurt?" Yadin asked her.

"A little."

"Want me to massage you?"

"I'm okay." She set the popcorn on top of a stack of magazines on her nightstand and readjusted her pillows. "Mary Wilkerson says they might give us panic buttons."

Yadin did not answer, because he had heard the sentence as, "Merry workers may kill some manic lessons," and he was trying to parse it.

"Are you listening to me?" Jeanette asked.

"Yes."

"Did you take your hearing aid out?"

"I hate the thing," he said. He seldom wore it; usually he could still hear well enough to get away without it. While the threshold for his right ear was already at 55 dB, on the edge of moderately severe, the hearing loss in his left ear was only mild for the moment.

"I hate when you take it out," Jeanette said. "Put it back in."

The problem with the hearing aid, a beige plastic in-the-ear model, was that it was cheap. Everything sounded tinny, mechanical, and compressed, particularly voices. The mic picked up noises from all directions. It wasn't good when driving, or in the wind, or with music. It would occasionally whistle or squeal with feedback, and it was useless with a lot of background or competing noise, like a TV.

He dug into his pocket, turned the hearing aid on, and inserted it into his right ear.

"I never know if you're ignoring me or just can't hear," Jeanette said.

"My plan all along, keep you guessing. What were you saying?"

"Corporate might issue us panic buttons. You know, the portable ones you wear around your neck, like for old people who can't get up."

"Why?" Yadin asked.

"The French guy."

"What French guy?"

"The rich French guy, the one who raped the housekeeper in New York."

"I didn't hear about this," Yadin said.

"How could you not? It happened last week. It's been all over the news."

Jeanette was forgetting: he didn't watch the news on TV, nor did he read any papers. "He raped a housekeeper?"

"Some sort of assault. I don't know exactly," she said. "But it was bad. And he'll get away with it because he's a diplomat or something with loads of money."

Now he was concerned. "Anything happen to you thus far?" he asked. "A guest ever proposition you or, I don't know, expose himself?"

"I'm sworn to secrecy," Jeanette said, unperturbed. "Remember, I had to sign a nondisclosure agreement the day I was hired. It's like the CIA. If I told you, I'd have to kill you."

"Oh, yeah? How would you kill me?"

"Well, first I might have to tie you down, like this." She grabbed his wrists and, rolling halfway on top of him, pinned his arms above his head. She looked down at him, then kissed him lightly on the mouth, tasting of wine.

She had a wide face, with small eyes spaced far apart. Her mouth was small as well, framed by lines. When she smiled, she did not like to open her lips, embarrassed by her crooked incisors. She swept her hair—parted on the side in a shaggy, layered bob, longer in back—across her forehead and kept it tucked behind her ears. He thought her pretty, even though she did not consider herself pretty. She had done something odd to her eyebrows, however, since the last time he'd seen her. It appeared she had plucked the hairs almost bare and was now penciling them in.

As was their custom, they made love during the Andy Rooney segment of *60 Minutes* and finished just before *The Amazing Race* began, a window of thirteen minutes, and, as was customary, Jeanette did not have an orgasm.

"Should I keep trying?" Yadin asked.

"It's okay," Jeanette said.

"Isn't there something else I can try?"

"No, it's all right."

"I wish there was something I could do for you."

"Don't worry. I'm fine. I'm happy. Come up here. The show's beginning."

Before Yadin, Jeanette had been celibate for at least ten years, perhaps longer. She wouldn't say, exactly. He had wondered at first if she had once been abused or raped—maybe by someone like the French guy—but she refuted it. It was only when she told him about Étienne Lau, her long-ago fiancé who'd died in a car accident, and the baby she'd miscarried, that he had begun to understand somewhat.

He didn't mind that they had sex so infrequently. Sex—except with his first girlfriend, Mallory Wicks, née Wickenheiser, when he was twenty-three—had never really mattered to him. As a musician, he had had no-name flings with groupies and barflies (if you were a singer and guitar player, even an ugly one, there were always women willing to fuck you), but even in those encounters, he could never lose the feeling that it was a performance, that he had to measure up to vague yet ever-present expectations, and he never drew any real pleasure from the act, just relief that he hadn't made a fool of himself, that the women had not been repulsed by him. Of course, since alcohol and drugs were usually involved, he sometimes did make a fool of himself, impotent or premature, and the women did end up repulsed. Over the years, he could do just as well without sex, and that was what he chose—not seeking it, trying not to think about it.

His Sunday routine with Jeanette was deeply satisfying to

him. He didn't care that their lovemaking was less than spectacular. He didn't care that overall they had little in common. They didn't share many interests or hobbies. They didn't discuss politics, or books, or art, or sports, or music—notably, his music (he was pretty certain Jeanette had listened to his albums only once through, as a courtesy). They didn't discuss religion—just updates about her committee work and gossip about church members (he was scared, with her devout atheism, to bring up the religious conversion he seemed to be undergoing). They didn't talk about anything, really, other than the quotidian: tidbits about her job, the town, Joe. Yadin didn't think there was anything wrong with that. It wasn't perfect, but what relationship was?

He did not want to be alone. It haunted him with a squashing sadness, the thought of being alone, never having anyone to take care of him or missing him, wondering where or how he was, waiting for him to come home. Before moving to Rosarita Bay, he had been convinced that he would be alone forever. Often he'd realize that he had not talked to anyone in days—even weeks. The telephone wouldn't ring. No one would knock on his door. He had no friends. All he did was go to his job—whatever job—during the day and write songs at night. When he got sick with Ménière's and started losing his hearing and couldn't work or play music anymore, he wouldn't bother to shower or get dressed or leave his apartment.

Jeanette was his reprieve. She had saved him. She had given him a community—the church and her family ("You're practically family," Joe had said)—and she had supported him during the worst of his financial woes. Without her, he was sure he wouldn't have survived. She was his last chance at something approaching normalcy, belonging to someone and some place, having a life that was no longer provisional.

Yet there was something holding her back from him—not just sexually, but emotionally as well. He felt it most keenly at the end of their Sundays together, when she would send him home, no longer making any pretense that she wanted him to spend the night. It made him terribly sad, having to leave.

He gathered his laundry and Costco sacks and tubs of salad, and he loaded his van while she changed into her pajamas and arranged her accoutrements for the night: eyeshades, earplugs, night guard, and a thin, flat pillow for her head.

At the door to her bungalow, she hugged Yadin, and they kissed good night.

"I love you, Jeanette," he told her.

"I love you," she told him.

He stared at her penciled eyebrows, which made her appear skeptical. "Are you sure?" he asked.

"Yes," she said. "Of course. Why?"

Yadin removed the hearing aid from his ear, switched it off, and put it back in his pocket. "I guess sometimes I'm not so sure," he said.

—◌◌—

He began losing his hearing eight years ago, in 2003, when he was on tour for his last album. In the middle of a show in

St. Louis, he became dizzy and nauseous. He wandered to the side of the stage, puked, and tried to negotiate the steps to the green room but tumbled down the stairs and broke his left wrist. He thought he'd been sick because he was drunk and high—he always got drunk and high to perform. He was taken to a nearby ER and was discharged in the wee hours of the morning. After sleeping in his van for a bit, he drove back to Portage, Michigan, since the rest of his tour would have to be canceled. He couldn't play guitar with a cast on his wrist.

A few days after getting home, he was walking out of a 7-Eleven, and he felt something odd happening. His right ear stopped up, as if he were descending in an airplane, and the pressure kept building as he was overcome by a whooshing sound, like from a conch shell, only much louder. He began to sweat profusely, and the horizon started to spin, turning on an axis, the sky and the ground awhirl, as if he were on a rapidly listing ship. He fell to the asphalt, splitting open his forehead, and vomited repeatedly. He believed he was having a stroke. Someone called 911. The EMTs transported him to the Bronson ER, where he stayed for ten hours, mostly passed out from an IV of Antivert for motion sickness, until the vertigo faded. The attending physician kept asking Yadin what he had taken, what he was on, but at the time he had been absolutely sober.

During the next few days, he had an excruciating headache that no amount of aspirin could relieve. He was weak and unbalanced on his feet, needing to prop his hands against walls and furniture to walk. His right ear continued to block up. He couldn't hear anything out of it other than that mysterious whooshing noise. He'd swallow and yaw his jaw for thirty minutes, finally pop his ear, but then it'd stop up again. The following week, just as he was beginning to feel better, he was hit with a more severe episode, this time at the laundromat. Once again he was hauled to the ER, and once again the attending physician was dismissive, releasing him without an explanation or prescription or referral.

Worried he had a brain tumor, Yadin took it upon himself to see a neurologist, who ordered a CT scan for him, but it turned up negative. He then made an appointment with an internist, who said it could be a number of things: stress, allergies, anemia, something metabolic, low blood pressure, high blood pressure, migraines, diabetes. He removed the wax from Yadin's ears with a curette and ordered a batch of blood tests, all of which came back negative.

He had three more episodes, spaced about a week apart. They'd arise like panic attacks, and all of a sudden he'd be on the floor, vomiting. The internist then said perhaps it could be MS or Lyme disease or even syphilis (he was a musician, after all), but those tests, too, came back negative. The internist suggested he go to an ear, nose, and throat specialist.

The ENT ordered an audiogram, a basic hearing test, and Yadin sat in a tiny booth wearing a headset as the audiologist whispered words for him to repeat: "cupcake," "hot dog," "ice cream," "river," "father." Often he only caught the hard consonants of the words. Sometimes he did not hear them at all. The ENT ordered a more sophisticated test, electrocochleography, and Yadin's hearing in his right ear was found conclusively to be impaired. The ENT said perhaps it could be an acoustical neuroma (benign tumor pressing against his auditory nerve) or otosclerosis (abnormal bone growth) or vestibular neuritis or labyrinthitis (infections), any of which could explain the combined occurrence of vertigo, tinnitus, and hearing loss. The tests—with no health insurance, the bills were enormous for all these doctors' visits and tests— came back negative. And, confusingly, a subsequent audiogram showed his hearing had *improved* in the interim.

He spent another six months trying to find out what was happening to him, going to two more ENTs for second and third opinions, getting more tests, all the while having near-monthly attacks. By this point, he could tell when an episode was in the offing, his ear and hearing closing up, the tinnitus ramping into a howl, his vision tunneling, the geometry of the world suddenly slippery and tenuous. Usually he had a minute or two before the spins would arrive, and he'd pull over if he was driving, or sit on the ground if he was walking, or lie down on his bed if he was in his apartment. Then the vertigo would engulf him, everything unspooling, pulsing, rupturing. It'd last anywhere between five minutes and several hours, and he'd be retching and heaving, and then afterward, drenched in sweat, he'd have to sleep for twelve hours straight, and he'd wake up the next morning feeling as if he'd been pummeled with tire irons.

For a while his manager would check up on him, inquiring how Yadin was faring, when he might be ready to resume his canceled tour, when he'd begin thinking about a new album. There was no way Yadin could make it onto a stage or into a studio in his condition. Nonetheless, he asked his manager if he might be able to get a small advance from his record label. His manager hooted in laughter. Eventually he stopped calling Yadin altogether.

He couldn't resort to his usual day jobs. He couldn't go on ladders or scaffolding or operate tools or machinery. He could barely manage to leave his apartment. He had to walk with a cane, his equilibrium was so off now, and he wore sunglasses even when it was raining, because changes in light would make him reel, subtle shifts feeling abrupt and magnified, like exiting a movie theater on a bright day. He couldn't watch TV or look at a computer. He couldn't read a book. He kept his apartment pitch-dark, the shades drawn. He had to apply for disability. Welfare. Food stamps.

His hearing deteriorated further. Perplexingly, some days he could hear perfectly fine, but overall, during the recovery periods, the effects were worse and more prolonged and, most distressing, were beginning to migrate to his left ear.

He was losing the edges, the lower frequencies. Everything sounded metallic and distorted. People on the phone seemed to be speaking underwater. When receptionists called to him in doctors' offices, their voices would be patchy walkie-talkies. It was embarrassing, not realizing that he was being addressed, having to ask people to repeat themselves. He would try to guess words. It helped if he could watch lips. But often he'd be mistaken. He'd answer questions that hadn't been asked, or restate what the person had just said. He began to simply nod as if he understood. Entering into any conversation—even the most innocuous exchanges, like with a kid taking his order at Burger King—made him feel uncomfortable and vulnerable. It was easier just to withdraw, not talk to anyone.

Then his hearing oscillated to the other extreme. Certain things—crying babies, car alarms—he began hearing too well, the volume piercing. Even softer noises, like water pouring from a faucet, were agonizing. For several weeks, he couldn't shower without wearing earplugs. Soon, tones doubled up. He'd pluck the D string on his guitar, hear a C or D-sharp or both, then a D. It was like having a tremolo bar—hooked up to a chorus pedal and a ring modulator—that would randomly bend and release on everything. It was impossible to play music, much less listen to it.

At last, one of the ENTs gave Yadin a diagnosis. He said Yadin probably had Ménière's disease, a disorder linked to an imbalance in inner-ear fluid pressure. He couldn't be sure, since there were no specific blood tests, scans, or X-rays for Ménière's, but it fit all his symptoms.

Ménière's had no known cause. Theories about its roots varied from viruses to immune reactions, head trauma, and herpes. But the ENT speculated that playing music, the construction work, chemical exposure—they could have all been contributing and cumulative factors. It was hard to predict a prognosis. Ménière's affected patients in different degrees and durations. His vertigo and tinnitus symptoms could dissipate or disappear entirely in time, or be episodic, dormant for months or years before recurring. His hearing loss could fluctuate, but overall would likely get worse. The enlargement of the endolymphatic sacs had damaged his auditory hair cells—damage that was degenerative, and would be permanent. There was no cure. All Yadin could do, the ENT said, was manage his symptoms. Cutting back on salt, caffeine, and alcohol seemed to help people, as did certain medications: Dramamine, Serc, Valium, Natrilix. But basically Yadin would just have to learn to live with it. Almost certainly, the ENT said, he would have to give up his music career.

Yadin refused to believe him. He couldn't stop making music. It was his entire life—the only thing that gave him succor and purpose. There had to be something that could be done.

He turned to the Internet, where he discovered a dizzying (and often contradictory) wealth of information about Ménière's. It was comforting to find allies online, where they called the disease MM, after its German name, *Morbus Menière*. There were tens of thousands of fellow MM sufferers out there, going through the same misery.

Probing deeper into forums, Yadin read some encouraging reports. For many MMers, the vertigo attacks subsided substantially after two years from the onset of the disease, and the tinnitus became less acute. It was true that once MM went bilateral to affect both ears, the hearing loss was usually progressive, but miraculously, some people had been able to reverse it, regaining their hearing. Indeed, there were stories of complete remission. The first step, Yadin under-stood, was to stop smoking, go completely sober, and make rigorous, wholesale changes to his diet and lifestyle. The next was to try out various drugs to curb the attacks and preserve his ears' remaining health.

After a few duds, he settled on Meclizine (anti-vertigo), Prednisone (steroids), and Dyazide (diuretic). In short order he knew more about Ménière's than his ENT, who would wearily prescribe whatever Yadin asked for. There were side effects. The diuretic made him need to pee all the time and threw him into electrolyte imbalance, causing his fingers to tingle. The steroids gave him stomach acid and insomnia. Yet, as hoped, the vertigo all but disappeared.

A lot of posters on the forums touted a holistic, alternative-medicine approach as a long-term solution, and he experi-mented with an assortment of supplements. Then he ran across an antiviral regimen devised by someone known only as "John of Ohio." People said it worked wonders. He followed the pro-tocol of homeopathic remedies, and he was fully symptom-free for three months, until he had an unexpected relapse. Still, he thought he was on the right track, and consulted a naturopath. After much trial and error, his Ménière's finally stabilized to the point where he could ditch all of his prescriptions, just tak-ing daily doses of L-lysine, vitamin C, and a natural antifungal called pau d'arco. As long as he kept hydrated, kept his stress low, ate clean, and got regular sleep, he could work again.

Since moving to Rosarita Bay, he had experienced just two mild episodes: once when he accidentally ate something splashed with soy sauce, another time when he had a bout of insomnia. The aural fullness and the tinnitus returned, and he got a bit of the spins, but it wasn't so bad, and the symptoms vanished in a couple of days. He wasn't cured by any means, he knew. This was a lifelong illness, and he would have to remain vigilant. But for the moment, his condition was tolerable, except for one lingering, major issue.

His hearing never rebounded. It still came and went— deaf one day in certain situations, clear the next. He'd halted a precipitous slide, but every year, he went in for an audiogram, and every year, he was told that his hearing had become a little bit worse. Slowly but surely, certain sounds, certain frequencies, were receding from him forever. He was losing parts of himself, note by note. The ENT had been right, after all. Yadin had to accept that, for all intents and purposes, his music career was over.

She caught a glimpse of her on Thursday morning. Fleeting, just a phantasmal blur from around a corner, but Jeanette was sure it had been Mallory Wicks walking down the hallway on the third floor.

The actress was staying in one of the Centurion's best suites, and Jeanette had heard about some of her Charisma notations, despite strict guidelines about their confidentiality. Ms. Wicks was being permitted to smoke on her private terrace and provided with ashtrays, when the entire resort property was supposedly smoke-free. She was being allowed tee times as a single, when, as a general rule, the starters at the club always tried to pair singles with other golfers to make up a foursome, threesome, or at least a twosome. She was being supplied with a bottle of twenty-year-old Pappy Van Winkle's Family Reserve, a coveted small-batch bourbon, as well as a stock of Tasmanian rainwater. Apparently the list went on.

Jeanette was tempted to follow her down the hallway. Perhaps Ms. Wicks would have a question or a request for her, and they'd ease into incidental conversation, get chatty, even friendly. Jeanette could learn what she was like in real life. She had a weakness for celebrities. She liked hearing gossip about them, reading about their lifestyles. But when she turned the corner and looked down the hallway, Ms. Wicks was not there.

She began cleaning No. 331, a standard room with a mountain view, facing the foothills instead of the ocean. Still nice, still very expensive, but not extraordinary, not a VINP room that merited any Charisma notations.

As she made the bed, Jeanette thought about Yadin, the way he had questioned her last Sunday, asking whether she truly loved him. She had been ruminating about it all week. What had prompted him to ask that night? Because she didn't invite him to sleep over? Because she didn't have an orgasm? None of this was new. She used to fake it once in a while, but stopped when Yadin began to suspect and reassured her that she shouldn't.

She hadn't always been so unresponsive. She used to love sex, and even had had a reputation in high school for being promiscuous. She and Étienne Lau—her boyfriend the summer before she was supposed to go to the Corcoran School of Art in Washington, D.C.—couldn't fuck enough. He had been the love of her life. Yet no one ever understood how she could let herself be defined by a relationship, as tragically as it'd ended, that had lasted a mere two months when she was eighteen. That was why, when pressed, she sometimes lied, and said that they had been engaged, and that when she became pregnant, they had intended to keep the baby, and that she had suffered a miscarriage after learning that Étienne had been killed in a car crash. The truth was, she and Étienne were never engaged, and she didn't miscarry. She had had an abortion.

Whatever the embellishments, she had been devastated by Étienne's death—so much so, she'd suffered a breakdown, and her parents had her hospitalized for a week. She thought about enrolling at the Corcoran the following year, or maybe the year after that. But then her mother was diagnosed with colon cancer, and Jeanette took care of her throughout the surgeries and chemo and radiation. Then she died, and Jeanette had to raise her little sister and hold things together for her father, who had been undone, and Jeanette felt compelled to stay in the house until her sister went to university, and then she was thirty years old.

She went out on a few dates—not many. In the seventeen years between Étienne and Yadin, she had sex twice, one-night stands with two different men. Both times, it was sort of date rape and sort of not. She didn't say no, she didn't say yes. She just lay there. She couldn't imagine having to cope with another unintended pregnancy, and had her tubes tied.

Somehow, that part of her—erotic, desirous—had disappeared, lost amid the years packing lunches and cooking dinners and cleaning house, driving to hospitals and parceling out pain meds and changing colostomy bags. She felt as if everything sentient about her had been erased. Was any of it retrievable? Was it dormant but still there? She wanted it to be, especially for Yadin.

She finished cleaning No. 331. She wanted to work on No. 342, but it was a DND (Do Not Disturb), which she worried might throw her entire day off-schedule. In the hallway, Anna, uncharacteristically in a frenzy, scrambled up to Jeanette and asked, "Can you help me with something?"

The problem was in No. 363. There were black scuff marks all over the marble bathroom floor. "I've tried everything," Anna said. "I can't get them out. Do you have any ideas? I don't know what kind of shoes this guy had, what he was doing in here. I mean, was he tap-dancing or what? This will really fuck up my QCs."

"I know something that'll get them out," Jeanette said.

"Let me guess," Anna said. "Alberto VO5."

"No, even better." Jeanette went back to her cart and got a tennis ball that had a hole poked in it. In No. 363's bathroom, she inserted the end of Anna's broom handle into the hole, flipped it upside down, and, pressing hard, rubbed the tennis ball against the scuff marks, magically erasing them.

"That is amazing," Anna said. "Damn. What other tricks you got up your sleeve?"

—◎◎—

She had a lot of tricks. She knew how to do things, take care of things, get things done. She prided herself on being someone people could depend on. She had been considered indispensable at city hall, and she was regarded that way now at the church, where she'd recently been elected president of the board of trustees, in spite of her continual astonishment that she had joined the church in the first place.

Thirteen years ago, a woman who worked as a coordinator in the city recreation department, Gabriela Flores, had invited her to a potluck at her house, not telling Jeanette that she was trying to start a UU fellowship in Rosarita Bay. Jeanette had never heard of Unitarian Universalism before. She wondered if it was associated with the Unity Church, or the Unification Church, and if Gabriela was trying to recruit her into a cult. Even after being told UU's principles, she was not assuaged. Her mother, an atheist, had raised her children to be wary, if not contemptuous, of all religions. What drew Jeanette back for another potluck, however, was that she was lonely. She had no life outside of her job in the clerk's office and her family. It was an excuse to get out of the house, a respite from caring for Joe and her siblings.

They started slowly, using a Church in a Box subscription from the Unitarian Universalist Association. In each box was a sermon written by a UU minister and program materials. Someone would read the sermon, they'd talk, and they'd sing songs—a simple exchange of fellowship that grew enlivening to Jeanette. Without knowing it, she had been seeking a purpose, and she found it within this fledgling congregation. UU's commitment to social justice, in particular, aligned perfectly with her residual liberal ideals. She worked indefatigably with Gabriela and the other founding members to establish the church, and in time they signed a lease for their current building and became a chartered congregation of the UUA.

They'd had some setbacks along the way, such as when Gabriela—as well as several other members—got laid off and had to relocate, but Franklin Kuchenbecker had brought new life to the church. He had been their part-time pastor for a year and a half now, and conducted the worship service in Rosarita Bay on the first and third Sundays of every month.

For most of their history, their services had been lay-led, interspersed with the occasional guest speaker or visiting minister—circuit riders who traveled to various congregations. Before Franklin, they'd never had the means to hire a minister on a permanent basis. Without a Chalice Lighters grant from the UU Pacific Central District office, they wouldn't have been able to afford even the paltry sum they were paying him: twenty-six thousand dollars a year as an independent contractor, with no benefits (albeit he was given much of the summer off). On alternate Sundays, he was the consulting minister of a UU fellowship in Aptos, just south of Santa Cruz, and he supplemented his income further by presiding over weddings and funerals.

Jeanette was grateful that circumstances—Caroline being

offered the library manager job—had brought Franklin to town. He was a popular minister, smart, eloquent, and charismatic. Often, during his sermons, Jeanette found herself nodding her head in agreement and tearing up in recognition, as if he were speaking directly to her. "We can't eliminate pain," he would say, "but we can be there for each other."

It gave her a lift whenever she saw him, on or off the pulpit, as it did this evening, after work. She was in the church office, printing out the order for service, feeling a little blue, when, without notice, Franklin dropped by, and his appearance immediately cheered her.

"What are you doing here?" she asked him. "It's your off-week."

"Needed a book," he said. He scanned the shelves and pulled out a paperback, *The Phenomenology of Spirit*, and tucked it into his messenger bag. "How's Stephanie? Nervous?"

For the lay-led service this Sunday, one of the members, Stephanie Weiler, would be giving a talk—her first—entitled "How My Dog Taught Me to Be a Better UU."

"A basket case," Jeanette said. "She's already made Siobhan listen to her rehearse three times."

"I'm sure she'll do great," Franklin told Jeanette. He was wearing jeans, a suede jacket, and a pair of spiffy ankle boots—leather and walnut-brown, buffed to a high sheen.

Forty-one years old, he had dark brown hair, thick and wavy, which he kept mussed and somewhat long, wisping his earlobes. His eyes were his best feature—green and alert, above sharp cheekbones and a straight nose—accentuated by his habit of glancing at things askance, sideways peeps that made him appear boyish, mischievous. He seemed taller than he actually was, five-nine, because he was lean and athletic, the muscles on his forearms ropy and veined.

He had the beginnings of a potbelly, however, and his shoulders were too narrow for his body, his chest concave, topped by a sinewy, equine neck. His head, too, was small, as was his chin, and he was badly nearsighted, requiring chunky silver-rimmed eyeglasses. He could be comely from certain angles, yet stringy and queerly proportioned and hollowed-out from others. All the same, when they had been interviewing ministerial candidates, his looks were noted, sotto voce, by several women (and a few men) in the church, and Jeanette had been among his admirers.

He lingered in the office, leaning against the doorway and smiling awkwardly, as if he wanted to discuss something with her but didn't know where to begin. "Listen," he said finally, "you almost done here? Want to get a drink somewhere?"

She was surprised. They had gone out for lunch a few times on Saturdays if they both happened to be working in the office, but otherwise they never socialized together, just the two of them.

"Do Buddhists drink?" she asked.

"There are all sorts of Buddhists," Franklin said.

In separate cars, they drove to the Memory Den—Jeanette's suggestion—which was near the harbor, an outpost for fishermen, surfers, and ne'er-do-wells. Franklin had never been to the bar before, and, actually, neither had Jeanette, reminded of it only because Anna had proposed going there the other day. No one from the church would see them in the dive. She wasn't certain why, but she thought it best for them to seek seclusion. It felt like they were doing something illicit, and the idea excited Jeanette.

The fact was, she had become a little infatuated with Franklin in the last few months, meeting with him regularly in her new role on the board—feelings she kept to herself, and which she considered fundamentally innocent. It was a commonplace, a cliché, for a woman in her position to have a tiny little crush on the minister, and she knew she would never, ever think to act on it.

They entered the Memory Den together. There were only a handful of people inside the dingy, windowless building, all older men, playing pool.

"You run in glamorous circles," Franklin said.

There was no table service. They ordered at the bar—a beer for Franklin, a glass of Merlot for Jeanette—which he insisted on buying. When he got his change, he laid down a dollar bill, hesitated, then added another single. "I never know what to tip," he said as they settled into a booth near the back. "Especially in hotels. Until I was in my early thirties, I didn't even know I was supposed to tip the housekeeper."

"A lot of people don't."

"But the guests at the Centurion, I imagine they're pretty generous," Franklin said. "Or is that indecorous to ask?"

"I'll get a ten now and then, but two, three bucks is more typical."

"I would've thought they'd be bigger tippers at a high-end resort like that."

"At this motel where I used to work," Jeanette said, "I was lucky to get spare change, if anything. Sometimes people would leave religious pamphlets for me on the nightstand. Once in a while, used tampons."

"No."

"And used condoms." She had no compunctions discussing such matters with Franklin. He might have been her pastor, but he wasn't the least bit puritanical. He seemed, in fact, a little titillated.

"Where was this?" he asked.

"The Holiday Breeze in Pacifica."

For six months, she had cleaned twenty-five rooms a day at the Holiday Breeze. She'd find porn magazines underneath beds, the pages swollen and warped; straps hanging from headboards; forgotten dildos and vibrators in drawers. Couples would have period sex; blood would be everywhere; it'd look like a murder scene. Biohazards were a daily occurrence: syringes, razor blades, bent and blackened spoons, crumpled tinfoil, cans of whipped cream, menthol chest rubs, cotton balls, glassine bags. The sheets and furniture and carpet would be stained with bong water, burned with holes, littered with cigarette butts and roach ends. Someone once used a room as a mobile meth lab, and they had to call the fire department to remove the leftover chemicals. Regularly there'd be vomit, piss, and shit to clean up. Dog shit, cat shit, people shit. Turds deposited in coffeepots. Used toilet paper thrown on the floor instead of flushed. Teenagers would have parties, tear apart the rooms, spray beer and soda on the walls, fling pizzas against the ceiling, puke in the shower, take shits in the sink.

"Holy crap," Franklin said. "Excuse the pun."

Just as appalling had been the attitude of the motel maids. They'd pop the sheets, not changing them between guests. They'd pick trash up from the carpet but wouldn't bother to vacuum. They'd run a washcloth over spots in the tub but wouldn't scrub the whole thing. They'd clean glasses with Pledge and a toilet rag. They'd blot semen stains on the bedspreads with a wet sponge until they were marginally blended.

"No wonder you'd get tampons for tips," he said.

"That was never me," Jeanette said. "I always cleaned everything."

"I know, I know," Franklin said. "You're one of the most conscientious people I've ever met, Jeanette. I would've left you a ten-spot for sure."

Was he flirting with her? She thought he might be, and she was enjoying it. She had been curious why he'd asked her out—if this was just a casual drink, or something else—and she still wasn't certain, but she felt safe. She knew that neither of them had any designs beyond banter.

Franklin bought them another round of drinks and, coaxed by Jeanette, told her stories about his Peace Corps days in Togo, West Africa. She hadn't heard them in such detail before, and she was fascinated. She was having fun. She couldn't remember the last time she'd had so much fun.

A few more people trickled into the Memory Den. "You see those two guys over there?" Jeanette said. "Tank and Skunk B. They were pals with my brother in high school. You'd never know it, looking at them now, but they used to be hard-core surfers."

"At Rummy Creek?" Franklin asked.

"Yeah." Rummy Creek was a famous big-wave break just north of town.

"Your brother was a surfer, too?"

Jeanette glanced over to Tank and Skunk B again. When they'd come into the bar, they'd given her the once-over, but didn't recognize her. "No. Tank and Skunk were major pot-heads, and so was Jeremy. It got him sent to prison."

At once she regretted the gaffe. There was an unspoken agreement in their family to conceal Jeremy's record. More so, she was sorry to have broken the mood. Franklin had been lounging against the backrest of the booth, relaxed, but now he sat up, solemn and alert, ready to dole out ministerial empathy.

"Substance abuse?" he asked.

"That's the ironic thing—he'd pretty much stopped smoking weed, and he never got into anything more serious."

At the time, Jeremy was beginning to make a name for himself as a chef in San Francisco. Yet in culinary school, he had worked as a bike messenger for a company that delivered pot door-to-door, and had kept a stake in it. When the company got busted, Jeremy was indicted on federal charges for conspiracy. He served ten months in Lompoc, which was no Club Fed. He was now making grilled cheese for a food truck in Portland.

"I didn't even know you had a brother," Franklin said. "You have an older sister, too, don't you?"

"Younger. Julie. She lives in San Diego. She was an accident. My mother had her when she was thirty-nine." The exact age Jeanette was now.

"I'm ashamed to say this, but it occurs to me I don't know a lot about you, Jeanette."

The frivolity between them had perforated. "I bet you want to know why I've never been married," Jeanette said. That was what everyone always asked her. *Why are you single? What's wrong with you? How'd you end up an old maid?*

"I wasn't going to ask that," Franklin said.

"No?" Jeanette said, because it was impossible to answer, to explain all the heartaches and disappointments that divided who she had once been and who she was now. She didn't understand it herself, as often as she turned it over in her head. She had thought she was going to have a life, and then one day she had looked up and it was over, and she'd become a person who lived in the past, not in the present or future.

She had had a scholarship to study documentary photography at the Corcoran School. During high school, she had gone to the town of Watsonville—just inland from Monterey Bay—to volunteer after the Loma Prieta earthquake, and she had shot photos of the farm and cannery workers who were encamped in tents in Callaghan Park. One of the photographs was published in the *Santa Cruz Sentinel*, and it was picked up by the Associated Press and reprinted in hundreds of newspapers. She had brimmed with ambition. Once she got to the Corcoran, she had planned to intern at *National Geographic* or the *Washington Post*, and then, after graduating, land a job with *Time* or *Newsweek* or *Mother Jones* and travel the globe.

She never received her degree. She never attended a single class. She never stepped foot on campus. In time, she quit taking photographs entirely.

"You and Yadin seem to be a good match," Franklin said.

"Do you think?"

"Things are good between you two?"

Why was he asking this? she wondered. Did it seem like she and Yadin weren't getting along? Had Yadin said something to Franklin? She knew that Yadin had been going to him for pastoral care.

"Things are good," she told Franklin.

She excused herself and went to the bathroom. After peeing, she washed her hands and checked her face in the dimly lit mirror. She thought she looked haggard. At least her eyebrows were beginning to grow back in. She had been trying to follow a makeover tip from a magazine last week and had gotten overzealous plucking the hairs. She didn't know why she got so absorbed reading about beauty treatments and fashion trends. It was silly of her, wasting her money on these magazines. She wanted to improve herself—look prettier, more stylish, younger—but she never really did anything about it. She never changed her hair, which she cut herself. She didn't diet or exercise. She was too much of a

penny-pincher to ever buy any of the clothes or accessories in
the magazines, and she was too modest to bring attention to
herself with a lot of makeup, always preferring, for instance,
clear gloss to lipstick, eschewing perfume, never straying, as
it were, from the Centurion's grooming standards. She'd be
better off, she thought, if she just accepted that her destiny
was to be dowdy.

She returned to the booth. Franklin was hunched over the
table, scratching the corner of the label from his beer bottle. She changed the subject to the UUA's General Assembly.
In three weeks, Jeanette, Franklin, and the president of the
Aptos fellowship would be traveling together to Charlotte,
North Carolina, for the national conference—Jeanette's first.
Over four thousand people were scheduled to attend, and she
was looking forward to the trip. The only other times she had
been out of the state were to visit Jeremy in Oregon and Julie
in Seattle, when she had been in university there.

"Do you think we'll have any free time for sightseeing?"
she asked Franklin.

"I don't know what there is to sightsee there."

"I'm a little worried about the flight, the layover in Minneapolis. It's only thirty-eight minutes. I'd hate for us to miss
our connection. I wish we could've afforded the nonstop
flight."

Franklin didn't answer her. He was staring at the ball
game on the overhead TV, Technicolor flashes reflecting
off his glasses. She hadn't known he was a sports fan. She
segued to questions about the church's own annual meet-

ing, which would occur just before they left for the General Assembly.

"Did Vivian say when the membership committee will give us the final survey?" she asked. "I can't get a straight answer from her. We should've gotten it a week ago."

He didn't respond.

"Franklin?"

He shifted his gaze toward Jeanette and looked at her—steadily but without expression—for at least eight full seconds. "Look," he finally said, "there's something I need to tell you, but I'm going to ask you not to share it with anyone else. It needs to stay between us for the time being. Can you do that for me?"

Jeanette was unsettled. She had no idea what Franklin was about to reveal to her. "Yes."

"I'm only telling you this because, as the board president, you deserve fair warning, even though—and please believe me about this—nothing's for sure yet. These are purely contingencies. That's why I'd rather not have anyone else know. I'd hate for people to get upset and then have all the fuss for naught."

"What is it?" Jeanette asked. Her immediate thought, of course, was cancer—something detected in a checkup, waiting on the results of a biopsy.

"LMS submitted another proposal, and the city council's been reviewing it, and there's the possibility—"

"Wait. What's LMS?"

"Library Management Services, the for-profit that runs

municipal libraries, the company the city council got a bid from, back in February. They submitted a revised proposal last week and flew up from Riverside on Monday and met with the council in a closed session. It's like a secret cabal. So much for the transparency they promised. It's Gerry Lowry who's undermining everything and pushing to privatize."

Gerry Lowry was the city manager, the chief administrative officer of Rosarita Bay, to whom all department heads and employees reported.

"But I thought they decided to leave the library alone," Jeanette said.

"They did, but Lowry put it back on the table. How much you want to bet there's a kickback in the offing? Now the council's leaning toward accepting their bid."

"What would that mean?"

"What would it mean?" Franklin said. "It'd mean the city would no longer have to pay for the library staff's CalPERs and health plans anymore. It'd mean that *if* LMS opts to keep the current employees, a big if—you know they won't keep everyone—they'd have to take salary cuts and make monthly contributions for medical and a 401(k). It'd mean, in short, they'd get screwed. And the person it'd affect most would be Caroline."

"Would she be let go?" Jeanette asked.

"She doesn't know," Franklin said. "Having to subsidize family health coverage, losing that pension, it'd be crippling for us, especially with how little I make. Caroline anticipated something like this might happen. She wanted a backup plan, so she sent out some applications, and she's been offered the county librarian job in Mariposa. If the council goes with LMS, she'll probably take it."

"You would move?" Jeanette asked, panicked by the thought. How would she manage without Franklin? What would happen to their church? She knew that small UU congregations like theirs often collapsed when a well-liked minister left.

"Mariposa's in the Sierra Nevadas in the middle of nowhere, a town of two thousand," Franklin said. "There's not a single stoplight in the entire county. It's a tourist stop for people driving to Yosemite. There're no UU churches there or in Oakhurst. There's a small fellowship in Merced, a bigger church in Fresno, but nothing's available right now. I checked. I called."

"What would you do there?"

"Work in a gift shop? Maybe a motel? I don't know. I'd probably have to give up being a minister altogether."

"We could picket city hall," Jeanette said, "start a lobbying campaign. We could ask everyone in the congregation to get signatures on a petition. We'll have them all show up at the council meeting and speak."

Franklin tore off more bits of the label from his beer bottle. "Caroline's been working on this round-the-clock since January. She's come up with all sorts of studies and projections and external evaluations. She's collected testimonials and letters and signatures. She's gone in front of the council six times. But it's a puny issue to them, a triviality. Everyone in town's much more concerned about the police department. At this point, there's really nothing more that can be done."

"I can't accept that."

"You'll have to. Besides, there's a deeper issue," Franklin said to Jeanette. "I'm not sure Caroline wants me to go with her."

"What do you mean?" she asked.

"She didn't tell me she was applying for these jobs. We've been— Things haven't been good between us. Not for a long time. I think she's been having an affair with someone."

"Who?" Jeanette blurted. "Someone at the library?" Of all marriages, all families, she had assumed Franklin and Caroline's was among the strongest. There never seemed to be anything amiss, no tension in evidence when they were together. And they were so patient and attentive with their children, Lane, Peyton, and Rebecca. They seemed happy.

Franklin took off his eyeglasses and grabbed a napkin, as if to clean the lenses, but then placed the glasses down on the table. "I thought, for a while," he said, "she might be having an affair with Yadin."

"Yadin?" Jeanette almost laughed. "Seriously?"

"Have you noticed anything lately?" Franklin asked. "Yadin acting strange or canceling plans, making excuses, things like that? Has he, I don't know, seemed nervous or edgy?"

So this was why Franklin had invited her out for a drink, why he'd asked about Jeanette and Yadin's relationship. He wanted Jeanette to confirm or contradict his suspicions.

Sometimes she was miffed that Yadin had become closer

to Caroline, supposedly because of his interest in this long-dead poet, Hopkins. She saw them chatting together, getting chummy, during coffee hour at the church. Caroline could be condescending and irritable—frankly, at times, a bitch—but she was sexy. Skinny, even after three children. She had extraordinarily good posture—the spine of a former ballet dancer or yogi—and long legs. Her skin was milky, her hair dark, her features sharp. Jeanette could see how someone like Caroline, with her looks and education, would appeal to Yadin, but the idea that something untoward could be going on between them had never occurred to her until now. Was it possible they were sleeping together? Was that why Yadin seemed so restless lately?

"Have you confronted Caroline about this?" she asked Franklin.

"She denies it. She denies everything. She says she's not having an affair with anyone," Franklin said. "I don't know. Maybe she's not. We fight constantly—mostly about money. Splitting these two part-time jobs, commuting to Aptos, it's taken a toll. There's no security in either of them, no bene-fits, and the pay's not sustainable. People wonder why the ministry's such a high-burnout profession. This is why."

There were two reddish dents from the pads of his glasses on the bridge of his nose. His eyes were rheumy. He was one of those people who looked better with his glasses on than off.

"She wouldn't really leave you, would she?" Jeanette asked.

"I don't know. Either way, I'd have to follow her to Mariposa if I want to see my kids. I love my kids so much," Franklin told her, and his voice cracked with the last word. "Let's hope it doesn't come to that. Let's hope the council votes next Friday to keep the status quo, and this will all be moot. We can stay here, and we can work on our marriage, figure things out."

"I wish there was something I could do," Jeanette said.

"Me, too." He slipped his glasses back on, tucking in the temples. "You know what I'd miss most if I had to leave? I'd miss working with you, Jeanette," he said, and he reached across the table and placed his hand over hers and held it. "I really would."

The latest counselor at the Community Credit and Housing Program was named Joel Hanrahan—lanky, in his thirties, wrinkled shirt, dark curly hair with a strange springy half goatee. The beard was disconcerting to Yadin. It wasn't the type of facial hair he expected on a bureaucrat. There was no mustache, nothing around Hanrahan's mouth, just a thick divot of hair on the end of his chin that tufted out two inches and looked as if it'd been glued on as a joke.

"I've been hearing about refinancing and mortgage modifications," Yadin told him. "I see interest rates going way down. I'd really like to lower my monthlies. You think there's any way I'd qualify?"

"Honestly?" Hanrahan said. "Probably not a chance

in hell. After a BK7, it'd be implausible at best. They might laugh just taking a gander at your application."

Yadin had declared bankruptcy a little over two years ago. By that point, he'd accrued over forty thousand dollars in medical bills and credit-card debt. He was continually getting harassed by collection agencies and, to stave them off, was hawking everything he could to pawnshops and scavengers on Craigslist: his grandmother's furnishings, dishes, and appliances, down to her stove and refrigerator, her jewelry, his stereo system, his extensive vinyl collection. Then he began receiving letters threatening foreclosure of his house. In desperation, he sold nearly all his guitars and musical equipment, including his prized 1957 Martin D-21. The letters and calls persisted, becoming more ominous. At last, he confided in Jeanette and spelled out to her just how bad his situation was. She took him to CCHP in San Vicente, where a counselor told them that a foreclosure action was unlikely, because those particular lenders would get nothing from the sale. Yet he could always be sued by them. The counselor recommended Yadin file for Chapter 7 bankruptcy.

His grandmother's property did not come, beyond taxes, without encumbrances. She'd had two mortgages. Yet at the time of the bequest, Yadin had been assured that he had plenty of equity. No one foresaw the housing bubble bursting, after which the value of the house plummeted.

Chapter 7 was a liquidation process. Yadin could wipe away all of his unsecured debt in one fell swoop. And because the balance of his mortgages was greater than the value of the property, minus California's homestead exemption, he could keep the house. But almost everything he owned, which wasn't much by then, had to be auctioned.

Bankruptcy seemed like a disgrace that was not only financial, but moral. Yet Jeanette stood by him, as did Joe, who lent him, against his future wages, most of the two thousand dollars he needed to hire an attorney.

Now that it had been two years since his official discharge date—a decisive legal milestone—he wanted to examine his options. The problem was, every time he went to the Community Credit and Housing Program, the counselor he'd seen before was no longer there and he had to start from scratch with someone else, always beginning with how to pronounce his first name correctly: *Ya-deen*, not *Yay-din* or *-dine*. (More than once in clubs before a performance, he had been introduced as Yannich, Yadda, and Yanni.)

Hanrahan flipped through Yadin's file. "You have your pay stubs?"

Yadin dug into the manila envelope on his lap and pulled out the stubs. "I've been with Matsuda Wall to Wall almost three years now," he said, "and sometimes I pick up shifts at the Brewing Company."

"Doing what?"

"Washing dishes." This was how he had ended up repaying Joe ahead of schedule. "I've done everything the other counselors told me to do."

"Which is very admirable." Hanrahan leaned back in his chair and put his feet up on the desk. "Ideally what you'd like to do is consolidate your mortgages with an FHA-insured refi, but you'd have to go through all the hoops—even more, with the BK7—of applying for a mortgage, and lenders are pickier than ever these days. Your FICO's 618 right now. You'd be considered a subprime borrower, so even if, by some sort of miracle, you managed to get approved, your rate would be astronomical. The first step, I suppose, would be a property reappraisal. Maybe your FMV has rebounded enough so you're no longer underwater. But I can't imagine your LTV will get below seventy-five percent anytime soon, and with your BK7 to boot, a refi, I would venture, would be damn near impossible."

Yadin could barely decipher what Hanrahan was saying. "Is there any way I could get a cheap loan?" he asked. "I could really use some extra cash."

"You want a loan or a refi? They're two different things."

"Both, I guess," Yadin said.

"A HELOC?"

"What?"

"Home equity line of credit," Hanrahan said.

"That'd be cheaper than a personal loan, right?"

"By miles. But there's a catch. You default, they can foreclose. What do you want the money for?"

"I want to release a record," Yadin said.

"A record," Hanrahan said. "What kind of record?"

"Music. I'm a musician." When he'd informed other counselors that he had been a musician, they had scrutinized him with new suspicion, assuming he was a junkie. Joe did, too, at first, which had been understandable, considering Jeremy's history.

"Professional?" Hanrahan asked. "Or wannabe?"

"It's been a while, but yeah, I used to have a label. Inland Records. I put out four albums with them. But this would be an indie self-release."

"What kind of music?"

"Alt-country," Yadin said. "I've recorded some other stuff, under different names: Ajax Montage. The Falconer. Pelvic Mischief."

In his younger days, he had not been able to stop himself from making music. One year when he'd been signed to Inland Records, he produced enough material for three albums, the last of which could have been a double CD. (Inland told him he needed to be more selective.) To expend his restlessness, Yadin had ventured into side projects—lo-fi synthwave, electronic beats, organ riffs, and metal jams, mixed with found sounds and field recordings. These albums he released under other monikers on cassette tape. He had learned that in many prisons, particularly in New York and Illinois, inmates could only listen to music on screwless, clear cassettes from an approved vendor, primarily a distributor in Van Nuys, California. Yadin contacted the company, and they had put his cassettes—which proved to be surprisingly popular—in their catalog, selling them to correctional facilities and the general public by mail order.

Since Inland had dropped him, and since his manager was no longer returning his calls, Yadin figured he could record his new album on the TASCAM machine he had used for his side projects and self-release it. He intended to sell the album through his own indie label on CD, vinyl, digital, and cassette. That was, if he could ever secure enough money to produce it.

Hanrahan was typing into his computer and scrolling through pages, presumably Googling Yadin's name. He didn't know what was on the Internet about him these days—he never bothered to check. He didn't have his own website, but he assumed there were still links to his albums, music guide entries, some reviews, perhaps a Wikipedia page—enough to confirm he had once been a legitimate recording artist.

"I could do it pretty cheap, the album," Yadin said. "Ten thousand. Maybe seventy-five hundred." He extracted a handwritten budget from his manila envelope: rough estimates for mixing, mastering, pressing CDs and vinyl, and miscellany like cardboard eco-wallets stenciled in one color.

Hanrahan pushed his keyboard aside. "Why don't you just do a Kickstarter or Indiegogo campaign?"

"I'm not very good with computer stuff," Yadin said. He could do searches and order items, but invariably needed the reference librarian's help to do anything else online.

"That's no excuse. It's not that hard. You could learn. Or get someone to do it for you."

"Maybe. If it comes to that," Yadin said. "I'll be honest. I've been out of the industry a long time. I don't know what kind of a following I still have out there. It could be no one remembers me."

"You realize you don't have to cost out separate masters for CD and vinyl?" Hanrahan said, scanning the budget sheet.

Yadin saw the serendipity of having Hanrahan as his counselor today. "But the compression, the signal-to-noise ratios, the dynamic range—they're all different," Yadin said.

"I know that," Hanrahan said. "I mean most engineers these days will give you both for the same price. You tracking this yourself? You don't have studio rental time on here."

"Home recording," Yadin told him. He watched Hanrahan combing his fingers through his weird half goatee, stroking it forward, not inward. "So," Yadin said to Hanrahan, "you're a musician, too." He knew not to ask professional or wannabe.

"Give me a few days to look over your case," Hanrahan said. "I still think a HELOC's out of reach for you, and inadvisable, anyway, but maybe a refi's viable somehow. I strongly doubt it, but if you could reduce your rate even just a little bit, you might be able to save some money in the long run— maybe enough to release your album someday."

He never made a formal announcement to anyone that he was quitting. He simply fell away from the music business. With the twin despairs of his finances and his Ménière's, his hearing becoming so spotty that sometimes he couldn't tune his guitar by ear anymore, it had seemed unimaginable to him that he would ever be able to make music again. When he was dismissed by his label, it seemed the decision to retire had been rendered for him. He knew that Jeanette was secretly relieved his career had ended. She was practical, and she had made it clear that she thought being a musician was impractical.

If not for the happenstance of visiting the library three months ago, on the first Saturday of March, he likely would have never begun writing the songs for his new album. As he walked by the community room, he had heard Caroline reciting a stanza of a poem:

My aspens dear, whose airy cages quelled,
  Quelled or quenched in leaves the leaping sun,
All felled, felled, are all felled;
  Of a fresh and following folded rank
        Not spared, not one
        That dandled a sandalled
      Shadow that swam or sank
On meadow & river & wind-wandering weed-winding
  bank.

Intrigued, Yadin took a seat in the back of the room, and he learned from the slides being projected onto a screen that Caroline was lecturing on a nineteenth century English poet named Gerard Manley Hopkins.

"What's notable to me," she said, "is how the melancholic subject of the poem—the chopping down of a stand of beloved trees to make way for a development—is conveyed with language that's so full of music and percussion and surprises, beginning with the collocation of 'airy cages,' juxtaposing freedom and entrapment, wildness and industrialization."

Caroline discussed Hopkins's background, how he had converted to Catholicism and become a Jesuit priest, never publishing any of his poetry during his lifetime, so as not to violate the humility of his position. "He believed that all the temporal pursuits and indulgences of everyday life, especially ambition, should be left behind. He advocated asceticism, or a sort of poverty, in order to be more attentive to God's voice and encounter Him more deeply. Only by reining in your selfish desires could you truly get in touch with your spirituality."

It turned out that Caroline, before getting her master's in library science, had been pursuing a Ph.D. in Victorian literature at Boston College, and the lecture on Hopkins had been requested by a Catholic group, timed for the start of Lent. At the end of the session, Caroline offered the group a packet of Hopkins's poems and writings to reflect upon; she suggested they might use them to embark on a quasi-Ignatian spiritual exercise, going out into nature in silent meditation and keeping a journal on what they experienced.

"Are you Catholic?" Yadin asked Caroline after the lecture.

"I'm not a practicing Catholic anymore, but I once was."

"You believe in God?"

"I do," Caroline said. "But don't tell anyone."

He was pretty certain she was kidding. Wasn't she? She could be prickly, and her sense of humor always threw him. "Does that cause a conflict with Franklin?" he asked.

"Not as much as I'd like."

As far as Yadin could determine, Franklin was mostly a Buddhist (like many UUs, he was reluctant to profess a particular creed). He often referred to the teachings of Thích Nhất Hạnh, the Vietnamese Zen Buddhist peace activist, though occasionally, too, to David Steindl-Rast, the Benedictine monk.

Franklin's sermons largely revolved around mindfulness, inclusion, and empathy—all pretty much in line with Unitarian Universalism's Seven Principles. "UU is about deeds, not creeds," he would say. "Faith doesn't have to be synonymous with doctrinal belief. It's simply about keeping a place of hope and meaning at the center of our lives."

All of this had reassured Yadin at first. Unitarian Universalism had allowed him to draw the benefits of fellowship, yet avoid what UUs called "The God Issue." In the last year, though, he had become strangely fidgety. The services—and Unitarian Universalism as a whole—had begun to feel too amorphous, even somewhat empty to him. Franklin's sermons sounded good on delivery but were, upon further reflection, often circular, repetitive, and touchy-feely.

Even adherents acknowledged that UU's lack of strong denominational beliefs was a problem. Its Seven Principles were sometimes referred to as the Seven Dwarfs or Seven Banalities, indoctrinating UUs to walk the fine line between confusion and indecision. There were other jokes: What's the Holy Trinity for UUs? Reduce, Reuse, and Recycle. Why is it dangerous to piss off a UU in the South? He might burn a question mark on your front lawn. How does a UU begin a prayer? To Whom It May Concern. Why do UUs have trouble singing in the choir? They're always reading ahead to see if they'll agree with the next verse. What do you get when you cross a Jehovah's Witness with a UU? Someone who knocks on your door, then says, "I don't know why I'm here."

Yadin tried to talk to Jeanette about it. During each worship service, there was always a juncture where Franklin would say, "If you pray, please pray; if you meditate, please meditate," and everyone would bow their heads and close their eyes.

"What do you feel in those moments?" Yadin asked Jeanette.

"What do you mean, what do I feel?"

"Do you feel anything? As an atheist?"

"I feel at peace. I feel gratitude for the people around me."

Supposedly forty-six percent of UU members considered themselves agnostics or atheists, and the UUA explicitly welcomed them. In addition to people of all faiths, they embraced those with no faith. Yet Yadin suspected that many members of their church were closet theists of some sort, privately beholden to a deity, sustained by the promise of an afterlife or rebirth. During the moments of prayer, he felt them radiating serenity; he imagined they were communing with a larger spirit or essence, and were being transported or touched or consoled by it. He wished he could join them.

Yadin went to see Franklin.

"This is very common, what you're feeling," Franklin told him in his office. "You should think of it as an encouraging sign, actually. It's all part of the process. You and you alone should choose what you want to believe. Brother David reminds us that *I believe* means *I give my heart to this*. What do you give your heart to, Yadin?"

Franklin handed him a workbook for a program called "Building Your Own Theology." It contained various exercises, and the culminating assignment was to write your own credo statement, a few hundred words declaring your personal convictions. It took Yadin days to pen. In the end, he stooped to clichés about treating others as he wished to be treated and making a difference in other people's lives.

He wanted something more definitive—a clearer direction or path to follow. He wouldn't have minded creeds, rules, if they could furnish him with some reassurance and tranquillity. He wanted a religion with more structure, more vigor. He wanted, he realized, to believe in God.

Hearing about Gerard Manley Hopkins—not just his poems, but about his life—stimulated something in Yadin. Two days after the lecture, he returned to the library and asked Caroline for a copy of the packet she had distributed to the Catholic group.

"Don't tell Franklin I'm giving you this," she said.

"Really?" he asked.

"No. That's the maddening thing. He wouldn't mind at all. He'd applaud it. He's polymorphously perverse—at least when it comes to religion."

"I'm going through something," Yadin said. "I'm kind of having doubts about UU."

"A crisis of faith?"

"I guess."

"You want answers to all those epistemological questions: Who am I, why am I here, what's it all about, why do I feel so alone, is there any meaning to the things I've gone through."

Disquieted, Yadin said, "That's exactly right."

"And UU isn't cutting it for you, so now you're looking for the transcendent, the numinous, the ecstatic. Would that do it for you?" she asked.

"Maybe," Yadin said. "What's numinous mean?"

"Suggesting the presence of a divinity or strong spiritual quality."

"Oh. I thought it was more like luminous."

"Similar connotations. The UUA commissioned a self-study a few years ago," Caroline said. "It concluded that in order for a religious organization to grow, it needs clearly defined boundaries. But you can't put a boundary around a vacuum. That's why UU keeps losing members. People drift away because they don't see the point to it anymore."

"Do you?" he asked her.

"I'm married to Franklin," she said. "We have three children."

"That's not really an answer."

"Isn't it?" Caroline said.

That night, Yadin tried to read the photocopied poems in the packet she had given to him, then went back to the library.

"Could you explain some of these lines to me?" he asked Caroline.

"Explicate, you mean," she said.

He faltered. "Okay."

"Don't look so scared," Caroline said. "Tell me what you want to know."

He pointed to the second line of "Pied Beauty" and asked, "What's 'couple-colour'?"

"It just means the sky's two colors—blue, 'dappled' with white clouds."

"What about 'brinded'?"

"Same as 'brindle'—brown fur streaked with another color," she said.

He moved his fingertip to the third line. "How about 'rose-moles all in stipple'?"

"The reddish dots on a trout, as if they've been stippled or painted on. Are you going to make me do this with every line?"

He pretty much did. She accommodated him for the rest of "Pied Beauty" and most of "God's Grandeur," then told Yadin that, for the other poems, he would have to fend for himself.

"But I can't even make heads or tails of what these poems are about," he said.

"There are only two subjects in lyric poetry: love and death. You figure it out."

She lent him a dictionary and a thick academic book on Hopkins's poetry, most of which was indecipherable to him. He had never done well in school, and he was aware that, in general, he wasn't very smart. Yet he began to understand that it wasn't absolutely necessary for him to know what every word meant—they were so strange and funny, the words, combined so queerly—or even what was being discussed in each poem. It was only important for him to give in to the sound of the words, their rhythms and rhymes and proximities.

"You again?" Caroline said.

She was standing in the periodicals section. The library, as usual, was bustling. There were just fifty seats and twelve computers in three rooms, and kids often had to sit on the floor between stacks to read.

"I want to do what you suggested to the Catholic group— the spiritual exercise," Yadin said. "When does Lent begin?"

"Tomorrow," Caroline told him. "Ash Wednesday."

"How do I go about it? What's the first step?"

"I wasn't suggesting anything formal. Just take a walk. One step in front of the other."

"That's it?"

Caroline gathered a newspaper and put it on a shelf. "Saint Ignatius of Loyola originally designed his spiritual exercises for thirty-day retreats. Then it got spread out to cover the forty days of Lent. It's serious work, and no one has the time or patience for anything like that anymore. I certainly don't have the time or patience to guide you through it, nor is it my place. But if you must know, the key theme is discernment, observing what Ignatius called motions of the soul, the interior movement of thoughts, emotions, desires, imaginings, which he said can manifest themselves in two ways: consolation or desolation."

"Explicate for me," Yadin said.

"It's 'explain,' in this case," she said. "Consolation is being able to feel the presence of God, seeing God's grace in the everyday world, having a deep sense of gratitude for His love and mercy and companionship, which makes us, in turn, more alive and connected to others."

"And desolation?"

"The absence of God. Darkness and emptiness. Moving through life without any purpose or meaning. Being constantly assailed by doubts and regrets and temptations and selfish, materialistic preoccupations. Always feeling anxious and restive and cut off from everyone, leaving you without hope or the ability to love or think past yourself."

Yadin felt himself tingling with inchoate recognition. "How do you move from desolation to consolation?" he asked her.

"I can't tell you that. No one can. It's an individual journey." She nudged several magazines on a rack so they were spaced evenly apart. "Someone whose teachings appealed to Christian-leaning UUs, Forrest Church, he once said that religion is the human response to the dual reality of being alive and having to die. He had terminal cancer, but he didn't blame God or ask for healing. He said knowing he would die, each day became more precious and beautiful to him. He said, 'You walk through the valley of the shadow, and it's riddled with light.' Replace 'riddled' with 'dappled,' and you have Hopkins. He was inflamed by the beauty of the natural world, which he believed was not only God's gift to us, but also God incarnate."

"So just take walks?" Yadin asked.

"Not that complicated, is it?" she said. "Franklin and I used to go hiking all the time. That's how we met—the Boston chapter of the Appalachian Mountain Club. I was at BC, he was in seminary at Andover Newton. It used to be our favorite thing to do, rambling into the woods, camping back-country, following each other on single-tracks. I can't remember the last time we did anything like that, the two of us."

She looked down at the magazine in her hand, an edition of *Newsweek* covering the Arab Spring protests with the headline "Rage Goes Viral."

"Yes, just take a walk," she told Yadin, lifting a hinged display shelf and sliding the magazine on top of the back issues.

"Where should I go?" he asked.

"Anywhere. A beach, the woods. Look at the birds, the sky, the stars."

"And meditate? Or pray?"

"Read the poems aloud, see where they take you," Caroline said. "I've always thought poetry and prayer are similar engagements. They both speak in apostrophes." Before he could ask, she explained, "A speech or poem addressed to someone in the second-person—*you*, opposed to the first-person *I* or the third-person *she*."

He had never thought about it before, but that was what he did in lyrics. He nearly always wrote songs in second-person. Sometimes first, but never third, which he found awkward.

"I don't necessarily mean praying to God, or reflecting on God or the grandeur of God's presence," Caroline said. "Forget God entirely, if you want. Think of it as 'the other' or whatever you want to name it. Or don't name it at all. The numinous can be anything—nature, life, the mystery of existence, whatever you perceive as an essence or abstraction outside of yourself. Enter into deep listening by entering into deep silence."

"What should I be trying to hear?"

"Not an answer, if that's what you mean. Don't expect a voice calling to you, anything like that. The answer, if there is one, has to come from you."

She loaned him field guides for the flora and fauna in the area, and told him to keep a journal of his ruminations.

The next Saturday, Yadin set out to Pismo Beach, near the harbor, with the guides and the packet, and walked along the shore. It had rained most of January and all of February. It was mid-March now and dry, but cold, gray, windy. He sat down on a mound of sand, and gusts from the northwest buffeted the pages of his packet as he held them on his lap. He read some of the poems out loud to himself and tried to let Hopkins's words swirl and unfurl in his head. He peered up at the *chevy* of *silk-sack clouds* as they *moulded and melted* across the *wild world-mothering air*. He watched the *teeming thrills* of the swell, listened to the *thunder-purple* of waves as they *bleared, smeared* onto the *mazy sands*. He wanted to be inflamed, like Hopkins. He felt only frigidity, his face, fingers, and feet numb from the piercing wind.

A week later, a warmer day, he headed south, down Highway 1, to the Bidwell Marsh Preserve. On foot, he followed a path along a creek bordered by willows and cattails and bobbing yellow catkins. Eventually the creek widened into an estuary, where he spotted a great blue heron and several snowy egrets. *Song-fowl. Wippling wing.* A little ways onward, there was a meadow of *louched low grass, sunsplurged* with wildflowers. He crested the sand dunes and trekked down to an area of rocky shale reefs and explored the *water-wattled* tide pools. Breathing in the beach wrack, he watched a sea otter on its back in the golden green kelp beds and the *fawn-froth* of the incoming surf. He tried to meditate. He tried to observe the motions of his soul. He felt nothing.

On moonless nights, he drove along Skyview Ridge Road, following the contours of the hills until he was at a remove from any houses or streetlights, and goggled the stars, those *circle-citadels, shining from shook foil,* the *firefolk in the air, airy abeles set on a flare.* He tried to quiet his mind and invoke awe. He wanted to be shaken alive with

God's majesty, with the mystery and beauty of this world, with its infiniteness.

"Nothing's happening," he told Caroline at the library.

"It could be that nothing will ever happen," she said. "Or maybe you're just trying too hard. You can't force it or manufacture it. Even Hopkins struggled at times. Near the end of his life, he wrote six poems that came to be known as the Terrible Sonnets, or the Sonnets of Desolation. He agonized he'd failed as both a priest and a poet. He felt distant from God all of a sudden. He didn't have that direct colloquy with Him anymore, and he blamed himself for that failure—indulging in self-pity and ego. So you see, it's not a simple trajectory, a neat little upward path without dips and deviations."

The following Saturday, Yadin took to the redwood trails. The path was covered with damp, spongy topsoil, everything vibrantly green after the winter rains, the creeks rushing with runoff. He climbed into groves of live oaks and old-growth redwoods, many of them over three hundred feet tall. In the *thicket and thorp*, he sensed mischief, mirth, insects and little animals scampering about, peeking boo—*the diamond delves, the elves'-eyes.* Flitting overhead were thrushes and warblers, woodpeckers and western tanagers, their *trickle of song-strain* wringing *through the echoing timber. Weedio-weedio!*

He sat down and leaned against a redwood and, after several minutes, began to pray. *Dear God, I want to feel closer to you. I want to feel your grace. I want there to be a purpose and meaning to this life. I want to feel connected to you and be worthy of your companionship and mercy. Please, God, give me consolation.* He heard nothing in response, felt nothing. He wondered if he was doing something incorrectly—maybe he sounded too self-serving with all those *wants*—or, worse, if he was somehow ineligible for God's grace or even His acknowledgment.

He kept trying, going on excursions into the woods, on walks on beaches, on hikes in the hills, hoping to see what Hopkins saw, and one early morning he even crept into Our Lady of the Pillar, the Catholic church downtown, genuflecting and crossing himself as he entered, lurking in the rear pews as Mass was being held. Yet he kept failing. Weeks passed. Lent ended, Easter came and went. It was nearing the end of April. And still, whenever he opened his spiral-bound notebook to write down what he was experiencing, he had nothing to say.

The Sunday before Memorial Day, May 29, Yadin saw Jeanette, as always, before the service for choir rehearsal. Darnell had them go through two hymns from *Singing the Living Tradition*, and also a third song that Stephanie Weiler, this week's lay leader, had chosen: Simon & Garfunkel's "Bridge over Troubled Water."

There weren't many people in the sanctuary for the worship, less than twenty members, which was typical when Franklin was not preaching. Caroline and their three children usually traveled with him to the UU fellowship in Aptos on these alternate Sundays, but surprisingly they were here this morning.

The congregation moved briskly through the service, and Stephanie, nervous as she was, gave a funny and ultimately moving speech about how her dog, who'd died last month, had taught her to be a better UU.

After coffee hour, Yadin and Jeanette set off on their usual post-church run to Costco, Yadin driving them in his van, the engine straining as they climbed up Highway 71 toward San Vicente.

"How come Caroline and the kids didn't go to Aptos today?" Jeanette asked him.

"Someone said something about Peyton coming down with a cold."

"He looked fine to me."

"Maybe it was a migraine?" Yadin said. "I didn't catch the particulars."

"You didn't talk to Caroline?"

"No." It had been a month since he'd last solicited Caroline's help. His spiritual quest had taken a strange turn in late April—a metaphysical detour that didn't have much to do with Hopkins or even, perhaps, religion, yet had conveyed him to the new songs.

"I saw you at the food table together," Jeanette said.

"I said hello, that's all."

Caroline had been smearing strawberry jam onto a bagel half at the table, and her youngest child, Rebecca, had run up to her and asked for a bite. Caroline had feigned irritation, then said maybe she'd allow her a nibble. Yadin had watched as she slowly lowered the bagel, moved it toward Rebecca's mouth, then thrust it forward as if she were going to cram it into her daughter's face. Rebecca jumped back and giggled, as did Caroline—identical *heh-heh-heh*'s.

The hill was steepening, and Yadin pressed down harder on the accelerator, which seemed to have no appreciable effect.

"Is something going on between you two?" Jeanette asked.

"What do you mean?"

"Are you having an affair with Caroline?" Jeanette asked.

"What?" He thought for sure he had misheard her.

"Are you in love with her?"

"With Caroline?" Yadin asked. "That's ridiculous."

"Is it? Do you see her outside church or the library?"

"No, of course not," Yadin said.

"But you're attracted to her."

He was, a little, but his attraction was purely reflexive, and he knew not to admit it to Jeanette. "She used to get annoyed with all my questions about Hopkins. That was the biggest feature of our . . . conversations." He had almost blundered and said *relationship*. "I annoyed her."

"That's not an answer. Are you or are you not in love with Caroline?" she asked.

"Jeanette, I am not in love with Caroline. We are not having an affair. There is nothing going on between us. I am not attracted to her. Okay?"

She stared through the van's windshield. "Okay," she said.

She didn't say anything more the rest of the drive. At Costco, they split off with separate carts, Yadin going to the organic section. The place was more crowded than usual—people gathering supplies for Memorial Day barbecues, presumably. Not long ago, the bustle and bright lighting in a box store like this would have triggered a Ménière's episode in him. Supermarkets, even small ones, had always scared Yadin, and he had preferred doing all of his food shopping at 7-Elevens. Being able to weather Costco on a weekly basis represented significant progress. Yet today Yadin felt agitated as he navigated the aisles. Did Jeanette really think he could be having an affair with Caroline? Where had she gotten that idea?

It made him all the more apprehensive to confess what he'd actually been concealing from her—that instead of building an emergency fund and getting ahead on his mortgage payments, he had replaced his musical gear and intended to go seven to ten grand in debt for a self-released album that would, in all likelihood, never break even. He hadn't mentioned anything to her about seeing the credit counselor at CCHP. He'd said he was taking the afternoon off to get his teeth cleaned at a community dental clinic.

Truth be told, he was just as worried about how she would respond to his spiritual journey these past few months—the full extent of it, reading the Bible, buying a rosary. For Jeanette's sake, he was willing to stay on at the First Unitarian Universalist Church, but he was thinking of getting baptized.

They chanced upon each other in the produce section, and

Yadin girded himself for Jeanette to ask him more questions, make further accusations.

Instead, she looked down at the case of mineral water on the bottom rack of his grocery cart and said, "I heard there's a machine to make your own sparkling water. Maybe for your birthday?"

On the drive back to Rosarita Bay, she was in a softened mood, preoccupied now with his van, which was making even more of a racket struggling up the hill.

"That doesn't sound strange to you?" she asked.

"It always makes funny noises," he said. "It's old."

She crossed her legs and inadvertently shifted the worn floor mat with her foot. "You know you've got a hole in your floor? I can see the road."

He glanced over at the quarter-sized rupture in the rusted-out floor. Jeanette opened the passenger-side window and said something.

"What?" he asked.

She rolled the window back up halfway. "You're never going to pass your next inspection," she told him. "The exhaust's coming in through the floor. Something's loose or cracked under there."

The white cargo van was a 1997 Ford Econoline E350 with over 169,000 miles.

"You need to get it checked out," Jeanette said. "It's not safe."

Yadin ran through the repair costs for possible problems, none of which he could afford right now: the muffler, a bad gasket, the catalytic converter—he wasn't sure what else could be going awry.

He didn't know as much about automobiles as he should have. Every summer, his father would make Yadin and Davey go out to the driveway and rotate all four tires on his car and check the air pressure. Their father thought this would be good practice for them, a useful thing for a man to know. But it was a grueling undertaking for little boys, jacking up the car and torquing the crowbar and lifting the tires on and off. Lug nuts would be stuck, the crowbar would slip off, knuckles would crater-bleed. Worse, they had to take turns and do the job alone, one by one. Yadin always volunteered to go first so he could leave the lug nuts loosened for his brother.

The traffic slowed ahead of them, and they edged up to a Mercedes-Benz SUV. There was a sticker on its back bumper that read ROT IN HELL, OSAMA BIN LADEN. FROM AMERICA WITH LOVE. The Navy SEALs had killed bin Laden less than a month ago.

"We have a guest who has a new Mercedes-Benz, a convertible," Jeanette said. "I heard the valets have been washing and waxing it every day. She's been tipping really well. Everyone's falling over their feet for her. She's a celebrity. Or a former celebrity."

"Anyone I would know?" Yadin asked.

"I'm not supposed to say."

"You'd have to kill me first," he said. She smiled at this, which reassured him that she had tabled their earlier argument.

"All right, it's Mallory Wicks," Jeanette said. "Have you ever heard of her?"

Internally, Yadin halted, hearing the name. "Mallory Wicks?" he asked. "Mallory Wicks is at the Centurion?"

Long ago, in Raleigh, North Carolina, when they were in their early twenties, Yadin and Mallory had formed a band called Whisper Creek with a few friends, although often it had been just the two of them as a duo, Yadin on guitar, Mallory on fiddle, sharing the vocals. They had been lovers and bandmates for a year, and it had ended badly—his doing, his fault. They never spoke to each other again. Mallory absconded to Nashville and cracked the Country Top 40 with her first single, "Beds & Beer," and had kept going from there, all the way to Hollywood.

"I didn't think you'd know who she was," Jeanette said. "Or care."

It was impossible to fathom. "When'd she get to the hotel?" Yadin asked.

"Wednesday," Jeanette said. "She has the Miramar Suite. She got both the Spa and the Stay & Play packages—she's a golfer, wouldn't you know."

"Did you get assigned her room?"

"No. Clarisa, one of the floor supervisors, did."

He had never, not for a minute, ever imagined that Mallory might visit Rosarita Bay. "How long is she staying?" he asked.

"I think she's checking out tomorrow," Jeanette said. "Why?"

He took a shower, then inspected his face in the bathroom mirror. This was something Yadin used to despise—having to look at his face—and he still tended to avoid it, though there was no longer any reason to.

From the time he turned thirteen, he began having acne. Every morning, he'd awake to find new horrors on his face, red papules forming, whiteheads flowering. He'd pop the pimples with his fingers, squeeze until not only the pus but also the blood was expelled, kneading until the blood stopped flowing and had turned into a watery fluid. Then he'd fold up tiny squares of toilet paper and dab the centers against the ruptured pimples, trying to get the toilet-paper squares to stick on them (occasionally Scotch tape was required) and blot up vestigial fluid. He'd let them dry for thirty minutes to an hour, where-upon he would peel the squares off slowly and carefully. If all went well, the pimples would be flat and no longer open and oozing. The skin flaps would be beginning to bond together, and there wouldn't be too much surrounding redness. The timing was critical. If he popped a pimple too soon, the pus would not entirely burst out, and the whitehead would re-form. If he waited too long, the pus would turn rancid and yellow and harden and leave a hole in his skin after it was hollowed out. If he wasn't meticulous enough with the toilet-paper squares, there'd be a scab, which might break open inadvertently or spontaneously (just yawning could do it), and he'd have a seep of blood trickling down his face. Frequently, he would stay home from school rather than risk humiliation.

He tried applying various home remedies to his pimples: baking soda, toothpaste, oatmeal. He bought special creams and cleansers. He subscribed to an expensive mail-order treatment kit. He pleaded with his mother to take him to a dermatologist, and finally got a prescription for antibiotics. Nothing worked. His face remained greasy, as if his pores were secreting cooking oil, and the zits appeared unabated. And then, he didn't think it possible, but his acne worsened exponentially. He began developing cysts.

They were hard, painful bumps, embedded deep within the epidermis. They'd incubate for days, becoming larger and more inflamed. He would feel his face with his fingers, praying for them to go away, praying not to find any new cysts. Once in a while, he could stave them off by wrapping an ice cube in a paper towel and pressing it against the nodule, twenty minutes at a time. More often than not, though, it'd keep growing and swell into a massive pus-filled lesion.

He would have to perform surgery. He would sterilize a sewing needle with a lighter and lodge it into the cyst until it pierced the underlying abscess. Then he would pinch and squash and mash it between his fingers, and if he was lucky, the whole thing would explode out, squirting the viscous white pus against the mirror, and there would be just a small dot on his skin where the needle had been inserted. It never went that well. He nearly always had to lance it again, leaving a huge boil, residual scab, and leprous crater.

Besides on his face, he got cysts on his forehead, neck, and back. Worst was when they bloomed on his nose. The bulges could not be concealed, even with pancake makeup. Occasionally he would affix band-aids and lie that he had walked into a tree branch or collided against the corner of a cupboard door. Sometimes the band-aids would be justi-fied. The hard knobs and ridges on his cheeks and chin made it impossible for him to shave without slicing himself. (His beard came out thin and scraggly, and it would be years before he could grow out a full one.) And the scars—they were awful. After each cyst or pimple was excised, it might heal, yet it would add to the other discolorations, indenta-tions, pockmarks, and furrows on his face, riddling his skin with cavities and whorls and trails. Throughout his teens, he spent every waking moment agonizing over his face, inventing reasons for why he was hiding in his bedroom, wishing his cysts would somehow disappear.

Not much of his acne was in evidence anymore, a change that still seemed miraculous to him. To this day, he could not get used to having clear skin, although he had been free of blemishes since his late twenties. He was always afraid the cysts and pimples would reappear, much like he fretted about a recurrence of Ménière's attacks, and he continued to view himself as an unattractive person, although Jeanette claimed the contrary. It was all in his head, she said; everyone, including her, thought he was perfectly nice-looking.

This morning, he shaved without mishap and dressed in his Sunday khaki pants and white button-down shirt, garnishing the ensemble with an old striped rep tie he'd once picked up at a Salvation Army store. He was supposed to go with Jeanette and Joe to the big Memorial Day observance at the national cemetery in San Bruno. He had asked Joe what he should wear, what Joe himself would be wearing, and he had said a suit. Yadin didn't have a suit. This was the best he could do.

Out on the street, he turned the ignition to his van, and there was an alarming clatter, but it seemed drivable, certainly capable of reaching town, less than three miles from his house. He headed north on Highway 1, and several minutes later passed by the Centurion Resort on his left, then the employee parking lot on his right. He still couldn't believe that Mallory was at the hotel. He had told Jeanette, when she'd asked why he wanted to know how long Mallory would be there, that he was merely curious, but of course there was more to it than that. It had been all he could think about throughout the night, unable to sleep, brooding about it.

He had been tracking Mallory's career from its very start. For a while, she had been everywhere: three albums in five years, arena tours, then a major role on the prime-time drama *City Empire*, followed by several TV movies and a miniseries. He viewed every episode. He saw every music video. He read everything he could find about her in supermarket tabloids and in *People* and *Us*. He had stacks of old magazines in his bedroom closet—anything with a photo of her, a little mention. He had watched countless celebrity gossip shows, just in the hopes of hearing something new about Mallory. Now she was right there, a few hundred yards away. She had already been in town for four days, and she would be leaving any moment, and once she departed, he would never have another chance to see her.

He steered the van to the side of the highway and rolled to a stop. He sat there for a good ten minutes, the engine running and burning gas, trying to decide what to do.

His cellphone rang. He took it out of the pocket of his khaki pants, saw that it was Jeanette calling, and flipped the phone open.

"Are you on your way?" she asked him.

He knew he shouldn't do it, that he should just proceed to Longfellow Elementary School, where they were meeting to carpool, but he also knew that he would forever regret not taking this opportunity to see Mallory.

"I might be late," he told Jeanette. "I'm having a little van trouble."

"You broke down?"

"I guess you were right about those noises."

"You're never going to find a garage open today," Jeanette told him. "It's a holiday. And they'll charge you time and a half if you need a tow."

"I'll see if Rodrigo's around. He knows cars. Maybe it's nothing. I'll try to catch up with you guys in San Bruno."

He was sorry to lie to Jeanette, but after her outburst about Caroline, he thought it best. He fully intended for the visit to be brief—fifteen to twenty minutes at most—and join Jeanette and Joe for much of the observance ceremony.

He got back onto the highway, made a U-turn, and swung down the road to the entrance of the Centurion Resort, where a young man in a uniform stepped out of the security booth.

"I'm here to see a guest, Mallory Wicks," Yadin said.

The guard stared dubiously at Yadin, at his dented, rusting, rumbling van, at the gray smoke curling up from the undercarriage.

"Could I get your name, sir?"

"Yadin Park."

The guard went inside his booth and tapped on the keyboard of his computer and then came out again. "I'm sorry, sir. We don't have a guest named Mallory Wicks at the resort."

"Did she check out already?"

"No one by that name was or is registered as a guest at this Centurion."

Yadin was surprised by the hotel's discretion. She wasn't that famous anymore. "I know she's here," he said. "I know you're supposed to protect her privacy, but I'm an old friend of hers—a musician."

A car pulled up behind Yadin's van. "Sir," the guard said, "we don't have a guest named Mallory Wicks here."

"Look, I'm not a fan or a stalker or anything. Honest to God, I'm an old music buddy."

"I'm afraid I'm going to have to ask you to leave the property."

Yadin considered taking out the cassette tape that was in the pocket of his windbreaker and asking the guard to have it delivered to Mallory. It contained all the songs he had recorded for his album. It seemed vital and momentous to him, getting her imprimatur on the new songs. That was why he had woken early and compiled the separate tracks onto a single cassette. Hers was the only opinion that mattered to him, even after all these years—or maybe it was precisely *because* of all those years, the passage of them, what they had missed and what they could've had and what they had each gone through in the intervening time. He wanted to come to a rapprochement with her about the way things had ended, closing a circle that had been left agape in regret, and the cassette, her approval of the new album, seemed—without his being able to articulate exactly why—a means to do that.

Yet he knew how pathetic the request would appear to

the security guard, asking him to deliver the tape—another aspiring musician desperate for a break. The guard would surely drop it in the rubbish the minute he left.

"My girlfriend works here," Yadin said. "She's a house-keeper."

"What's your girlfriend's name?"

Yadin thought better of it—he didn't want to cause Jeanette any trouble. Moreover, if he used her name, she might find out about his visit. "Never mind," he said.

"Turn around before the fountain, please," the guard said.

Yadin drove forward. In his side mirror, he saw the guard speaking into his walkie-talkie, and as he neared the fountain, a second uniformed guard—holding his own walkie-talkie—stepped out toward the road. Yadin steered his van around and exited the resort, watched by the two guards the whole way.

He turned left onto Highway 1, then made another left into the Colony Estates, the development of McMansions surrounding the resort's golf course. When he first moved to Rosarita Bay, he had carpeted some of the houses for subcontractors. He thought he could park inside the development and cut through a fairway on foot to the hotel, but there was a guardhouse here, too.

He went south to another development called Cypress Point, spotted a security booth, and didn't bother going to the gate, circling around at the stoplight.

He had made a mistake. He shouldn't have mentioned Mallory's name at all to the guard at the Centurion Resort.

He should have simply said he was going to one of the restaurants, or the golf course, or the coastal trail. The Centurion was supposed to allow everyone access to the latter. There was an ongoing lawsuit about it, Yadin now recalled. The California Coastal Commission had sued the hotel over stipulations in the Coastal Access Initiative, which required the Centurion to provide the public with not only beach access but also a couple dozen parking spaces that were on-site and non-valet.

It was too late to insist on this now. He drove up to the edge of town, traversed the outlying neighborhood of Rio Rancho via Montecito Avenue, and went down Vista Del Mar Road until it dead-ended in a dirt lot. He parked and started walking toward the coastal trail, but then returned to his van. He grabbed his aluminum clipboard case, hard hat, and an orange safety vest that he'd been issued when the church was picking trash for Adopt-a-Highway. With his tie, he thought he might be able to pass for some sort of utility official.

He hiked down the path along the ocean. After three-quarters of a mile, the trail began to border the golf course, and he kept an eye on the golfers in the fairways, on the off chance that Mallory was out playing a round. It was a protracted walk. He hadn't known the course was so long. Eventually he came across a driving range, then a putting green, then the clubhouse, where people were eating breakfast on the patio.

Finally he reached the grounds of the hotel proper. It was an impressive, mammoth structure, cresting a cliff. He had never seen it before, even from a distance. He stepped onto the walkway near the bluff. Hesitant to go inside, he lurked around the windows of the restaurants and various rooms on the ground floor, trying to peer through the panes. Around a corner of the hotel, a gardener was trimming hedges, and he stopped and straightened up when Yadin approached.

Yadin held up his clipboard. "Routine inspection," he said.

He slipped through a side door and went down a corridor. It appeared he was outside of the spa. Guests were coming and going through a doorway, wearing identical white robes with hoods and pockets, resembling monks, though very pampered ones. Yadin drifted through the lobby, near the openings to the restaurants, down hallways. He wished he could just pick up one of the house phones and ask for Mallory Wicks's room, but he knew the operator would tell him no one by that name was registered at the hotel. He continued roaming down corridors. He wasn't sure what he had been expecting. What, really, were the odds that he would run across Mallory this way?

A man in a black suit nodded to him as they walked past each other in the hallway. Yadin took a few more steps, then heard behind him, "Excuse me, sir." He turned around slowly, and the man asked, "Could I ask what your business is in the Centurion?"

"I'm doing an inspection."

"What department are you from?"

"PG&E," Yadin said after a moment, perhaps sounding a little too hopeful. He realized he had made another blunder.

Without the clipboard, hard hat, and safety vest, he could have gone incognito as a guest or visitor.

"Has there been a report of a problem?" the man asked.

"No. Just a routine inspection."

"I'm the chief of security. May I see your ID?"

Yadin glanced down at the breast of his safety vest, as if genuinely perplexed that an ID badge was not clipped to it. He patted his pockets. "Must've left it in the truck."

"Why don't we go to your truck, then. Is it down near the loading dock?"

"You know, I'm finished with the inspection," Yadin said. "Everything seems fine. I'll see myself out. Sorry to trouble you."

"Could you follow me, please?"

He took Yadin down to the lower level, where the guard who had stepped in front of the fountain was in the security office, reviewing a bank of closed-circuit monitors.

"Is this the fellow who tried to see Ms. Wicks?" the security chief asked him.

"I'm a friend of hers. I swear," Yadin said. "Can't you just call her?"

They called the police department instead, and in due course an officer arrived. It happened to be Siobhan Kelly. "Yadin?" she said. "What're you— Doesn't Jeanette work here?"

"Jeanette who?" the chief of security asked.

Yadin subtly but vehemently shook his head at Siobhan.

"I was thinking of someone else," she said.

"But you know this man?"

"He belongs to my church," Siobhan told him.

"I see," the chief of security said, momentarily mollified—perhaps he was a religious man. "We won't press charges, but I'm afraid I'll need you to issue him a formal trespass warning." Then, to Yadin, he said, "Sir, your name has been entered into our global database. You are not welcome at any Centurion property ever again. Is that clear?"

The security chief and the guard led Yadin and Siobhan up the stairs—they didn't insist on handcuffs, at least. They entered the lobby, and Yadin could see Siobhan's white and blue squad car parked out front. She would take him, he assumed, to the police station. He didn't know whom he could call for a ride back to his van. Jeanette and Joe, obviously, were out of the question. Rodrigo? Esteban? His only friends—if they could be considered friends; they were more like acquaintances, he had to admit—belonged to the church, and he dreaded having to explain to any of them why he had been at the Centurion. He was anxious enough about Siobhan, whether she would agree to keep this incident between them and not tell Jeanette.

"Yadin?" he heard in the lobby.

They all turned around, and there, standing beside the concierge's desk, was Mallory, dressed in a golf outfit and running shoes, holding a tote bag.

"Mallory," he said.

She came up to Yadin, stared at him for a moment, then dropped her tote bag and embraced him.

Involuntarily, his hands rose and encircled her waist, and he felt her body, sylphish yet strong, the knobs of her breasts pressed against his chest, his fingers on the ridges of muscle that ran down her spine, the curve in the small of her back that scooped to the edge of her butt. He smelled her shampoo, her lotion—or was it perfume? Some sort of supernal amalgam of rosemary, jasmine, chamomile, and perhaps evening primrose. He was overcome by all the sensations of holding Mallory again, after all these years. He clung to her, and didn't want to let go.

He had been unsure how she would react to seeing him again today. He had been prepared for hostility or histrionics, even for Mallory to slap him and have him thrown out. He hadn't been prepared for unmitigated affection.

"Please accept my apologies for the misunderstanding," the security chief said to them.

"We're very sorry, sir," the guard said. "We're very sorry, Ms. Wicks." He picked up her tote bag and held it out for her.

Siobhan, mystified, stared at Yadin and Mallory, said, "All right, then," and trundled to her car, her flashlight and baton swinging from her gun belt.

"What on earth?" Mallory said when they were alone. "What was that about?"

"They didn't believe I knew you," Yadin said. "I heard you were in town. I wanted to see you before you left."

"You live here?"

"For the last four years."

She knocked her knuckles against the top of his hard hat. "Is there an explanation for this getup?" she said, and laughed. "Let's have breakfast and catch up. Do you have time?"

He needed to hurry off to the cemetery, yet Mallory was being so relaxed with him, so warm, it made him want to linger. "Maybe I can stay for a cup of tea?" he said.

She took him to La Barca, one of the three restaurants in the hotel that overlooked the ocean. They were seated at a table near the windows, and Yadin removed his safety vest and windbreaker and placed them, along with his hard hat and clipboard, on the adjoining chair.

A waitress attended to them immediately, and, without consulting the menu, Mallory ordered coffee, black, two egg whites scrambled with spinach, olive oil only, no butter, one slice of applewood-smoked bacon, baked, not fried, and no potatoes, no toast. When Yadin asked the waitress only for decaf herbal tea, Mallory insisted he get something more. "I'm pigging out," she said. "It'll make me self-conscious if you don't eat with me."

Yadin looked at the selections on the menu—uncertain what would be safe for him to ingest—and their prices. Everything seemed to be over twenty-five dollars. He ordered the seasonal fruit and berries.

After the waitress left the table, Mallory appraised him happily. "You look good. Older, obviously, but it suits you. You've lost so much weight." Her voice was the same, still inflected with her childhood Georgia accent.

"I've been on sort of a special diet," he told her.

"And your skin is so smooth."

"They made me get some work done a while back."

Before the release of his second album, his manager, prompted by hints from Inland Records, had Yadin submit to a five-month regimen of Accutane, originally a chemotherapy drug, that was prescribed to treat cystic acne. The medication was extremely powerful, with the possibility of dangerous side effects, including suicidal tendencies, Crohn's disease, and birth defects. To prevent the latter, Yadin was advised not to let women accidentally handle or touch his pills, even the slightest brush, and never to have unprotected sex with anyone while on the Accutane. He got headaches and joint pain during the protocol, and he was sometimes woozy, but it was worth it. His acne vanished. He was cured. Before the release of his third album, his manager had Yadin undergo a series of cosmetic procedures—dermabrasion, laser skin resurfacing, collagen injections, and chemical peels—to flatten out his acne scars.

"I thought they were just airbrushing your promo shots," Mallory said. "Like mine."

"You saw photos of me?" he asked. There hadn't been many.

"I've kept track of everything you've done, Yadin. I have all your albums. They've all been magnificent."

For twenty-three years, he had been following Mallory's every move. He had never imagined she was keeping tabs on him, too.

"You're not going to say how I look?" she asked.

"You look fantastic, Mallory."

"Well, I should. I've had a lot of work done myself."

She was unrecognizable from the girl he had known. At the time, she had been intrinsically pretty, but not remarkable—a little overweight, flat-chested, a bit awkward and mousy. Her transformation began the moment she signed with MCA in Nashville. All of a sudden she was dyed and blow-dried, waxed and polished, heavily made up and watting a shimmering smile. She got breast implants, though thankfully not grotesque ones. Underneath the pudge, she had always had a petite frame—only five-three, with small bones—and the surgeons were careful to make the new boobs proportional to her body, somewhere between a B and a C cup. They might have given her butt implants as well. She became renowned for showing off her sculpted tush, wearing bodysuits and hot pants onstage. In addition, she must have subjected herself to an extreme weight-loss and workout program. On the red carpet for premieres and award shows, in stilettos and dresses with slits, she was toned, her muscles long, not a nip of body fat on her.

The images changed over time. Her weight and shape fluctuated. There were paparazzi shots of Mallory looking bloated, inadvisably walking down a beach in a bikini, corpulent thighs pitted with cellulite. There were further photos of her as she entered and left courtrooms over her four divorces and multiple lawsuits (breach of contract by a former manager, failure to pay a plastic surgeon). At one point, she had to file for bankruptcy herself. She was in and out of rehab. There were mug shots of her as she was booked twice for DUIs and once for domestic violence (she split open the back of her husband's head with a woodcarving of an elephant). For a while, she was regularly caught misbehaving. There were photos of her in dark sunglasses and low-slung hats after trashed hotel rooms and tantrums and the dissemination of a sex tape with a married costar.

She became someone who was unreal to Yadin, a cartoon. Yet he hadn't seen much of Mallory in the headlines in the last decade, as much as he searched. The sole exception had been six years ago, when she released a new album, another cheesy pop country record that was viciously, universally panned ("a true disappointment," "unlistenable," "a maudlin, lugubrious piece of tripe," "an insult to musicians everywhere," "possibly the worst album in the history of recorded country music," "can only hope, for the sake of all of us who would like to preserve our hearing, never mind our sanity, that Mallory Wicks will never release another album"). Granted, it sold over a hundred thousand copies.

The hiatus, it seemed, had been good for her. She looked healthy, fit, and trim, almost waifish. Yes, like him, she was older now, but her skin was supple and pearlescent, as if it had never seen the sun, and she exuded the sort of luminosity that made it unmistakable she was a celebrity, even in her stretch-polyester golf pants and jacket.

"You came here to play golf?" he asked her. It wasn't a sport he would have ever predicted for her.

"It's a terrific layout," she said. "It could be a championship course." She had become a bit of a fanatic, she told

Yadin, often playing two rounds a day. She had bought a house in Thousand Oaks, just outside L.A., to be next door to Sherwood Country Club, but liked taking vacations to other courses to mix up the routine.

It seemed lonely to Yadin, the idea of Mallory going on these golf trips by herself. "When did you start playing?"

"One of my ex-husbands got me into it. It was the only productive thing to come out of that particular union."

From tabloid articles, Yadin knew the complete history of her marriages. First had been an actor, who'd been on the receiving end of the woodcarving of the elephant (he'd been an incorrigible cheat). Second had been a singer, whom she met at a Farm Aid benefit concert, where they had shared the stage for "Hallelujah" (that one was actually an annulment, since they were married for only sixteen days). Third had been a venture capitalist (after the actor and singer, she swore off men in the industry). Fourth had been a cable-TV tycoon (according to *People* magazine, he had been petrified of aging; for fifteen minutes a night, he wore a halo contraption that pulsed electromagnetic waves to his brain in the hopes they would forestall Parkinson's and Alzheimer's). She had wangled large divorce settlements from the last two men. She would never have to worry about money again.

"You never had children," Yadin said.

"No," she said, "just stepchildren," and he couldn't tell whether there was remorse in her answer. In Raleigh as a twenty-two-year-old, she had wanted a gaggle of children someday, and Yadin had daydreamed they'd have them together.

She told him she was still on good terms with an ex-stepdaughter who was now a freshman at Kenyon College and an ex-stepson who was in med school at Harvard. The others—younger—never really cared for her.

"And you?" Mallory asked Yadin. "Married? Kids?"

Was there anything freighted in those questions, or were they just two old acquaintances having a casual reunion? It was so very strange, talking to her like this, after obsessing over her for so many years.

"Never married," he said. "No children."

"A partner?"

"She works here at the hotel, actually," he said.

"Really?" Mallory asked. "What does she do?"

He gazed around the restaurant. The Centurion was even more opulent than he had expected, the panorama from their table breathtaking—scorching clear sky, sun glistering the ocean, the blues riotously acute. "She's in housekeeping."

"Oh."

"There's no shame in it."

"I didn't say there was," Mallory said. "What about you? Are you making enough off your music to . . . ?"

"I think you know the answer to that," he told her. "I haven't put out anything new in nine years."

"I've wondered about that. You used to be so prolific."

"I had some health issues," he said to Mallory, "then

some money issues, and along the way I got dropped by my label."

"You're all right now? Your health?" she asked.

"It's under control. I'm a carpet installer—that's how I'm making a living these days," he told Mallory.

"There's certainly no shame in that," she said.

"No, there isn't."

Their food arrived, his fruit and berries arranged on the plate as artfully as sushi. Mallory pecked at her breakfast, forking very small bites into her mouth, chewing thoroughly and lengthily, setting her utensils down and taking a sip of water before allowing herself another bite.

"It's called mindful eating," she said, noticing Yadin's inquisitive glances. "If you slow down, you'll consume fewer calories and feel full faster and longer. What sort of diet are you on?"

He recited the things he could no longer eat or do.

"Good God, even to me that seems extreme, and I've been on a diet for over twenty years," she said. "You can't imagine what it's like, being scrutinized every minute of the day, every day, everyone feeling they have the right to comment on your weight, your hair, your clothes, every little thing you do and say."

Of course, Yadin knew that feeling well, believing throughout his music career that he was being eyeballed and judged, becoming self-conscious to the point of reclusion.

"Apparently, though," Mallory told him, "I'm no longer relevant enough to be scrutinized. I haven't had a paparazzo follow me in I don't know how long. It's an indication of how far I've fallen. I'm old news. I can't even get myself invited to the Pebble Beach Pro-Am. Hardly anyone recognizes me anymore. A few people will think I'm familiar and ask if we went to high school together. That's what I like about places like this, partly why I go to these posh resorts on golf excursions. Here, I'm still treated like a VIP. You really stopped drinking and doing drugs?"

He nodded.

"Did you go to rehab?" she asked. "Or AA?"

"No." In truth, it had not been very difficult for Yadin to quit. He had only gotten wasted when he had to perform. Otherwise, he could go weeks without a drink.

"You used to be legendary on show nights," Mallory said.

"Not in any way that was helpful," he said.

"Do you remember how much coke we used to do? I miss those days. Everything was so simple then. It was just about having fun and playing music. What we did was pure."

It had been, to Yadin, magical—the best year of his life.

"Are you working on any new material?" Mallory asked.

He had been waiting all morning for her to inquire, waiting for a propitious moment to hand over his cassette. He just wanted her to listen to the songs and tell him if they were any good, yet it felt like an immense thing to ask of her, fraught with abrasions from their past. "I'm pretty much done with a new album," he said.

"That's great. What type of stuff? More electronica? Black metal?"

He was dumbfounded that she knew about his side projects. "You really have been following my career," he said.

"I still have those tapes somewhere."

"If you can't find them, I have stacks of leftovers in my bedroom," Yadin told her.

They finished eating, and Mallory wanted to take a walk and smoke a cigarette. She asked the waitress for the check, and when it was placed on the table between them, Yadin reached for his wallet, but Mallory waved him off—a quick flick of her fingers—and charged the meal to her room.

Going through the lobby, she stopped by the concierge's desk and requested a late checkout of an hour or two.

"I'm going to try to get in at least nine more holes before I have to hit the road," she told Yadin. "Don't you miss the road? I used to love being on the road."

The road was glamorous, Yadin thought, when you had a five-star hotel awaiting you at the end of each night.

On the coastal trail, a northwest breeze was ruffling, which made it pesky for Mallory to light her cigarette. He didn't think smoking was allowed on the trail, which was part of the state park system. A middle-aged couple on the path stared at her belligerently, but they said nothing, and neither did Yadin. One did not cavil to a woman who looked like Mallory.

She began walking south on the trail. "So what is it you're working on?" she asked. "You're being so coy."

"Simple, quiet stuff," he told her. "No frills, just slow, raw songs."

"Are you going to look for a new label?"

"No label's going to pick me up at this point."

"I don't know about that," Mallory said. "What do your people say?"

"What people?" He kept to her right side as they walked so he could hear her better.

"Well, your manager, for one."

"He dropped me, too," Yadin said. "I'm going to self-release the album."

"Wouldn't that be risky?"

"I don't have much choice in the matter."

He noticed rows of chairs set up before a gazebo on the lawn of the hotel. A wedding? The coastal trail here was wide and paved concrete, winding alongside the sandstone bluffs, and as they went farther along, it became more crowded with joggers and dog walkers. Everyone kept staring at Mallory's cigarette.

"Don't sell yourself short," she said to him. "There are a lot of new indie labels that have come up recently. They might not have much promotional power, but at least they have distribution channels."

"I've made up my mind on this. I'm going to do it myself."

"What about a producer?" she asked.

"You're looking at him," he said.

"Well, where are you going to record the album, then? I'm assuming there're no studios in this town."

"I put together a studio in my house. I've been recording the songs analog on four-track cassette."

"Quaint." Mallory tossed the butt of her cigarette, which was still lit, and Yadin watched it wobble midair before the wind took it over the edge of the bluff. "You know, there's software for these things now," she said. "You should hear what kids are doing these days on their laptops. Never mind laptops—their *phones*."

He peered down the bluff, expecting the tinder of dry grass to be ablaze.

"What about backing instruments?" she asked. "Are you going to hire session players to lay down the rest of the arrangements?"

The bankruptcy trustee had only allowed Yadin to keep a small portion of his leftover musical gear, cheaper odds and ends, as tools-of-the-trade exemptions. A little over three weeks ago, when he decided to record the new songs, he spent a frenzied weekend visiting pawnshops and scouring eBay and Craigslist, driving all over the Peninsula and Bay Area to replace his instruments and equipment; sometimes people were willing to give him stuff for free if he just came and got it. He thought he could play everything on the album himself. He was okay on keyboards, he could keep time on snare drum, he was decent on bass. Yet, in the end, he decided against having any backing tracks and didn't use the majority of the gear he'd acquired—a waste of money that would appall Jeanette if she knew.

"No arrangements," he told Mallory. "It's just me—solo acoustic guitar and vocals, two mics, that's it. Straight to tape, live, no overdubs."

"I guess that's what you've always wanted, isn't it?" she said. "Full control. Do everything yourself without having to compromise or listen to anyone."

"No, that's not true," Yadin said, alert to the shift in her tone.

"Isn't it? Seemed that way to me."

They returned to the lobby of the hotel, where Mallory picked up a pen and a notepad from the concierge's desk. "Give me your contact info?" she said to Yadin.

They exchanged addresses, phone numbers, and email. "Will you send me the songs you've finished?" Mallory asked. "I'd love to hear them."

Yadin looked down at her address on the sheet from the notepad. Her handwriting had changed; he remembered it being smaller and narrower. He didn't know why he was hesitating, why he didn't simply fish the cassette out of his pocket and hand it over to her, and it occurred to him that maybe her opinion wasn't what he had been seeking after all, that it wasn't the real reason he had come. "They still need to be mixed and mastered," he said.

"I don't care about that. Send me the raw recordings."

It didn't feel right to him anymore. "You'll have to wait for the finished product."

"Really?" Mallory said. "I can't get a sneak peek?"

"No," he told her.

"But I'm dying to know what you're doing."

"You might be the only one," he said. "But still, you're going to have to wait."

"This is very unfair, Yadin. I hate being made to wait."

"You'll get over it."

"Like I had to get over other things?" Mallory asked—that shadow of edginess again. But it seemed to pass quickly, and she said, "I wish we could talk more, but I have to get back to L.A. today."

"It was wonderful seeing you again, Mallory."

She hugged him, hooking her arms around his head and bending him down to her height—an old habit of hers that he recalled. She would hang her weight off his neck, tweaking his back more than once.

They released each other for a moment, and then, in front of the concierge, in front of everyone in the lobby, the passersby and staff, Mallory kissed him, a prolonged kiss on the mouth, lips exploratory and on the verge of ardent, and this, too, was viscerally familiar to Yadin.

"It's funny," Mallory said after letting him go, "how, after so long, you can still remember the taste of someone's mouth."

In town, at a flower shop that was open early for Memorial Day, Jeanette bought a premade bouquet of red carnations, white lilies, and blue statice. The arrangement was a little tacky, and the flowers weren't very fresh, but she didn't think anyone would mind. The gesture was what mattered. Twenty years ago, her cousin Atticus had been killed in the First Gulf War, and Jeanette had agreed to accompany her father to mark the anniversary with Atticus's family, with whom she had never gotten along.

From the flower shop, she drove down Main Street past city hall, where she expected to see a banner or sign hanging out front commemorating the town's veterans, but there was none. Presumably another victim of budget cuts. She had heard that her old office, in which she had spent all those years as the assistant records clerk, had been moved recently to the annex down the block.

Like all cities in California, Rosarita Bay was obliged by law to respond to any and all public requests for documents and information. Most of those records—archived since 1957, when the city had been incorporated—had been handwritten, typewritten, drawn, or printed on paper, and stored in closets and filing cabinets in various municipal buildings. It took hours, often days, and a great deal of guile, to find anything, to answer the esoterica of questions that arose. Jeanette had taken great pride in her ability to track things down, being a sleuth, a detective. She had developed a feel for which person in which department to query and which drawer or file or tub to crack open first. But a new mayor insisted they bring the town's operations to the modern age and budgeted fifty thousand dollars to have every piece of paper scanned by an outside vendor as a PDF, and for every PDF to be indexed with keywords that could be searched in an electronic management system. Jeanette was trained in using databases and spreadsheets and spent four years working on the project, at the end of which her old position became obsolete.

Joe was waiting for her in the parking lot of Longfellow Elementary School, which was closed for the holiday. He was leaning against his Wall to Wall van, dressed in a suit, the only one he owned. It was black wool, originally purchased for Jeanette's mother's funeral, altered several years ago—

allowing more room in the waist and chest—for her sister Julie's wedding.

"Aren't you going to be hot in that thing?" Jeanette said to him. It was unseasonably warm today.

He shrugged. He had on a pair of sunglasses, wraparound with mirrored lenses, that she had never seen before. "Open," he said. She pulled the lever to pop her trunk, into which he deposited his mini-cooler. He settled into the front passenger seat, lowering himself gingerly. Clearly he'd aggravated his back again.

"Where's Yadin?" she asked.

"Beats fuck out of me."

She tried calling Yadin's landline, got the answering machine. She rang his cellphone, and he picked up.

"Are you on your way?" she asked Yadin.

"I might be late," he told her. "I'm having a little van trouble."

She stowed her phone in her purse and restarted the car.

"What's up?" Joe asked.

She explained, and added, "He's going to try to meet up with us in San Bruno."

"Fat chance of that. Looks like it's just you and me today, babe."

For a moment, Jeanette thought about what Franklin had asked her—if Yadin had been canceling plans, failing to show up when he was supposed to, making excuses. Was it at all possible that Yadin was cheating on her with Caroline? Jeanette still could not envision it.

She drove out of the school's empty parking lot and turned east onto Highway 71. As they began to climb the hill, the sun blinded Jeanette, and she flipped the driver's-side visor down. Her father didn't follow suit with the visor on his side. "Those new sunglasses?" she asked him.

"I look cool, don't I?"

"You have never looked cool in your life."

"You never knew me when I was young."

Jeanette had seen photographs. He had been a fetching young man, muscular but not yet barreled. His hair had been quite long then, and he had sported a full beard; he'd favored skintight shirts, hip-hugger jeans with bell-bottoms, and desert boots. In many of her parents' photos before they got married, her mother, Joanne—or Jo, as she liked to be called—wore a leather headband and a silver pendant of a peace sign.

It had never ceased to amuse her parents, their same-sounding nicknames, Joe and Jo. Whenever someone called out to one of them, they'd chime, "Which one?" and laugh. They gave all their children first names that began with *J* so everyone would have the same initials.

Jo's illness and death had changed everything for their family. If she had lived, even just a few more years, maybe Jeremy would not have been reckless enough to land in prison, and maybe Joe would not be drinking himself to sleep every night. Maybe Julie would be closer to her older siblings, and maybe Jeanette would have had a normal life—stopped thinking about Étienne and left town and gone to art school and become a photographer and gotten married and had children and been happy, perhaps with someone like Franklin.

She still didn't know what to make of the other night at the Memory Den, the way Franklin's hand had lingered on top of hers. They hadn't said anything more after that moment. They had left the bar, and they didn't kiss or hug good night in the parking lot. "Thanks for listening," was all Franklin had said to her. But his hand on hers—had he been making a pass at Jeanette? Was he signaling his attraction for her? It was confusing. He was distraught over Caroline, and ostensibly he had sought out Jeanette to glean if Yadin might be sleeping with his wife. But maybe there had been something else going on. He had been flirting with her—she was sure she hadn't been imagining it. He had said that what he would miss most was being with her. Perhaps, all along, he'd been aware that she had a crush on him. Perhaps he felt himself being drawn to Jeanette, and a part of him yearned to venture beyond banter with her. She hadn't considered any of these possibilities until that night, but she had to admit that their emergence provoked her. Whatever the case, she knew that the stakes for her long-standing infatuation with Franklin had been dramatically altered. Now nothing could be called innocent.

Joe was trying to brush some lint off his pants leg.

"Glove box," Jeanette told him.

He opened the glove compartment, where she kept a lint roller.

"You ever thought of getting a dog?" she asked her father.

"What?"

"A dog. Dogs are great companions."

"I don't need a companion," Joe said.

"Don't you ever get lonely? Or depressed?"

"I am never depressed. Being depressed is a hobby only rich people can afford."

"There's a woman at church," Jeanette said, "Stephanie Weiler—you know her? She used to work in the inspections department."

"No."

"She used to have a dog."

"So?" Joe asked.

"She's a widow. I was thinking yesterday, you guys might like each other."

"What the hell," he said. "You trying to set me up?"

"Why not?" As far as Jeanette knew, her father had not dated anyone in the last fifteen years. She wondered if, sometime in that duration, he'd had a secret lady friend, or if he had not had sex at all since Jo died.

"Forget it," Joe said.

"What could it hurt? It wouldn't have to be like a blind date. You could come to a church event, maybe the annual picnic. You could meet her and see how you feel."

"You are deranged. Now you want me to go to your church? Fuck that."

"Chew on it for a while," Jeanette said.

"I will not."

"Now that I think about it, there's another woman at

church who's single, our pianist, Siobhan Kelly. She's a police sergeant."

"I know her. She gave me a goddamn speeding ticket once."

"She's kind of cute, don't you think?"

"I am not having this conversation."

Jeanette took the ramp north onto Interstate 280, and they didn't speak again until they entered the Golden Gate National Cemetery in San Bruno. As they drove down the Avenue of Flags, they passed underneath a banner that read SERVING GOD AND COUNTRY: A MEMORIAL DAY SALUTE TO OUR HEROES.

"Thanks for coming today," Joe told her. "I know it represents everything you hate."

It'd represented everything Jeanette's mother had hated, too. Jo had protested against every American military conflict in her adult life, from the Vietnam War to the Gulf War.

"You used to be such a little hippie," Joe said to Jeanette. "I kind of miss that hippie."

"You do not."

"Okay, maybe not."

In high school, she had embraced a certain style: gypsy skirts with tiered ruffles, peasant blouses and embroidered tunics, thick belts with large buckles riding low on her hips, lots of bracelets and rings and multi-stranded, beaded necklaces. The vintage bohemian clothes—some of them remnants from Jo's youth—had reflected Jeanette's burgeoning activism, inspired by her mother and her eleventh-grade ethics teacher, Mr. Rojas.

She walked with her father to the base of the big hill—topped by a huge flagpole flying at half-mast—in the middle of the cemetery, where Joe's brother had saved seats for them for the observance ceremony. Mike, four years Joe's junior, was in his old Army uniform, which must have required prodigious alterations to fit, many more than his older brother's black suit. He had served two tours in Vietnam, enlisting immediately upon his high school graduation. Joe had drawn a high draft number and was never called.

Mike's wife, Patsy, was of course at the cemetery with him, as was their daughter, Amyra, and her husband and two kids, Maggie and Meg, nineteen and eighteen, and their husbands, and Maggie's newborn. Incredibly, Mike and Patsy, in their early sixties, had become great-grandparents last month.

Growing up, Jeanette never spent much time with that side of the family. They were evangelical Christians, members of a megachurch in Modesto, and at family gatherings, Jo (and, in time, Jeanette) had gotten into horrific arguments with them over politics and religion. Mike and Patsy believed in the Second Coming, and distorted news headlines as signs that the Great Tribulation, the Rapture, was near at hand. They were creationists, and condemned the theory of evolution and its adoption in textbooks. They were, of course, for school prayer and against sex education. They backed the Moral Majority, and lobbied against the ERA. Most vehemently, they denounced homosexuality and abortion. There was not a single barbecue or holiday dinner that Jo did not leave apoplectic.

The observance ceremony began with a musical pre-lude by a brass band, then a bagpiper played "Amazing Grace." There were speeches from the cemetery director and a retired general, interleaved with an invocation and benediction from a chaplain, the recitation of the Pledge of Allegiance by a former POW, songs from two vocalists, the laying of the Gold Star Wreath, the reading of a poem, a rifle salute, and a bugler playing taps while the color guard marched. A pair of Coast Guard jets did a flyover, then the vocalists sang "God Bless America" to close the pro-ceedings. It felt interminable to Jeanette, the ceremony, but when she looked at her watch, she saw that it had clocked in at almost precisely one hour.

"Well, that wasn't so bad, was it?" Joe said to her.

They got back in her car, and Jeanette drove them to Atti-cus's plot. Each of the cemetery's 112,700 graves had a small American flag in front of the headstone, planted in advance, Joe told her, by three thousand Boy and Girl Scouts.

Ahead of them, Atticus's family was parking along a curb. Jeanette stopped behind the line of cars, and she and Joe took out two folding chairs and his mini-cooler from her trunk. With the others, they walked to Atticus's grave, and they helped set up a picnic underneath a stand of trees while Mike and Patsy cleaned the marble headstone.

Jeanette watched them from afar. They were doing it all wrong. They had simply mixed some Spic and Span with water in a bucket and were using the scrub side of a kitchen sponge to soap up the headstone. Household cleaners were corrosive and deposited salt. They should have been washing the marble with a non-ionic, biocidal cleaning solution.

After Mike and Patsy put away their cleaning supplies, they called to the others, saying they were ready. Everyone placed flowers at the foot of Atticus's headstone, and they formed a semicircle and joined hands.

"Let's begin with Psalm 23," Mike said, and he and his family started reciting, "The Lord is my shepherd." Neither Jeanette nor Joe partook. She doubted her father knew any prayers. His parents had not been religious. Mike had found Jesus after leaving home, through Patsy.

The headstone had a cross in a circle on it, and was engraved: ATTICUS NATHANIEL MATSUDA, PVT, US ARMY, PERSIAN GULF, APRIL 29 1972, FEB 26 1991, DESERT STORM, PATRIOT, WAR-RIOR, LOVING SON, PURPLE HEART. A tome, especially com-pared to what was on Jo's gravestone—just her name and the years of her birth and death. Jeanette and her father had agreed, when deciding what to put on the bronze marker, that there was dignity in simplicity. Together, they visited the grave in Rosarita Bay's Capistrano Cemetery on Jo's birthday, the anniversary of her death, and Christmas. Jeanette didn't know how often her father dropped by the cemetery on his own these days. The first few years, he had gone weekly.

It was a bright, crisp day, and Jeanette gazed at the rows of identical white headstones glimmering in the sun. For a moment, she thought about Étienne. He was buried some-where in Canada—she didn't know exactly where, and it'd always bothered her that she didn't know.

Mike took out a piece of paper and read a long tribute he had handwritten to his son. Patsy, in turn, gave a prayer, then Amyra and the rest of the family each offered testimony, invoking Almighty God and the heavenly kingdom and the faithful departed and the gateway to a more glorious life, pleading for Atticus's soul to be bound up with theirs forever through their Lord and Savior, Jesus Christ. By the end, they were all crying.

"Where's my cooler?" Joe asked Jeanette as they made their way toward the picnic table. "I need a beer."

Under the trees, after loading up a paper plate with food, he took a seat at the end of a folding table with his brother and tipped a bottle of Anchor Steam. No one else was imbibing. Mike and his family didn't drink. Joe had put his sunglasses back on, and he was sweating, fat beads on his forehead after standing in the sun. He and Mike had matching buzz cuts, though Joe's was looking a little ragged.

"How are you doing, Jeanette? It's been so long," Patsy said.

She had aged badly—gotten fat and gray and wrinkled with deep grooves and puckers.

"I heard you now belong to a church?" she asked. "Is that right? And you're one of the elders?"

"I'm on the board. There are no elders," Jeanette said.

"I'll tell you the truth. I could hardly believe it when I heard."

Jeanette wanted to say, "Will wonders never cease," but didn't, because often she could hardly believe it herself.

"Although can it really be considered a religion?" Patsy asked. "Unitarian Universalism?"

"According to the IRS, yes."

"As if the IRS can be the judge of such matters. Well, irregardless, I'm glad you found a flock of your own," Patsy said, with too much satisfaction.

When Jeanette had been in her teens, Patsy had tried to persuade her that, as a young woman, her sole objective was to prepare for a future husband, learn to cook and clean and sew and keep house, that she should pray for a man to select her and take care of her and lead her to fulfill her purpose as a dutiful Christian wife and mother—which naturally had led to heated fights. "I'm going to see the world. I'm not going to depend on a man for anything," Jeanette would jab at her aunt. "You have too much pride. It'll be your ruin," Patsy would jab back.

What would Patsy say now, Jeanette wondered, if she knew everything that had happened to her in Watsonville? Would she have any sympathy for her, or would she simply conclude that Jeanette had gotten what she deserved?

Her high school ethics teacher, Mr. Rojas, had been from Watsonville. For generations, his family had worked as *piscadores*, strawberry pickers, and he'd related stories to the class about the *piscadores'* working conditions there, and about the farmworkers' movement led by César Chávez, Dolores Huerta, and Maria Elena Serna. After the Loma Prieta earthquake on October 17, 1989, Mr. Rojas organized a caravan of students to go down to the city with him to assist in the disaster relief efforts. Jeanette, seventeen at the time, was among the first to sign up.

The city was decimated. The epicenter had been less than ten miles away. More than thirty percent of downtown and one in eight houses were in ruins. The destruction was incredible to witness—façades of historical buildings disintegrated, the steeple to the main Catholic church toppled, piles of crumbled brick and splintered wooden beams on sidewalks, glass broken in jaggy panes and shattered fragments, branches and bark sheared off trees, streets and pavement cracked and buckled, telephone poles tilting sideways, cables and power lines strewn in crazy serpentines, detritus and pieces of paper fluttering everywhere, houses pancaked with collapsed roofs and knocked off their foundations, red tags taped to front doors. There was no electricity or running water. Roads were impassable. Part of Highway 1 had caved in. Traffic lights, gas pumps, and ATMs did not work.

The situation in Callaghan Park, where Jeanette and her classmates were stationed, was a mess. Residents were living in jerry-built tents, and they would not move to the shelters that the Red Cross had set up at the convention hall and the National Guard armory, afraid of going inside any buildings, spooked by the continuing aftershocks. They rebuffed, too, the outdoor aid centers that had been erected at Ramsay Park and the Santa Cruz Fairgrounds. A number of them were in the country illegally, spoke only Spanish, and were fearful of government workers. They also didn't want to relinquish their possessions. Inside and around their tents, they had mounds of clothes and personal belongings in trash bags. Some had lugged their sofas, bicycles, and TVs to the park. They were cooking meals on charcoal barbecues and keeping warm with fires in rusty fifty-five-gallon drums. The conditions were growing squalid. There were real safety, sanitation, and health concerns for those who remained. Plus, the weather was miserable. It was pouring rain.

There was one volunteer in the park who was able to break through the refugees' mistrust. He looked to be in his early twenties, and he was bilingual (actually, quadrilingual, Jeanette would learn later), and he had an easy charm. As he went from tent to tent, people readily smiled and laughed, talking to him. It didn't hurt that he was so good-looking. He was slim, lanky. He moved with loose limbs, arms flaring out at the elbows, and a jouncy stride, unencumbered by any stiffness, doubts, or worries. His skin was suet-smooth, his face a whittling of sharp, angled planes. He had a widow's peak on his forehead, his hair straight and jet-black and finger-swept.

Someone told Jeanette his name was Étienne Lau—a first-year law student at Boalt Hall in Berkeley. She watched him for days. During breaks from handing out supplies, she took photographs, and every once in a while she furtively snapped a few shots of Étienne.

He caught her in the act one afternoon, and walked over to her. "Hey, shutterbug," he said.

She was paused by his mellifluous voice. He had a British accent.

"Are you the one who took that picture, the one syndicated by the AP?" he asked.

The appearance of the photo in the *Santa Cruz Sentinel* had happened by chance, through one of Mr. Rojas's connections; Jeanette hadn't expected anything to transpire when she'd handed over her canisters of film to him. The one chosen had been of a long line of people waiting to get water from a truck, toting any containers they could find. At the front of the line was a boy, maybe seven or eight, clutching an empty gin bottle.

"Yeah," she said to Étienne. "How did you know?"

"I asked around about you," he said, and she flushed—flattered. "Photos like that," he told her, "photos that good, have more impact in the court of public opinion than any amicus brief ever could. So kudos to you."

"Thanks."

They grinned at each other.

"I love your clothes. You carry that vintage look well," he said. "How old are you?"

"Seventeen."

"Oof," he said. "Young."

She asked what had brought him down to Watsonville, and he told her one of his professors had been involved in the landmark federal case *Gomez v. City of Watsonville*, which had argued that the system of at-large elections in Watsonville violated the Voting Rights Act. Étienne had been driving down to the city periodically to help with voter registration for the upcoming election, which would be the first under the new district-based system.

"It's history-making, what's happening here," he said. "Or what's going to happen. Not sure they'll hold the election on schedule now. Might be postponed a few weeks. But when they do, it'll be a watershed moment, a revolution. They'll finally get equal and fair representation. I think that's partly why these people won't leave the park. They see it as an act of civil disobedience. They don't want to be shuttled away, out of sight, out of mind. They want everyone to see how they've been marginalized and deprived. You have to admire them, don't you? ¡El pueblo unido, jamás será vencido! The people united will never be defeated!"

Jeanette was dazzled. They talked more that day during breaks, and she pieced together his background. His father was British, his mother Canadian (he held two passports). They were both economists and had started out in academia, but then decided to roam the globe as expats. They hired themselves out as international economic policy analysts, working stints for the IMF, the World Bank, and the UN and getting fellowships at think tanks and institutes. Étienne and his older sister grew up in London, Geneva, Hong Kong, Jakarta, Luxembourg, Frankfurt, Buenos Aires, and Vancouver. He had gotten his undergraduate degree in philosophy at McGill University in Montreal. Before coming to Berkeley, he had never lived in the United States. Jeanette had never met anyone who'd had such a glamorous life.

The election in Watsonville, as Étienne predicted, was postponed until December, and when the ballots were counted, the results were disappointing. Nothing much changed in the makeup of the city council. Jeanette wrote a letter to Étienne, commiserating about the outcome. She mailed it to him care of Boalt Hall's general address. He had asked for her telephone number and address, but hadn't given his in kind.

Almost two months passed, and she thought that the letter had been lost or, more likely, that he wasn't interested in corresponding with her. After all, he was twenty-two, a Berkeley law student, a globetrotter; she was a puppy-eyed high school student in Rosarita Bay who'd never been out of the country.

But then he replied. "So sorry for the long delay! The campus mail people here are not exactly paragons of efficiency. Of course I remember you!"

She was thrilled. It was a three-page letter, typed single-spaced on a computer. He rendered his postmortem on the election: "Unfortunate, yes, but I think the nagging effects of the earthquake had a lot to do with it. Still fifteen hundred people homeless, most from District 1, where Cruz Gomez lost to Milladin in a squeaker. I am not discouraged, however. The people will prevail!"

They exchanged more letters over the winter and spring. He told her about his desire to become a human rights activist after graduation, working for Amnesty International or UNESCO or WHO. She told him about her acceptance—accompanied with a scholarship offer—to the Corcoran School, and he said, "You are going to change the world with that Nikon of yours. And break a few hearts along the way. You'll be gentle with Étienne's heart, won't you?"

She wanted to see him. She was willing to drive up to Berkeley, yet he said, "I'd love it, absolutely love it, but I am so unbelievably *busy* these days."

She became frustrated with his evasiveness. He would send her long, impassioned, flirty letters, even call once in a while, but then would go AWOL for weeks. To make extra money, she had been planning to clean rooms at the B&B in town during the summer, but she learned that the *San Francisco Chronicle* offered thirteen-week paid internships and put in an application. Her chances weren't good for such a prestigious program. Usually they only took college upperclassmen. She was selected. "Isn't that wonderful news?" she said in her letter to Étienne. "I'm going to be a photo intern in editorial! We'll be right across the Bay from each other!"

She waited, and he didn't answer. She was ready to give up, but then she received a letter from him in early June. "I had a crazy semester! On top of exams, for a month I was in, of all places, Watsonville again. You know after the census was released April 1, they had to redistrict, and I finagled my way into working with Joaquin Avila on redrawing the maps. Anyway, I was going through the whole OCI cycle and was all set on being in New York this summer for my 1L internship, but you know what? I decided to go back to Watsonville and work at a tiny, tiny poverty law center called Central Coast Legal Aid. The city's still a debacle. They need all the help they can get. I've been here a couple of weeks already. So, sorry I'll miss you in the Bay Area this summer, agh, ships in the night, but I'll be in Watsonville for the duration. Come for a visit sometime?"

Jeanette contacted the *Chronicle* and withdrew from the internship program.

"What are you doing?" her mother asked her. "It's not just because of that boy, is it?"

She would not be deterred. The following week, the day after her graduation ceremony, she drove to Watsonville.

It was appalling, really, the state of the city. Buildings had been razed, but they hadn't been rebuilt, left as empty lots surrounded by cyclone fences. Many neighborhoods still felt like war zones, houses sagging on their foundations, windows boarded up with plywood, weeds proliferating. Highway 1 over Struve Slough was still closed. The tent cities were gone, but there were still hundreds of people living in temporary shelters and FEMA trailers.

Central Coast Legal Aid was in a strip mall on the outskirts of downtown, beside a discount clothing store. The office was just one open room, outfitted with rickety desks and chairs and yellowing posters on the walls. It was filled with waiting clients, weary-looking but silent, many with children on their laps. Étienne was at a desk in the back, interviewing two men. When he saw Jeanette, he seemed not to recognize her at first, but then he smiled broadly, rose, and ambled over to her in his cocky, marionette saunter. "She comes in through that door, and there's sunshine in the rain," he said, handsome and irresistible as ever.

When he could break for lunch, they went across the

street to a diner that served all-day breakfast. He ordered coffee and the linguica-and-eggs special. "What are you doing here?" he asked. "You just come down for the day?"

"I'm thinking of staying the entire summer," Jeanette said. "I want to volunteer. I want to help."

"You have something set up? An internship or a job?"

She didn't. For the past week, she had been making phone calls, but she had found nothing available thus far.

"Is there anything at Central Coast?" she asked him.

"Did you see the place? No, afraid not."

"I might have better luck finding something now that I'm here."

"Well, where you staying?" Étienne asked. "You have a place to stay tonight?"

She didn't.

"My roommate's away this weekend," he said. "You could stay with me."

They didn't leave his bed for the next three nights. They fucked, talked, and fucked some more. He confessed that he had been miserably lonely since arriving in Watsonville. "I'm really glad you're here," he told Jeanette.

Central Coast Legal Aid was staffed by two attorneys, an office manager, a couple of roving high school girls who sat in as receptionists, and two 1L interns—the other, Mikhail, was Étienne's roommate in the studio apartment that had been arranged by the clinic. They offered free legal advice and referrals to low-income clients, and also delved into community education and advocacy. The most pressing issue right now, though, was trying to get federal and state assistance for victims of the earthquake. Many of their clients had been sharing houses and apartments or living illegally in makeshift rentals such as converted garages and toolsheds. They couldn't produce lease agreements or canceled checks proving their residential status for a period longer than thirty days, and thus had been rejected by the Red Cross and FEMA for aid of any kind. The clinic had been filing appeals on their behalf. In the meantime, they were trying to secure temporary housing for them. Sometimes they had to resort to giving them motel vouchers.

Jeanette ended up staying in a motel herself for nearly a week when Étienne's roommate returned. She applied for every job opening in town. There weren't many. She settled for a part-time housekeeping job at the Days Inn off Highway 1 (where some of Étienne's clients had been placed), and lived in a boardinghouse for women, six of them in three bunk beds per room. Her things kept getting stolen. She found out that the manager took in girls who were on the waiting list for the halfway house down the street as they transitioned from treatment centers or prisons or institutions. Jeanette learned to keep her cash and valuables—especially her camera equipment—with her at all times, taking her backpack with her even when she went to pee.

It should have been depressing, her situation that summer, but it wasn't at all. She was, in fact, enthralled. She was in love. She saw Étienne every moment they had free. They took walks through the city, sat on plaza benches and bleachers

of soccer fields, and talked. They ate at La Perla del Pacifico and a superb restaurant called, plainly, Taco Burrito,
and watched movies at the Starlight Drive-In and the Pajaro
Showplace. They slipped into bars, where classic love songs
were on the jukebox, ballads like "La Nave del Olvido" and
"El Reloj," and they would slow-dance, pressing against each
other, Étienne whispering lyrics into her ear.

They embarked on long, aimless drives on weekends. Étienne had a red Alfa Romeo Spider convertible, and he loved
gunning it down the highway with the top down. It had a
five-speed and a burl-wood interior, a three-spoke steer-
ing wheel, and gray Italian leather seats with red stitching.
Sheepishly, he admitted to Jeanette that he had bought the
Spider because he had seen it in the movie *The Graduate*,
Dustin Hoffman zipping up and down the California coast in
the car, chasing Katharine Ross. The film was also where he
got the idea to attend Berkeley.

They couldn't go to the boardinghouse or his apartment
unless Mikhail, his roommate, was away, so they had sex in
his car or hers, on a blanket on the beach, in the woods—
which for Jeanette made it all the more romantic and erotic.

"I thought you were too young for me," Étienne told
her. "That's why I was dodging you last semester, not writing back. But there's something right about this, isn't there?
Right about us. I'm really becoming fond of you, Jeanette."

During the day, while he was at Central Coast Legal Aid,
Jeanette cleaned rooms at the Days Inn, two shifts a week,
but the work was easy. The families staying there, even with

so much of their property stacked in the rooms, were scrupulously neat and unfailingly polite. They always wanted to help her with the cleaning.

The rest of the week, she roamed around town, shooting photos. She had first become interested in photography in junior high—just a hobby then, something to do. Joe had a secondhand Nikon F2A that he never used anymore, and she began taking random shots with it of landscapes, horizons, buildings, and sidewalks. Eventually, though, she became more interested in people's faces, capturing their expressions and gestures and emotions, as she saw in photography books in the school library—portraits by Walker Evans, Gordon Parks, and especially Dorothea Lange, many of whose documentary studies of farmworkers were taken in California.

There were three lenses for the Nikon—35, 50, and 125 mm—and, except with her family, she mostly used the telephoto from a distance, shy about getting too near strangers. Once she switched to the shorter wide-angle lens, however, everything changed. She moved in closer to people and framed her shots level to or below her subjects, and suddenly her photographs had more dimensionality. Swapping Kodachrome for Tri-X black-and-white added further depth to her work. When she had her film developed, she was frequently startled by the photographs, by their intimacy. She didn't know exactly what she was doing at the time, but it was intoxicating.

The local paper in Watsonville, the *Register-Pajaronian*, didn't have an internship program, but the staff photographer, Sonny Guzman, agreed to let Jeanette tag along with him on assignment a few times. He was an old pro, fast and efficient. He didn't believe in flashes or reflectors or strobes, even at night. Photography was all about light, he said. Natural light, interesting light. "Be constantly aware how light is hitting things," Sonny told Jeanette. "Look at the light during different parts of the day, in different situations. Then you'll always know the right exposure. Shoot with a high ISO. Don't worry about the grain. Grain is beautiful, man."

She listened to him. She paid more attention to the light, and her compositions got stronger, her portraits more alive.

What really energized Jeanette, though, was the cause Étienne found for them. In May, Green Giant had announced that at year's end they would be laying off 370 of the 520 workers in the frozen-food plant on West Beach Street. The cutters and packers, who processed broccoli and cauliflower, were mostly women, and they had averaged fourteen years at the company. Some of their jobs would be going to Wellston, Ohio, most to Irapuato, Mexico.

Green Giant—which was owned by Grand Metropolitan, a British conglomerate—said they would do everything they could to ease the impact of the job losses on their workers. They were going to offer severance packages between three and four thousand dollars apiece, and they would contribute half a million dollars to a retraining program. The goal was to place eighty percent of the laid-off workers in new careers as auto mechanics, clerks, and technicians.

This was all well and good, yet it was, according to Étienne, merely a public relations gesture. The Green Giant
plant had not been losing money. The layoffs were just a way
for them to make more money and try to overtake Birds Eye's
position as the industry leader.

"It's avarice, pure greed," Étienne said to Jeanette.

He was puzzled that Teamsters Union Local 912, which
represented the workers, wasn't making more of a fuss about
the layoffs. He and Jeanette attended a meeting, and Étienne
asked Bobby Munoz, Local 912's president, why they hadn't
been holding protests.

"There's not a whole lot that can be done," Munoz told
him. "It's hard to fight a transnational conglomerate half a
world away. At least we were able to negotiate the severances
and retraining."

"Is eighty percent placement realistic?" Étienne asked.

"They're hardworking, skilled employees," Munoz said.
"Places like NorCal/Crosetti and Shaw's are looking for
workers like that."

Those were other frozen-food companies, which had few
openings. The current unemployment rate in Watsonville was
thirteen percent.

"Shouldn't you take a stand against Grand Met?" Étienne said.

"It's too late," Munoz said. "They're not going to change
their minds."

"Maybe not," Étienne said, "but even a symbolic protest
is better than nothing. What about the next plant, the next

conglomerate, the next time someone's deciding whether to move their operations? You want to make it easy for them?"

A woman behind them said, "*Cuando nos dan una cachetada, por lo menos tenemos derecho a gritar.*"

Jeanette's Spanish was rudimentary—tourist Spanish. "What'd she say?" she asked Étienne.

The woman translated for herself. "When we get slapped across the face," she said, "at least we have the right to cry out."

"Now we're talking," Étienne said.

Her name was Yolanda Aguilar. She and her husband, Lauro, had been packers at Green Giant for nearly twenty years.

Yolanda recruited her husband and several women from the plant to form El Comité de Trabajadores Desplazados, the Committee of Displaced Workers. For their first initiative, they put together a flyer detailing what was behind the exporting of their jobs to Mexico, the deplorable conditions in Irapuato. "People in this town need to know it's purely about profit," Étienne said.

They handed out the flyers downtown, posted them on bulletin boards in stores, tucked them into mailboxes. Jeanette documented everything with her Nikon. Sonny Guzman allowed her to develop the film in the *Register-Pajaronian*'s darkroom, and when he examined her contact sheets with his magnifier loupe, he said, "Not bad, not bad. What'd you say this committee's about?"

He talked to a reporter and the managing editor in the newsroom. They decided to interview Yolanda about El

Comité, and ended up featuring one of Jeanette's photos with the story. After the article appeared, Bobby Munoz and the officers in Local 912 became more supportive, and other Green Giant workers joined El Comité.

"You're changing the world already, babe," Étienne said to Jeanette. "Keep going."

He had his hands full at Central Coast Legal, often working nights at the clinic, and gradually had to curtail the number of hours he could devote to El Comité. Their contributions were largely up to Jeanette now.

Throughout July, she was fully and happily occupied, yet all along, she was thinking about the end of the summer. August was fast approaching. Étienne would be going back to Boalt, and she would have to leave for freshman orientation at the Corcoran. Already she grieved that they would be separated on opposite coasts. She couldn't stand the idea of being so far apart from him. She couldn't imagine being more in love with someone.

One night, they were eating dinner at Taco Burrito, and she said to him, "You never talk about the future."

"I talk about the future endlessly," Étienne said. "Even I'm tired of hearing me talk about my future."

"No, I mean our future."

"Oh."

"What's going to happen to us when I go to D.C.?"

He took a bite of his mole enchiladas. "Well," he said, "we'll write, we'll call. We'll see each other Christmas break. Or maybe—hey, this is a crazy idea, but maybe we could meet up in New York for Thanksgiving. Wouldn't that be wild?"

"I'm going to miss you so much. I'm going to die."

"Things will work out," Étienne said. "We'll make it work somehow. Trust me. We love each other, don't we?"

El Comité arrived at a course of action. They would hold five solid days of protests in Watsonville in August. Besides Green Giant, Grand Metropolitan owned Burger King, Häagen-Dazs, Smirnoff, J&B Scotch, and a slew of other brands. They'd list them on leaflets and picket Albertson's, Nob Hill Foods, Liquor Barn, and other stores, asking customers not to buy the products. They'd demonstrate in front of the two Burger Kings in town. On the final day of the protests, they'd carry a black coffin with a wreath of broccoli and cauliflower and lead a Jolly Green Giant, plastered with fake twenty-dollar bills, from Callaghan Park, along Ford and Walker, to the plant on West Beach Street. Then they'd return on Main Street to the park and hold speeches, songs, and skits. If the boycott campaign turned out to be successful in Watsonville, it might gain traction elsewhere in the country.

Two weeks before the scheduled protests, Jeanette missed her period. She waited another week, then took a home pregnancy test, then went to a clinic for a blood test.

She asked Étienne to meet her around the corner from Central Coast Legal Aid and told him the results.

"Really?" he said. "But you use a diaphragm."

"That night we drove out to Elkhorn Slough, we didn't have it with us."

"Oh."

"That's all you have to say?" Jeanette asked.

"Unfortunately, I don't think we have much of a choice here, sweetheart."

"You want me to get an abortion?"

"What else can we do?"

"We could get married," Jeanette said.

He laughed.

"Why are you laughing?" she asked, and began to cry.

"Oh, baby, I'm sorry," he said. He hugged her. "It's just that we've got our entire lives ahead of us. You especially. You're eighteen. You haven't even started college yet. It'd be harebrained for us to get married and have a baby right now. If we end up wanting to do that someday, okay, but this isn't the time. Don't you see?"

She knew he was right, but she was hurt by his quick dismissal, his laughter. She made an appointment at Clínica Paloma, a Planned Parenthood branch on Penny Lane, yet didn't end up going. Arguing with Patsy about abortion once, Jeanette had said that a fetus was no more alive than a frog. She questioned that now. Her breasts tingled. She felt nauseous. She was constipated and plagued by reflux. She realized it was probably too early to have these symptoms, that she might be inventing them, but she felt her body metamorphosing, preparing itself to grow and nurture this child. She wondered if she waited, Étienne might change his mind.

They didn't see much of each other over the next few days, Étienne working overtime, Jeanette preparing for the

El Comité protests. Finally, the first of the five days of rallies arrived, and Jeanette joined about ten other picketers in front of the Burger King on Main Street, holding up signs that read BURGER KING PIMPS FOR GRAND MET! SUPPORT WORKERS OF GREEN GIANT!

Étienne had promised to picket with her during his lunch break, but by two o'clock, he had yet to show up. Jeanette called Central Coast Legal from a pay phone. When she identified herself and asked for Étienne, the receptionist said, "Oh, oh," and warbled out what sounded like a sob. She abruptly put Jeanette on hold. She waited at least five minutes, a Spanish-language radio station playing on the line. At last, she heard, "Jeanette, it is Mikhail. Jeanette, I am so sorry. Jeanette, I have terrible news for you."

Étienne had been on his way to the courthouse to drop off some filings. He had tried to run a yellow light in his Alfa Romeo Spider, was too late, and had been broadsided by a flatbed truck. He hadn't been wearing his seat belt and was thrown from the car, and had died before the EMTs could reach him.

Somehow Jeanette ended up in her bunk bed in the boardinghouse—she didn't remember how. She only remembered keeling to the ground beside the pay phone. She stayed in bed, weeping, until the next morning, when she was able to gather herself enough to call Mikhail again. She needed to see Étienne. It seemed urgent and important, seeing him one last time. Mikhail told her that Étienne's body was being held at the county coroner's office, but since Jeanette wasn't related to him, she wouldn't be permitted inside. They would be transferring him to a funeral home soon, Mikhail said, and his parents were arriving the day after next from Brussels. They intended to fly his body home to Canada for burial.

His parents. Jeanette had not thought of his parents. Surely they would want to meet her, and learn that she was pregnant with Étienne's child, that a part of him was living inside her. It would provide some consolation for them during this awful week, and later it'd give them joy, welcoming a grandchild and Jeanette into their lives.

For some reason, maybe the mania of mourning, Jeanette felt it paramount to buy a dress—or two dresses—before Étienne's parents arrived. She didn't think it right to meet them in her vintage hippie-dippy clothes. She needed to get something more reserved, dignified, grown-up. And she would need a black dress, too, for without question, his parents would ask Jeanette to attend the funeral.

The next morning, she went to Target, and as she was combing through the clearance racks, a teenage girl approached her. "Hey, you're Jeanette, aren't you?" she asked. "I'm Elizabeth. I used to volunteer at Central Coast. Do you remember me?"

She was wearing a black crochet tank top that exposed her bra underneath. Her midriff was bared. She had denim cutoff shorts with a thick silver-studded belt riding her hips. A pendant of a tribal god hung from a leather string between her breasts. She was brunette, with dark red lipstick and eyebrows plucked in straight narrow lines. She wasn't exactly pretty—a pug nose and a downturned mouth marred what could have been a cute face—but she was undeniably sexy. Jeanette remembered her occasionally sitting at the receptionist's desk.

"I saw you on the street and followed you in here," the girl said. "I heard about Étienne. You were going out with him, weren't you?"

"Yes," Jeanette said, expecting words of commiseration—words she had already heard in the last two days from Mikhail, from Yolanda and Lauro and other members of El Comité and Local 912, from the manager of the boardinghouse and the girls who were rooming there, words that did nothing for her, that could not alleviate her grief or heartache the slightest bit and probably never would.

"I think I should tell you something," Elizabeth said. "I've been going back and forth about it, whether to tell you, but decided if it was me, I'd want to know. You won't believe this now, but I think it'll help you down the road—help you get over things."

She told Jeanette that throughout the summer, she had been having sex with Étienne. They had first met when he came down to Watsonville in April for the redistricting, and he'd sent her the same type of long, impassioned letters he had mailed to Jeanette—they might have been identical letters, copied and pasted. He'd seduced another receptionist, too—another high school student. Once Elizabeth found out, she had quit volunteering there. She hadn't known that he was seeing Jeanette until last month. The other 1L intern, Mikhail, was a dog, too, Elizabeth said. He'd hit on her more than once, knowing full well she was sleeping with Étienne. Mikhail told her that Étienne had never wanted to come to Watsonville for the summer. He had wanted to go biglaw in New York, working at a corporate firm, but he had been in trouble at Boalt, brought before the dean on suspicion of cheating. Nothing could be proven, but the allegation had blown his chances for a prestigious internship.

Jeanette found Mikhail across the street from Central Coast Legal Aid, sitting in the diner where she and Étienne had first eaten lunch.

"Is it true?" Jeanette asked him. "Is it true?"

He looked frightened, rooted in his chair. They had spoken four times on the phone in the past three days but had not seen each other until now. "Yes, I am afraid it is true. Étienne has passed."

"What?"

"He is gone from us, Jeanette. You must try to reconcile with this reality."

It seemed he thought she was in a dissociative fugue, unable to accept Étienne's death. "No, is what Elizabeth said true?"

"Who is Elizabeth?"

"The high school girl," Jeanette said. "The receptionist. Was Étienne sleeping with her?"

"What are you talking about?" Mikhail asked.

"She said you were just as bad. What about the other girl? What about Étienne almost getting kicked out of Boalt? Is it all true?"

"What? Jeanette, whatever those girls told you is a fabrication. That girl, Elizabeth, she is crazy. She is being vindictive because Étienne got her fired. I know you are not thinking right. You are in grief, in shock. But Étienne is not even in his grave yet. Could we give him a modicum of respect and mourn his passing before questioning his honor?"

Not knowing was what would haunt Jeanette. She would never be able to find out for sure what was true. She believed Elizabeth at first, believed that Étienne had betrayed her. All of his talk about integrity, justice, becoming a human rights activist, had been bullshit. He had been no crusader. He had been a fraud, a phony. And of course Mikhail would defend his buddy, and lie.

But then, later, Jeanette would wonder: perhaps it was Elizabeth who had been lying, seeking revenge for being fired, as Mikhail said, and Jeanette had made a mistake. If only Étienne had let a courier take the court papers instead of going himself; if only he had joined the protest at Burger King earlier; if only he had braked and not accelerated at the light—he would still be alive. He could have explained. He could have refuted everything. Or confessed. If he had been contrite, pleaded for forgiveness, they might have been able to work things out. They might still be together, traveling the globe. They might have gotten married. She might have kept Étienne's child, who'd be twenty years old now.

Then again, maybe not. He had wanted her to get an abortion, after all. Maybe to him it had just been another dalliance, and it would have ended in another week. Jeanette might have been wounded and inconsolable for a while, but eventually would have moved on, just like all the other women who seemed able to forget their first loves, their first betrayals.

After talking to Mikhail in the diner, Jeanette had gone to Clínica Paloma and waited two hours for a doctor to give her an abortion, then had left Watsonville that evening. For a long time, she obsessed about the fetus she had aborted. She wanted to know what they did with the remains. Was the tissue buried? Incinerated? Or simply dumped in a land-fill as medical waste, considered no different than soiled dressings, used syringes, and bloodied gloves?

She called Central Coast Legal Aid once, several years ago. She wanted to get in touch with Elizabeth and Mikhail. She thought maybe now, after all this time, if she could contact them, they'd be more forthcoming, and she could at last arrive at the truth, know one way or the other if Étienne had cheated on her, and if he had ever truly loved her. But she didn't know their last names or anything else about them, not nearly enough information to track them down, and, anyway, the archive for the legal clinic, she was told, had been destroyed in a fire a decade before.

Jeanette and Joe walked back to her car at the Golden Gate National Cemetery. Mike and Patsy had cut the picnic lunch relatively short. They had a long drive back to Modesto and were hoping to beat the holiday traffic.

As they were loading her trunk, Joe said to Jeanette, "You're not going to call Yadin?"

"Why?" Her cellphone had been on mute when Yadin had left his voicemails and texts, saying he was hurrying to the cemetery. She chose not to reply. She hadn't mentioned the messages to her father, and didn't feel like doing so now.

Joe took off his suit jacket, and Jeanette noticed his white shirt had yellowed sweat stains in the armpits. "You should tell him we're leaving," he said. "He might be on his way here."

"You said fat chance."

"Still."

She ignored her father. She had been worried about Yadin, worried he might be stranded somewhere on the highway, waiting for a tow, but once she knew that he was all right, she felt inexplicably angry with him, and wanted to punish him a little. She was irked that he hadn't listened to her about the van, the noises it was making. It had been irresponsible of him. He'd let her down by not coming today, helping her deal with her aunt and uncle. Mainly, she wasn't willing to dismiss Franklin's suspicions so quickly anymore. Maybe Yadin was lying to her. He was hiding something, she was almost certain. A secret. She thought he should be the one to keep trying to call her, appease her, grovel, not the other way around.

She took her father back to Rosarita Bay, and from the Longfellow Elementary School parking lot, Joe hustled home in his van to watch the Giants on TV—an away game in St. Louis. Jeanette went to her bungalow to soak in a bath, change, and get the groceries from her refrigerator, and by the time she reached her father's house, the game was in its final innings.

While Joe showered and napped, Jeanette prepared dinners for her father to microwave during the week. She always did this on Monday (every other Thursday, she cleaned the house for him). She assembled meals that her mother had made for the family: curry rice, breaded pork cutlets, thinly sliced barbecued beef, stir-fried noodles, and ginger pork. Jeanette had all of Jo's original recipes, which her mother had typed neatly on index cards, sometimes annotating them by hand ("only 1 tsp sugar," "touch more soy"). Jo had been a very serviceable cook, and she'd inspired Jeremy to become a chef. He made copies of the recipes, and then later enhanced them with French and Italian techniques he'd learned in culinary school.

His plan had been to open a restaurant specializing in haute stoner cuisine, with everything locally sourced, farm to table, his dishes imparting umami—a savory flavor—which was the last of the five tastes, rounding out salty, sweet, sour, and bitter. In some cultures, there was a sixth taste, piquant, and Jeremy wanted to infuse that into his menu, too, along with the option of having a fried egg on every item.

When he was released from Lompoc, Jeremy worked for their father for several years, learning to lay carpet for Wall to Wall. At one point, he considered starting a food truck, and he applied for a vendor permit and a business license in Rosarita Bay, yet was denied both. The applications required a criminal background check, and conspiracy to distribute drugs was regarded as a crime of moral turpitude.

For dinner tonight, Jeanette made teriyaki chicken thighs with sides of rice, broiled eggplant, and vinegared cucumber. She wished her father would at least attempt to learn how to cook for himself. Everything was spelled out in the recipes, and she offered time and again to go through them with him, but he always turned her down. When he ran out of the meals she'd stocked in Tupperware containers, he resorted to salami and cream cheese sandwiches. She wondered what he would do if she ever left town, how he'd manage without her attending to his every need. She supposed he would just microwave store-bought frozen dinners, like she did.

At the dining table, her father popped open another Anchor Steam. He was working on his second six-pack of the day. Not a good sign. On the other hand, Jeanette was drinking her third glass of wine.

"Here," he said, sliding a check to her. He always asked Jeanette to have the clerks at Costco ring up his items separately so he would know the exact amount to reimburse her.

He cut up a piece of chicken and chewed it, sampled each of the sides. "Good," he said.

"Thanks."

"Why didn't you make this for the picnic?" Joe asked. "Maybe with wings? I thought you were going to bring something."

"Didn't have time."

"I guess they had enough of a spread there."

"Why was it so important to you for me to go today?" she asked. "They wouldn't have missed me."

"You can't let bygones?" Joe said, his mouth full.

She disliked when her father talked without swallowing first—a habit of his. "Some things can never be bygone," she said. "Mom would be disappointed if I ever let it be bygone."

"You go to a church now. You're the president of it."

"There's no comparison. I'm still an atheist."

"Family's important," Joe told her. "It's the most important thing in life."

If he truly believed that, Jeanette thought, then why was he, for all intents and purposes, estranged from his only son? "They're virtual strangers to me," she said. "Might as well be to you, too. You never see them."

"He's my brother. He'll always be my brother, and this twentieth anniversary was a big deal to him."

They finished eating, and Joe helped her clear the table. As she was washing the dishes, she noticed that the edge of Joe's plate was chipped. The dish was a thin square, very delicate. It was made from clay that had been rolled into a slab and then hand-shaped and glazed with bright colors in an abstract pattern of dots and triangles. The set of plates and bowls was the last ceramics project her mother had completed.

For much of her married life, Jo had had a part-time job at the Moonside Trading Post, a gallery and gift shop that was also, for a while, a video store. The shop went through many iterations, remarkable only for the dependable mediocrity of the artwork and wares for sale. At one point, Jo had said, "I could do better myself." She began taking art classes at SVCC, first in drawing and painting, then in crafts, experimenting with various mediums, going from batik to decoupage to ceramics. Eventually the trading post put some of her work on display, and they sold respectably. She loved when tourists would point to one of her pieces and ask, "Who's the artist?"

Much of her artwork was still in the house, though not her personal effects. It had been gut-wrenching, sorting through her clothes, jewelry, and other possessions after she'd died. Joe and Jeanette could not stop crying. "You want this?" he would ask her, sobbing, as they cleared out Jo's drawers. "You should take this. It's still good."

She grabbed her father's white shirt from his bedroom and went into the den, where Joe was watching the MLB Network, catching up on highlights of other games.

"What are you doing with my shirt?" he asked. At least he usually did his own laundry, and even his own ironing.

"I'm going to take it home and try to get rid of these stains." She had several reliable methods—aspirin, hydrogen peroxide, vodka.

"I wonder if Alberto VO5 would work," Joe said. "I still have an old tube."

She laughed.

"What?"

"You ready?"

Joe aimed his remote at the TV and turned it off, stood up

slowly from his Barcalounger, and followed Jeanette across the hall into the bathroom, where she had set up one of the dining chairs for his haircut. The bathroom had a tiled floor, which made it easier for her afterward to sweep, vacuum, and lint-roll his shorn hair.

Once her father was seated, she wrapped a sheet around his neck. After cinching the sheet with a clothespin, she plugged in the clippers, attached a #2 guide comb, and began at the nape.

Joe, his head bent forward, asked, "How're you and Yadin doing?"

She heard an echo of Franklin's query from the other night. Why was everyone asking? It was particularly odd coming from Joe. He never inquired about their relationship. "Good," she said.

"Yeah?" her father said. "It was weird to me, the whole thing today about not calling. You guys don't seem to talk a lot for a couple, or even see each other much."

"We're both busy. We work a lot. We have our own lives, and that suits us just fine."

The thing was, she liked being alone. After living at home for so long, she had relished being alone, having her own place, the bungalow she had made beautiful. She had been fully absorbed with the church and working at city hall and decorating her little house, going to thrift stores and yard sales, crafting ornaments and knickknacks. The few times she had let Yadin spend the night, she had felt as if she were being crushed on the bed, not having space or air. As much as she tried, she couldn't get rid of that sensation—being suffocated by him.

She focused on making careful, concise strokes with the clippers, rhythmically arching them away from her father's head as she went upward.

"You've been together almost three years," Joe said. "The two of you talked about getting married anytime soon?"

The question caught her by surprise. "What's brought this on?"

"You think you guys might?"

"I don't know. Maybe."

"You could do worse," Joe said.

"Meaning I couldn't do better?" Jeanette asked.

Joe canted his head and peered back at her. "I didn't say that."

"He's still flat broke. He's going to be as stooped as you are in a few years, and he already has the hearing of an old man."

"Overall he's a good guy, though, isn't he? You have to admire how hard he's worked to get his shit together. He got out of debt, gave up that music nonsense, realized what it means to work for a living. He's been a good employee. He's responsible, honest, practical, he never complains. He doesn't drink or do drugs. He has a pretty good business sense. He came up with an idea to add carpet cleaning and repair to our services. I think we could make a go of that."

"He's not that practical," Jeanette said. "You know how much all his supplements cost? And he spends about twenty bucks a week on scratch tickets and the SuperLotto." She didn't know why, but the more Joe defended Yadin, the more compelled she felt to criticize him. "Then there's his food—everything has to be organic."

"Julie's pregnant," Joe said.

She stopped clipping his hair. "What?"

"Fourteen weeks. Her due date's November fourteenth."

"When did she tell you this?" Jeanette asked.

"Couple of weeks ago."

Jeanette should not have been hurt that her sister didn't tell her the news herself, but she was. Julie had been eleven years old when Jo died. From that moment on, Jeanette had raised her, fed her, taken her to school, to play dates, to sports practices. She had been her surrogate mother. Yet Julie grew more and more distant from Jeanette after she went to the University of Washington on a golf scholarship, and then to UCSD for law school, her tuition paid in large part by Joe, something he never offered to do for Jeanette or Jeremy. He had always pampered Julie, given her everything she wished—getting her braces, for example, when he had told Jeanette as a child that she would have to live with her crooked incisors.

"Is she going to give up being an attorney?" she asked her father.

"She'll go on maternity leave, and then see. Andy makes enough so she doesn't have to work."

Julie had been an associate in her law firm for only a year. Andy, a cardiologist, was twelve years older than Julie—an age difference that Joe had objected to, until he heard how much money Andy made. Her sister had always made it a point to say that she'd wait to have children, that her career would come first, but evidently circumstances had changed her priorities.

Jeanette resumed cutting her father's hair, tilting his head the other way.

"You know I've always wanted grandkids," Joe said. "I'd like to be around. I'm thinking I might move down there."

"To San Diego?"

"Not right now. In a year or two. I'll be sixty-six next January. I'll be eligible for full Social Security, and I've got some mutual funds."

She couldn't imagine her father not working. "You'd really retire?"

"I'd do something down there—I don't know what," Joe said. "First thing, they want to put in an addition and build a guesthouse in back for me, and I'd be the contractor for those. I was asking about you and Yadin because I was thinking, if you two got married, maybe I'd leave him my business."

"You'd just give it to him?"

"I'd expect a percentage of the monthly net while I'm still alive. I know he'll never have the money for a buyout."

"What about Jeremy?" Jeanette asked.

"What about him?"

"Shouldn't you consider leaving Wall to Wall to Jeremy? He worked for you. He knows the trade."

"Are you fucking kidding me?" Joe asked. "You know how much he still owes me in legal fees?"

She stared at the scar and lump on her father's scalp, now exposed with the shortened hair. The scar, two inches long, was from a childhood accident, climbing a cyclone fence. The lump, Joe could never explain. Sometime or another, he said, he must have smacked his head somewhere, he couldn't remember. When Jeanette first began cutting his hair and had noticed it, she worried he had a tumor and asked him repeatedly to have the lump examined. He never did.

"You talk about how Yadin's put his life back together," she said to Joe. "What about Jeremy? What about me? How about giving us some credit? We're your children."

"Jeremy doesn't give a shit about carpet. He hated every minute of it."

"He hated the way you made him feel," she told him. "You never let him forget how ashamed you were of him."

"You have no idea what it was like, having to tell people your son's in prison," Joe said. "Fucking right he should've been ashamed. I'd rather have said he was dead."

She stopped clipping again. "You don't mean that."

"No. You're right. I don't," he told Jeanette. "I don't know why I said that. It was a terrible thing to say. But you know the last thing he'd want is the business. He wants to be a chef. Yadin's the logical choice. The two of you could be set. It's not big bucks, with the way this town's dying on the vine, the fucking fad for hardwood, but if he ran it with a skeleton crew, it'd be a living. I wouldn't have to worry about you anymore."

She was at once touched and insulted, hearing her father say he worried about her. She had long assumed that she would have to take care of him in his old age. She'd always fretted that if something happened to her, he would have no one to cook for him, or clip his hair, or clean his house, or do his shopping.

She switched to a #4 guide comb and buzzed the top, cropping his thinning hair from front to back. "There's not a lot of passion between us," she said.

"Passion's overrated. That's not what marriage is about. You've always been a romantic, and it's never led you anywhere good."

"Étienne, you mean."

"You have these ideals, but you're thirty-nine now, almost forty," Joe said. "You're too old for ideals. People in our family, they don't live very long, you know. Yadin's nice to you, isn't he? You have some of the same interests. Your church. You trust him. Those are the important things."

Jeanette took off the guide comb and turned the clippers upside down. She trimmed his neckline, sides, and sideburns, pressing downward with the blades angled forty-five degrees. "We've never even talked about living together," she said. "Where would we live? My place is only big enough for one person, and his is a dump."

"I'm planning on giving you the house," Joe said.

"You are?"

"You were asking me before about going on a date," her father said. "I'm an ornery motherfucker. I wouldn't know where to begin, having to be nice to someone at this stage. I should've remarried when I still had the chance, while I was still relatively young. I didn't realize, there's nothing worse than growing old alone. I don't want that to happen to you, babe. It hurts, seeing you so sad all the time. It really hurts."

From the Centurion hotel, Yadin retraced his morning route along the golf course and the coastal trail, half running. By the time he reached his van in the dirt lot at the end of Vista Del Mar, it was almost eleven-thirty. The observance ceremony at the Golden Gate National Cemetery would be over soon, but Yadin thought if he was quick about it, he might be able to get to San Bruno for part of the picnic. He tried calling Jeanette to tell her he was on the way. It rang and rang, and eventually went to voicemail. He left a message.

In his van, he hurried across Montecito Avenue to Highway 1, drove through town, and turned east onto Highway 71. No one was on the road, and he was making good time. But then, just before the top of the hill, he came to a standstill. The traffic wasn't moving at all. His van rattled and shook on the incline. He texted Jeanette that there was a backup. It took over an hour and a half to travel the five miles to Interstate 280, and it wasn't until near the bottom of the other side of the hill that he understood why. The cab of a tractor-trailer was squashed against the embankment of a sharp curve. The truck driver must have been speeding or lost his brakes. In the process, he had taken out a sedan, which was partially flattened underneath the wheels of the truck. Yadin couldn't tell whether there had been any fatalities. By that point, the drivers and passengers, if there had been any, had been hauled away.

He phoned Jeanette again; he wanted to know how long she and Joe would be staying at the cemetery. Again she didn't answer, and again he left a message. He continued onto Interstate 280, rumbling the nine miles to the Golden Gate National Cemetery. After passing through the tree-lined entrance, he stopped at the office, seeking the location to Jeanette's cousin's plot. The people there directed him to a kiosk outside, which housed a computer. He typed in Atticus's name, and a letter and a four-digit number appeared on the screen. Confused, he looked around the kiosk, then saw a map with the cemetery divided into alphabetical sections and numerical rows.

As he drove to Atticus's section, he admired how clean and well tended everything was—the unblemished roads and curbs, the grass cut and trimmed immaculately, the neatness and symmetry of the headstones, all of them perfectly aligned in rows, a small American flag in front of each one.

He found the section and walked between the rows, following the plot numbers until he came upon Atticus's headstone. Jeanette and Joe and their relatives were nowhere in view. He was too late. The picnic was over. He stared down at the grave, which was surrounded by half a dozen bouquets of flowers, most of them still wrapped in cellophane. Engraved near the top of the headstone was a cross in a circle, the marble freshly scrubbed and glossy. He wondered if Jeanette had helped polish it. It was so quiet here, the mood of the cemetery hushed, reverential. The vastness and solemnity of the grounds moved him.

He had never met Atticus's father, mother, or sister. He thought it sad that Jeanette was so alienated from them, much as it pained him sometimes that Joe wasn't closer to his son. Family was family. If they could see things from his perspective—as someone with no family at all—they might not have taken their kin so much for granted.

His mother had died at fifty-eight—a heavy drinker and smoker. He hadn't seen much of her after he'd left home at seventeen. She had kept a shrine of his brother Davey's photos in whatever apartment or house she'd landed, and she had continued speaking of Davey—the golden one, the pretty one—in the present tense. Yadin knew she partly blamed him for his brother's death, bitter that Yadin's bone marrow had not been compatible for a transplant, resenting him for living when Davey had had to die. Yadin did not disagree with her. He, too, thought he should have died, not his brother.

His father was dead as well. Yadin didn't find out about it

until years after the fact. A former Goodrich sales rep who'd been friends with him happened to be in a club where Yadin was playing, and had told him. Apparently his father had remarried twice, but didn't have any more children.

In front of Atticus's grave, Yadin stood with his head bowed, eyes closed, hands together, and recited the Lord's Prayer. In the last few days, he had been learning the prayers for the rosary and had researched on the Internet how to make the Sign of the Cross. Squeezing the thumb, index finger, and middle finger of his right hand together, he touched his forehead and said, "In the name of the Father," and touched his chest and said, "and of the Son," and touched his left shoulder and said, "and of the Holy," and touched his right shoulder and said, "Spirit," and pressed his palms together and said, "Amen."

He thought he had done this correctly. He was a bit unclear about the horizontal sequence, which shoulder to touch first. On some websites, they instructed going the opposite direction, right to left, but he had read on one forum that you went from left to right to symbolize moving from misery to glory, and Yadin had liked that.

He headed back to Rosarita Bay. He wondered if Jeanette was intentionally not answering his calls or returning his messages. She could have saved him the trip. Was she upset with him? He felt guilty for lying to her about his van breaking down, about going to the Centurion, but he didn't think that could have been the reason she seemed to be in a pique. She couldn't have known that he was at the hotel, unless Siobhan had phoned her right away or someone else had spotted him entering the resort, which he thought unlikely. Maybe she was simply angry with him for bailing on her today, when she could have used his support. Or was she still thinking that he might be having an affair with Caroline? How would Jeanette react if she ever found out that he had gone to see Mallory?

And that kiss. What was he to make of that kiss?

He had thought, seeing Mallory again, that he would be elated, but he wasn't. He felt strangely disillusioned—not necessarily with Mallory, but with himself. He couldn't put his finger on why. Somehow everything felt different now. Fraudulent. Maybe that was why he had changed his mind about giving her the cassette of his album, especially after she'd alluded to his unwillingness to compromise, to the things she had been forced to get over. It made him forlorn, since with this record he had been trying to return to that place of purity they'd inhabited together in Raleigh, when they were starting out as musicians.

After they broke up, he had gone back to Ohio, to Elyria, where Davey was buried, for a few months, and then had moved to and fro along Interstate 80, working menial jobs and sending out demos to record companies, to no avail. Once in a while he busked on sidewalks and did open mics. He knew he would have to get better as a performer if he ever wanted to win a recording contract. After four years, when he was twenty-seven, the founders of a new indie label in Chicago, Inland Records, heard him playing a set in the side bar of a club called FitzGerald's. They asked him to record a song for a compilation of what they were then calling insurgent country, and later signed him as a solo artist. They didn't put any pressure on him initially. They knew he wasn't the type of singer who'd ever chart big sales, but they loved his music, they said, and wanted to support it. Even if he remained niched on late-night college and public radio, they told him they'd be satisfied.

As the company grew, things began to change. They started making suggestions here and there, particularly about his performances. They arranged for Yadin to get a manager (aka a handler, a babysitter, a noodge), who had a doctor prescribe him Xanax and Inderal for his stage fright, though he still needed to chase them with other drugs and liquor. They discouraged him from playing with his back to the audience and using light installations. They asked him to stand front and center instead of sitting off to the side in a chair, and to talk to the audience once in a while, try to be charming, personable, witty. Yadin didn't know how he could manage to talk to the audience when he could barely walk onto the stage without passing out. Already he had to have his lyrics in clear plastic pocket sleeves, spread out on the floor at his feet, because often he was so nervous and overwhelmed, he'd forget them mid-song. They expected him to do stage banter? He couldn't tell stories. He couldn't tell a knock-knock joke. Trying to be accommodating, he wrote out some stage banter to slip into a pocket sleeve. He always included a Townes Van Zandt cover in his set list, usually "Waiting 'Round to Die," and he used the song as a segue for a few stories about TVZ, like how he once lost his gold tooth in a card game—anecdotes he stole from Steve Earle and Guy Clark.

Then Inland's PR people—seemingly overnight, after they became a major-label subsidiary, they had a cadre of PR people—told his manager that something had to be done about Yadin's looks, his persona. He came off as sullen, burly, *scary*. That was when he was put on Accutane. They wanted him, too, to dress better. His flannel shirts and two-tone trucker caps and work pants and construction boots were so square, so hicksville, never mind the beard and matted, tangled hair. (Ironically, the ensemble later became standard hipster garb, boho chic. He had been fashionable before his time.)

After the mega-label merger, Inland said he could release a double CD, then reneged. They said he could put together an EP of downbeat love songs, then shelved it. Instead, they wanted crossover singles. They wanted hooks; foot-stomping beats; heavy guitar strumming; big, rollicking choruses; pounding, anthemic folk-rock. They hired producers and engineers for him, who, in the studio, would ask for take after take. They would listen to playbacks and insist on comping Yadin's vocals, patching together the cleanest segments from various passes for a pristine master. They'd have various session players drop in to record isolated tracks and assemble everything together on a computer with filters and plug-ins. The songs would sound nothing like what Yadin had played and sung. He despised everything about the process.

By that point, he had accepted that he would never win a Grammy or be anything more than a cult favorite. He no longer had any delusions about being a brilliant songwriter, or more than serviceable as a singer, or that he'd ever be anything other than an embarrassment as a performer. He knew there were tens of thousands of singer-songwriters out there who were just as talented as he was, if not more so. Some people made it. Most didn't. Not in any big way. It hadn't happened for him. That was just the way it was. But he was fine with being a journeyman. All he wanted was to be able to earn a living with his music and not have to succumb to day jobs between albums. Yet that proved impossible. Despite decent advances, after everyone from his manager to his booking agent had taken their cuts and points, after accounting for administrative overhead, expenses, and what were called packaging deductions, after subtracting his taxes and cross-collateralizing his royalties, whatever the hell that was, somehow Yadin was always in the hole with a negative balance. (It could have been, too, that his manager was embezzling from him, he realized later.)

It was a relief, really, to be out of the music business. He was glad to be done with it. He was satisfied with his life in Rosarita Bay—quiet and anonymous, with no ambitions other than to make an honest living and have a roof over his head and be with Jeanette and her family. He'd been certain that he would never return to making music again. That was why the emergence of the new songs had been such a surprise to him.

A month ago, in late April, he'd been driving past Chávez Field and had seen a Little League game in progress. Idly, he had parked and climbed into the stands to watch the game. It was several days after the end of Lent, and, ashamed and bereft, he was convinced he had failed in his spiritual exercise. He had stopped going on walks. He was no longer trying to pray. He planned to return the dictionary, academic book, and field guides to the library. He had all but given up.

The Little League game was between the Lions Club Twins and the R. B. Feed & Hardware Tigers. As a kid, Yadin had been an avid Detroit Tigers fan. Davey, too. Together, they had ridden the high of the Tigers winning the AL East in 1972, tumbled to heartbreak when the team lost in the LCS, then were stuck in the muck for the next four years, during which the Tigers were unable to rise above .500, true misery coming in 1975, when the team lost over a hundred games. The following season offered some hope, or at least some entertainment, with the debut of The Bird, Mark Fidrych. Yadin and Davey had loved the pitcher's antics, how he'd get on his knees to manicure the mound, smoothing it out with his hands, the way he would talk to himself and the ball. But before the end of the season, Davey would die, and Fidrych would be long gone by the time Detroit finally won the World Series in 1984, Kirk Gibson the star of that squad.

Yadin still followed the Tigers, though for Joe's sake he was trying to become a Giants convert. He had watched every playoff game with Joe last year, when the Giants had won the Series for the first time since moving to San Francisco. But

Yadin couldn't seem to get invested in the National League. All of his history was with the American League—the rivalries, the grittiness of the players and stadiums.

At the plate, a kid from the Lions Club Twins took a long, hard, looping swing, releasing his top hand from the handle of the bat as he rotated, which caused him to lose his balance and stumble out of the batter's box. He whiffed, struck out. When had they begun teaching Little Leaguers to hit like this, as if they were man-sized pros? Davey's swing had been short and quick and compact, and he had kept the barrel of the bat flat through the zone as long as possible. Not much ever got by him. After contact, he'd pronate and supinate his forearms, rolling his wrists, with both hands remaining on the handle, so he wouldn't lose any speed or control or power. It had been a sweet lefty stroke—not unlike Kirk Gibson's—even at ten years old.

"You didn't have any holes in that swing," Yadin whispered aloud, then, silently, he continued in apostrophe: *You would have made the high school team for sure, maybe gotten a scholarship to college. Who knows, maybe you would have made it to the show.*

For the next few days, he kept talking to Davey—first Davey as a boy, then Davey as the young man Yadin imagined he would have grown up to be, handsome and kind. He imagined Davey living with him in his apartment in Michigan and attending Kalamazoo Central High School, Derek Jeter's alma mater, and becoming a walk-on second baseman at the University of Michigan. He imagined Davey being drafted in the twenty-first round by the Orioles (alas, not the Tigers) and playing single-A ball with the Aberdeen IronBirds, the Delmarva Shorebirds, and the Frederick Keys before tearing the ACL in his left knee. He imagined that afterward Davey would have returned to college and gotten a job in supply chain management in the pet food industry, developing just-in-time delivery systems for Proctor & Gamble, rising to be an executive for Iams in Mason, Ohio, outside of Cincinnati. He would have married a former collegiate tennis player named Sissy who was now an assistant tournament director for the Western & Southern Open, and who—lithe and fast—could still kick Davey's ass on the court. They would have had four kids, Mickey, Dustin, Margot, and Rose, and two dogs and a cat, Oscar, Neon, and Popcorn, all of them living together clamorously in a five-bedroom, six-bathroom colonial with Brazilian cherry floors and an in-ground pool on four acres—bustling with barbecues and backyard touch football games and movie nights—to which Yadin was always welcome.

"What's it like there, Davey?" Yadin asked. "Is it nice?

"Yes, it is," Davey told him. "You shouldn't be afraid."

He imagined driving down a country two-lane in Montana with Davey, just the two of them, on an extended weekend getaway, the fishing trip they'd always dreamed of taking. Windows open in the car, they would smell the hard red wheat alongside the road, shoots waving and rustling in the wind, the fields—nearing harvest, green turning tawny-gold—running for miles until they met the Little Belt Mountains, ghost-blue in the distance, all under that boundless cerulean, white wisps and pulled puffballs of clouds high high in the sky. They would stop for gas, both getting out and standing beside the pump to stretch their legs, everything so quiet, Yadin aware of the engine tick-tocking, the dust of grain kernels sanding the air, water dripping from a basin in the garage and dinking the cement.

Back on the road, they would happen upon a station on the radio playing Gram Parsons's "A Song for You." Yadin would crank the dial, and they would listen to GP and Emmylou in reverent silence—those harmonies, the fiddle, the hymnal swell of Elvis's old sideman, Glen D. Hardin, on the Hammond B-3 organ. They wouldn't utter a syllable even after the song had ended, Yadin turning off the radio, driving another mile before the brothers would simply say, in unison, "Goddamn."

They would eat at a roadside diner, a shack, really, sizzles and clangs, cusses and burnt musks emanating from the smoky kitchen, but they would be served wonderful elk burgers, juicy, thick patties topped with caramelized onions, bacon, huckleberry sauce, and a fried egg on a toasted brioche bun, soft, chewy, crunchy raptures of flavor with each bite. Finally, they would arrive at their rental cabin, but would quickly set off again to fly-fish a section of the Judith River known for its rainbows, cutthroats, and cutbows. They would wade and cast and nymph for hours, and wouldn't catch a damn thing, which would not, really, make a bit of difference to them, just being out there together, brothers, in the sun and in the clear, glinty burbling water, the river currenting by them, surrounded by pines and junipers and cottonwoods that dangled over the banks.

Returning to the cabin, they would take turns showering and then sit on the porch and drink longnecks and watch the sunset, meadowlarks fluting out warble-whistles. Yadin would grill rib eyes while Davey made broccoli and York-shire pudding, popping open a bottle of hearty Grenache. After dinner, they would drink coffee and smoke cigars on the porch—oh, the splashed pinpricks of stars, the click pop chirp of insects, the hooing of an owl, the trembling leaves of aspens—then they would repair inside and arrange straight-backed chairs in the living room, and, facing each other, with Davey on their father's old Eko Ranger VI dreadnought and Yadin on his vintage Martin D-21, they would play duets of Townes Van Zandt's "To Live Is to Fly" and "No Place to Fall," alternating vocals on the verses, joining for the chorus.

Along with Davey, Yadin began speaking to his mother, to his grandmother, to relatives he never knew he had, to his father. In that club years ago, Yadin hadn't thought to ask his father's friend, the Goodrich sales rep who'd told him about his death, if his father had ever listened to his music, or had even known that Yadin had become a recording artist, and he had always regretted not asking.

These talks with "the other"—wasn't that how Caroline had phrased it? Was this what she had meant? Probably not. Yet Yadin felt different. Becalmed. Maybe he hadn't been touched, per se, by God, but he thought he had found a connection to the numinous. There was a movement within him toward what could be called grace, and this gave him comfort. The world around him slowed, but at the same time was in sharper relief. He was attentive to things now that he had long ago stopped noticing. Children laughing, birdsong, rain, the wind, his own breath.

The irony was not lost on him that he had never really learned to hear, to listen, until this moment, when he was losing his hearing. He rued all those years he had worn earplugs to bed to muffle the sounds of the world outside. Fire trucks. Barking dogs. Car alarms. Crickets. All those noises interested him now. He awoke to them. What he thought, for once, for the first time in many years, was that it was good to be alive.

"Something's happening," he told Caroline in the library.

"I'm glad."

"But I didn't do it right."

"It's not a test. There's no right or wrong way."

He started writing spontaneously in his notebook. Not reflections or thoughts or prayers. Songs. Very straightforward songs—plaintive, understated ballads, almost subversive in their simplicity, in their nakedness and sincerity. He remembered something Townes Van Zandt had once said: "There's only two kinds of music: the blues, and zippity-doo-dah." Then he remembered something Townes's friend Mickey Newbury had once said: "How many people have listened to my songs and thought, 'He must have a bottle of whiskey in one hand and a pistol in the other'? Well, I don't. I write my sadness."

That was what Yadin was doing. He was writing the blues. He was writing his sadness.

One after another, the songs presented themselves to Yadin, and he began to wonder what he should do with them, if anything. Maybe he would record them. But for what purpose? he asked himself. He had neither the desire nor the means to attempt a comeback.

April turned to May, more songs accrued. He kept thinking about one of Hopkins's earlier poems, "The Habit of Perfection," which began:

> Elected silence, sing to me
> And beat upon my whorlèd ear,
> Pipe me to pastures still and be
> The music that I care to hear.

There was something achingly beautiful to Yadin about Hopkins's commitment to asceticism and humility, his vow to leave all bourgeois pursuits behind, subscribing, as Caroline had said, to a voluntary silence.

He decided he would record this one last album, while he could still hear. Not as a comeback, not to try to revive his career, but as a coda, a valediction. A way to leave on his own terms, and say, *I was here.* Then he would sell all his instruments and equipment and never write another song. This would be his consolation. He would elect silence, and walk into the light.

When he returned home that afternoon from San Bruno, there was a silver Mercedes-Benz convertible parked in front of his cottage. He got out of his van and saw Mallory on his front steps, smoking a cigarette. Her hair was tied into a ponytail, and she wore large hoop earrings, a blazer with the sleeves rolled up, a black tee, tight capri pants, and ballet flats.

"What are you doing here?" Yadin asked her. For a second, he let his imagination flood with possible explanations, most of them absurd. "I thought you had to get back to L.A."

"I did. I postponed the meeting. I decided to stay another night. Where have you been? I've been waiting here all afternoon. Why'd you give me your landline? Don't you have a cell? Can I use your bathroom? Like, right this minute?"

He let her in his house. He stood in the kitchen, and through the closed bathroom door, he listened to her pee—a steady, splashy stream that felt, the longer it went on, too intimate to hear—and then to the toilet flushing and the faucet running. She said something to him through the door.

"You had a date with a WASP?" Yadin asked, for that was what he had heard.

"What?" she said, the water still burbling as she washed her hands. "No, can I take some of your floss? I've got something between my teeth, it's been driving me crazy."

After another minute, she came out of the bathroom and surveyed his living room and kitchen. "I like your decorating scheme," she said. "Very minimalistic."

He was abashed. After everything in the cottage had been pawned or auctioned, he had replaced only the bare essentials, not bothering with décor, just function. But now he was shamefaced, imagining what his house, his circumstances, must look like to Mallory, as if he were as indigent as he'd been in Raleigh before he met her. "Why are you here?" he asked.

"Curiosity got the better of me," she said. "I really want to hear the new songs. I've told you, more than once, I'm bad at waiting."

"Why? Why's it so important to you?"

"I don't exactly know myself. It just is," Mallory said. "Will you let me hear a track or two?"

Now that she was in his house, he could not say no. He needed her to confirm for him that this project was worthwhile, that it was as solid as he believed, and Mallory would be candid if she thought he was deceiving himself. He took her down the hallway into his studio.

"You weren't kidding when you said you were doing this DIY," Mallory said.

"There's something about the ambient sound in here," he told her, "something connected to the wood. You'll see."

He pulled out the straight-backed chair from the worktable for her. He turned on his studio monitors, slid the levels up on his TASCAM four-track recorder, and sorted through the cassettes in the cardboard shoe box on the table for the first track. The tape for the full album was still in the pocket of his windbreaker, but he wasn't ready to unfurl the whole thing to Mallory yet.

"That's the name of the album?" she asked. "*Lonesome Lies Before Us?*"

"What?" he said, then realized he had scrawled the title on the shoe box with a Sharpie. "Yeah."

She contemplated, then said, "I don't get it."

"What do you mean?"

"There are lies that are lonesome, and they're right in front of us?" she asked. "In front of our very noses?"

"What?" Yadin asked.

"Or there are people, other people, who made lonesome lies in the past, which still affect everything that's happening to us now?"

"What?" he said. "No. Lonesomeness, or loneliness, it's lying before us, laid out ahead of us, in our future, for everyone, no matter what we do."

"You might need to change that," Mallory said.

"Really?" Yadin said, unaccountably irritated.

"Wait, isn't that from a Rodney Crowell song?"

He found the tape labeled "Shades on the Window," jammed it into the TASCAM, and punched play. There was a fingerpicking intro in six-eight time, then Yadin singing:

> *It's astray inside of me*
> *That year so long ago*
> *When it all came undone*
>
> *You're a ghost so far away*
> *It's the same thing every day*
> *I only see you leaving*

Wherever were you going
It was never with me
It was only one for oneself

I'm outside your house
There's only darkness within
And I can't see a thing

Let me into the room
Show me just for once
Who you've always been

Let me see where you live
Part for me just once
The shades on your window

Yadin watched Mallory listening to the song, watched her
face, and he waited for her to react in some way—to narrow
her eyes or cringe or murmur or smile or nod or shake her
head. Nothing. She thought the song was hopeless. He had
been fooling himself. The whole record was a fiasco.

When the track ended, Mallory asked, "Can I hear
another one?"

He would let her hear them all, but he could not endure
staying in the studio with her while she did. From the shoe
box, he picked out the tapes for the rest of the album, stacked
them in order, and left Mallory to her own devices.

He went outside and paced in front of his house for a

while, then sat in his van. An eternity. It should have taken Mallory less than fifty minutes to listen to all twelve songs, but it was more than an hour and a half before she opened the front door.

She looked to be in a stupor, as if she had been up all night. "Do you want to go somewhere for dinner?" she asked. "I'm starving."

"I have some food," he said.

He sat her down at his café pedestal table, and, from a plastic tub, he scooped out a salad of Swiss chard, cabbage, garbanzo beans, broccoli stems, cottage cheese, grapes, and almonds onto a plate and a bowl.

"You sure you don't want to go out?" Mallory asked.

"This is easy enough," he said.

"To be honest, that doesn't look too appetizing."

"I think you can rough it this one time, Mallory."

He fetched the straight-backed chair from the studio and joined her at the table. They poked at their salads, and he gulped from his glass of mineral water, apprehensive, waiting for her verdict on the songs, growing impatient and despondent.

"The album's brilliant," she told him.

He had never been so relieved, nor grateful. "You really think so?" he asked.

"I really think so," she said to him. "They might be the best things you've ever written. They tear your heart out. They couldn't be sadder. It's a little punishing at times, but there's something beautiful in that. You're singing as if it's the last time you'll ever get the chance, the last show you'll ever play. Everything's tight and focused. There's not a single extraneous note. Every one of these songs is a gem, Yadin. There's not a filler or dud among them. Have you let anyone else listen to them?"

"No. Just you."

"You should," Mallory told him. "You could find a major label for this for sure."

"No one would want anything this bleak."

"I could give it to Ronnie, my music manager. He might have some ideas."

"None of this has any commercial potential," Yadin said. "Especially with me as the recording artist. If you're an alt-country singer, you're in no-man's-land."

"They're calling it Americana or roots now," Mallory said, "and they're big categories. There's an audience for it. What would it hurt to have Ronnie make a few calls?"

"Those days are over for me," he told her. "I'm done with that route, letting myself get ripped apart."

In many ways, the new world of the music industry— reduced to self-releasing—was liberating to Yadin. He wouldn't have to worry about the numbers or hope for a breakout or prove anything to anyone. The only person he had to please was himself.

Mallory mindfully chewed a tiny bite of salad. "You still have a fan base out there," she told him after swallowing. "You ever read the posts on that forum?"

"What forum?"

"The one dedicated to you."

"There's a forum about me?" he asked. "On the Internet?"

"How do you not know about these things?" she asked. "It's called the Yadin Park Preservation Society. That's how I found out about your experimental tapes. They've been waiting for another album from you, just as I have. It'd be a great story—your comeback. Who doesn't love a comeback? All the stuff about your sobriety, getting healthy, losing so much weight, that's a compelling media angle. Why won't you even explore getting a label?"

"I told you, Mallory, I've made up my mind about this."

"You know what's involved with a self-release?" she asked. "All the things you have to do these days as an indie musician?"

She told him that he would have to promote himself on Facebook, Twitter, Instagram, Bandcamp, Myspace, and YouTube. He would have to maintain a website and a blog and an email newsletter. He would have to manage accounts on PayPal and Rhapsody, SoundCloud, Amazon, iTunes, CD Baby, Pandora, and Spotify, and God knew what else.

"It's mind-boggling," she said, "all the details you have to attend to. Then, for tours, you can't just play in clubs anymore. There aren't enough venues left, and the economics—going to a city for just one show—don't add up when you have to split the door. You have to do house shows. You know what house shows are?"

He didn't.

"Shows in people's living rooms. Instead of tickets or covers, you get donations and a couch to sleep on, and you have to book the shows yourself, beg for hosts, drive all over tarnation trying to sell enough CDs and T-shirts and merch to gross a couple of hundred bucks so you can break even. Why deal with any of that? Leave the business side to the professionals."

The prospect of needing to do that sort of self-promotion and marketing, establishing all those Internet accounts and sales outlets, dazed Yadin. He had had no idea. He hadn't thought about anything beyond getting the album finished and manufactured. Quixotically he'd imagined that people would find his album through word of mouth and order it through the mail, maybe from the prison-cassette company in Van Nuys. Now he was thrown into doubt about the viability of the entire enterprise.

He said to Mallory, "Can we not talk about this anymore? I'll self-release the album when I've saved enough, and whatever happens, happens." He was still hoping the credit counselor, Joel Hanrahan, would figure things out for him with a refi or HELOC so he could put out the record sooner rather than later. Otherwise, he would moonlight for extra cash, wash dishes, maybe try to find demo or landscaping work.

Mallory set down her fork. "What do you mean, 'saved enough'?"

He had slipped.

"You don't even have the money to put it out?" she asked. "How much do you need?"

"Around seven grand."

"I'll write you a check this minute," Mallory said.

"No," Yadin said, pained by thought. He realized now this was, in part, why he hadn't given her the cassette at the Centurion. He didn't want her to think the only reason he had come to see her was for her connections or money.

"Why not?" she asked. "I don't want to be crass, but it's a trivial sum to me."

"I need to do this myself."

"Think of it as a loan, then."

"That doesn't make it any more appealing," he said.

"I'd be investing in you. It'd be a tax write-off. I have one hell of an accountant. He set me up so I'm my own Sub-S corporation—a movie and TV production company. The other day, I had someone from the San Vicente film commission come to the hotel and meet me for coffee. Twenty minutes, talking about a possible film that doesn't exist. But it'll allow me to deduct my entire trip, even the tips. Your album would be a wash for me. Why won't you let me help you? I really want to. Is it just pride?"

"Yes, pride," Yadin said. "I had to file for bankruptcy a while back, but I didn't have an accountant like you. I've been grinding it out for years to get back on my feet, not be in debt anymore, clear my credit. I want to do this on my own without having to rely on anyone for handouts."

"It wouldn't be a handout."

"Call it what you want. That's what it'd amount to."

He took her plate and his bowl and deposited them into the sink.

"It's that important to you?" Mallory asked.

"Yes," he told her. "Maybe I'll try Kickstarter or something, but I need to do this myself."

"All right," she said, "but if that's the case, you're going to have to do something about the sound quality of the recordings."

"What are you talking about? The sound quality is perfect. You can't say that room isn't special."

"The sonics in there are terrific—unbelievably so—but I'm not talking about that," Mallory said. "I can hear your chair creaking, your fingers squeaking on the strings. I can hear you licking your lips and taking breaths, your nose whistling. There are vocal pops—you didn't use a pop shield, did you?—and trucks going by. There're kids playing in the background of one song, crickets at the end of another."

"Some of that's intentional. I want to keep all that in there," he said. "I'm not going to have any of it filtered out. That's the whole point of tracking it live. It's more authentic when it's not all cleaned up."

"I get it," Mallory said. "I know that's the charm of lo-fi, keeping it loose and rough, but sometimes this drops down to the level of a bad demo or bootleg. It comes across as amateurish. The EQs on a lot of songs are off."

"They are?" He sat back down at the table.

"It's not obvious to you?" she asked. "You used to have such a great ear. In a couple of places, you didn't set the gains properly, so there's clipping. What kind of mics did you use?"

"SM58s."

"Too bad you didn't have 7Bs, at least," Mallory told him. "You got some phase and bleed issues, and, worse of all, there's tape hiss on every song."

"There's always going to be tape hiss with analog," Yadin said. "What you get in return is some life, some depth. You totally lose that 3-D effect with digital."

"The problem is, quieter stuff is harder to record," Mallory said. "All it takes is for you to have a dry throat to wreck everything. Did you have a little cold at one point? Even if you send the tapes out to be mixed and filtered, I don't know. I think you need to re-record a lot of the album."

"Really?" he said, profoundly disappointed. It wasn't the time it would take to re-record the songs that bothered him. Most of them had been first or second takes, all done in less than three weeks. Yet he had recorded the tracks on the album one by one, immediately after he'd finished writing each song, and he'd been in the moment then, fully immersed in the emotions of each performance. He didn't know if he would be able to re-create that kind of freshness.

"It might be just as well," Mallory said. "The arrangements of just you and the guitar, it gets too stark and monotonous when it's every song. You need to do something different occasionally."

"Like what?" Yadin asked.

She stared at his kitchen cupboards. "You don't have anything alcoholic hidden away for your guests?"

"No," he said. "Like what, Mallory? What do you think I should do differently?"

Looking down at the table, she pushed her bottom lip out and clamped it over her upper lip—a gesture he remembered. She did it whenever she was gathering herself to make a decision. "There's something I want to ask you, Yadin. Something I'd like you to consider. A personal favor."

"What?"

"If you re-record the songs, I'd like to work on a few of them with you," she said. "Sing backup or harmony, maybe play backing for you."

It was the last thing Yadin had expected her to say. "You'd want to do that?" he asked.

"I'm forty-five," Mallory said, "although my official biography has me at forty-one. Hollywood and Nashville are not kind to women my age. I blew my last shot at salvaging my music career with my last album."

"That's not true. It sold pretty well, didn't it?"

"You know that's not what I'm talking about. What a disaster. They've all been disasters."

"You've written some good songs," Yadin said.

"Not really. Not anything I've ever been proud of. I've always had a whole team of songwriters and producers behind me, and I let them dictate everything. On tour, the band would play to click tracks, and they'd Auto-Tune the fuck out of my voice. I might as well have been lip-syncing. There wasn't a single thing authentic about it. People know when a song's honest or not. You can't fake it. For once, I'd love to be involved, even in just a tiny way, with a project that has some integrity. Your project." She wrapped both of her hands around his left hand on the table. "Will you let me do that, Yadin? Would you allow me that privilege?"

Absently, lightly, she rubbed her fingertips over the calluses on his palm, around his fat fingers and thick, dry skin and bitten nails. Her hands were so soft.

"How long can you stick around?" he asked her.

She said Thursday. She could stick around until Thursday morning. It wasn't much time—just two days, discounting that Monday night, since Mallory didn't have any of her instruments with her—but it would have to do.

After Yadin washed the dishes from their dinner and Mallory had a cigarette outside, they went back into his studio and listened to the entire album, going through it song by song, and chose which ones they would redo together, agreeing they would aim for four. They talked about the arrangements, which vocal lines could use harmony, where they might add fiddle or rhythm guitar or slip in a riff or instrumental, and he gave Mallory the lyrics and chords to the first two songs so she could take them back to the hotel and familiarize herself with them.

What worried Yadin was how he would conceal the recording sessions from Jeanette over the next two nights. He couldn't tell her about them now, after deceiving her about seeing Mallory at the Centurion, after not revealing in the first place that he and Mallory had once been lovers—something he never divulged to anyone because he thought it would come across as pathetic, trying to boast that he'd once fucked someone famous. Besides, who would have believed him? Tuesday was also rehearsal night for the church choir. He would need to devise an excuse for why he wouldn't be showing up.

But in a sense Jeanette made things easier for him. For whatever reason, she was continuing to evade him, not responding to his messages. On Tuesday evening, after he got off work, he tried calling her, and, as he expected, she didn't pick up. He left her a quick voicemail, saying he felt too worn out to make it to choir practice that night, maybe he was coming down with something. Jeanette was ordinarily averse to communicating during the week, and considering her current mood, i.e., the silent treatment, it wouldn't have surprised Yadin if they didn't talk again until church on Sunday.

He returned home, and Mallory was waiting for him in front of the cottage, her convertible filled with gear. Her personal assistant had driven everything up from L.A. that afternoon while Mallory had been golfing.

"Are you putting her up at the Centurion tonight?" Yadin asked as he helped Mallory unload the equipment. It was a six-hour drive, minimum, back to L.A.—a long trip for the personal assistant to take twice in one day.

"It's a he," Mallory told him. "No, a B&B in town. I'm nice but not that nice."

The assistant had delivered Mallory's custom-made fiddle, Gibson J-45 guitar, a pair of Røde K2 condenser mics with pop shields, some high-end XLR cables, a dual-channel FMR Audio preamp, a pair of Sony MDR-7506 studio headphones, an Olympus handheld digital recorder, and a plethora of other items, most in their original packaging.

"How much did all of this cost?" Yadin asked, assuming the personal assistant, on Mallory's orders, had raided a music store that morning.

"They're not brand-new. Everything's from my house. I've been tinkering with Ableton Live on my Mac for a while now, recording snippets of things. That's why I know so much about self-releasing. I was looking into it for myself, crazy as that sounds, but everything I tried to write was shit."

It took them quite a bit of time to set up the equipment, and almost as long to sort out working with each other again. "You're going to sit in the chair the whole time?" Mallory asked. "You're not going to stand? I'm going to stand."

"I always sit."

"It'll feel awkward. I'll be looking down at the top of your head." She adjusted the height of a black aluminum conductor stand, on which she had propped the lyrics, and squinted at the words. "Fucking hell," she said, and pulled out a pair of reading glasses from her purse. "I hate these things."

Yadin did a run-through of the first song, "The Days As We Know Them," on his Martin D-21 Special, and Mallory tried to follow along on her 1965 Gibson J-45. It was a beauty of a guitar, sunburst in maple and wine, just like Dylan's, and it issued out a nice thump and snap. It'd been manufactured before the infamous Norlin era, when Gibsons were built heavy with double-X bracing, which had made the guitars sound utterly dead.

"Are you tuned down, like, half a step?" Mallory asked.

He had one song on the album in drop-D, but everything else was in standard tuning. As a general rule, however, he liked to loosen his strings down a semitone. It created a fatter tone, fit his vocal range better, and made his playing flow.

She had her own quirks. She had brought a fifth of Pappy Van Winkle with her and poured a couple of fingers into a Centurion rock glass to sip on, neat, but she also imbibed from bottles of Vocalzone and Nin Jiom Pei Pa Koa syrup—a tablespoon of each—to moisten her throat. On days she was singing, she told Yadin, she avoided milk, ice cream, citrus fruits, coffee, spicy foods, soda, and anything cold.

She launched into a series of vocal exercises: humming, lip-trilling, bumblebeeing, solfèging. He watched her queerly—this was all new.

"What? You don't warm up?" she asked him.

The only thing he ever had to do was clear his throat. That would be all Mallory required, too, Yadin thought, if she quit smoking.

They began rehearsing the song, but Mallory interrupted

him almost immediately. "Wouldn't it be cool to start with the chorus instead of the verse?"

"No."

They argued as well over the next song, "Tell It to the Angels."

"It's just 1-5-4, right?" she said, setting down her guitar and picking up her fiddle. "Can we raise the key a little?"

"No."

As they laid down the tracks in earnest, though, they eased into a familiar rhythm. Her voice was as good as ever, so expressive with her shadings and phrasings, and her fiddle sweetened and deepened the songs with her full-bow notes, melodic fills, solos, and rides. Their musical chemistry was still there, as if they had never stopped playing together.

"Now we're cooking," Yadin said, exhilarated.

This was what he had been chasing and missing all those years, before everything got corrupted by becoming a recording artist. It had never been about performing *for* others. It had been about playing *with* others—with Mallory, Whisper Creek, friends, in kitchens, garages, and barns—just jamming and finding synergy and congruence and chancing upon moments of improvisation. It was what he had loved, starting out as a songwriter in Raleigh—making music simply for the joy of it.

He dropped out of high school a week into his senior year. At the time, he had been living in Norfolk, Virginia, where his mother had gotten her latest job as a phlebotomist, drawing blood from dissolute sailors at an STD clinic. Lured by the music scene, he hitchhiked south to the Triangle and kicked around for several years, busing tables and washing dishes at the Rathskeller and the Circus Family Restaurant and doing demo work to support himself, sacking out on coworkers' couches, occasionally squatting in abandoned buildings or empty houses or renting trailers or storage lockers and showering at the Y.

He subsisted mostly on tomato sandwiches, a staple in the South. He'd get a bag of ripe, juicy heirloom tomatoes from a farmers' market or a roadside stand, cut them up, and lay them between slices of cheap store-bought white bread (Merita was his preferred brand), sprinkled generously with salt and pepper and slathered with Duke's mayonnaise—no substitutes allowed. All the while, he was trying to sharpen his guitar skills and write songs. He went to dive bars up and down Hillsborough Street—the Comet Lounge, Kisim's, the Brewery, Sadlack's Heroes, Boo's Hideaway—to listen to music, and along the way befriended other aspiring musicians.

There was a lot of talk then that Raleigh and Chapel Hill would be the next Seattle, a hotbed for new grunge acts. Punk bands like Superchunk abounded, but the Triangle would soon become more famous as a breeding ground for alt-country groups like Whiskeytown. Yadin was there for the first intimations of the genre, and gradually he found his affinities sliding from noise rock to alt-country. Nearly every free night, he participated in informal jam sessions at people's apartments and houses. One coterie in Raleigh called themselves the Siesta Club. They'd drink cans of beer and grill burgers and hot dogs and get stoned and play horseshoes until the sun set, then sit on the porch or around the kitchen table and strum guitars and mandolins and banjos and sing. They'd do covers, but more and more, they challenged each other to present their own compositions.

Yadin was too shy ever to take a turn with one of his songs. It was only after Mallory began showing up to the sessions that he collected the courage to perform one. He had seen her around, and desperately wanted to impress her. She was a double major in music and drama with a minor in English at NC State, and worked as a clerk at Schoolkids, the record store on Hillsborough across the street from the campus Bell Tower. A frequent browser at the store (he could never afford to buy much there), Yadin had overheard her talking to customers, and her knowledge of music, all kinds of music, her references and technical insights, had staggered him. She had learned the viola through the Suzuki method and had taken up country fiddle for fun. A multi-instrumentalist, she was better at guitar than Yadin at that age. Yet it was her fiddle that made the Siesta Club sessions soar. She had a wonderful voice, too, a sweet, ethereal keening.

Yadin waited for a night with a smaller turnout. At last, one rainy evening at a house in Five Points, just six of them in attendance, he took out a crumpled napkin and, sitting on an ottoman, laid it on his denimed right knee. "Key of G?" he said to the others. "It's 1-6-5-4." He was a bit chagrined.

I-vi-V-IV was one of the most banal, hackneyed chord pro-
gressions in music. "Chorus is 5-4-1."

He started strumming his guitar. He was trembling, and
the napkin on his knee—the ink of the lyrics bled felt-blue—
fell to the floor. He left it there, toeing it with his boot so it
was readable. He sang the first verse, playing G, Em, D, C:

> *We weep for lost youth*
> *And we weep for lost love*
> *We weep for old memories and*
> *Fallen stars*

Tediously, every line in the song contained the phrase "we
weep," even the chorus, with slightly harder strums for D, C, G:

> *Oh we weep*
> *All we can do is weep*

It was verse-chorus, verse-chorus, verse-chorus. No bridge.
Not long enough. Dull and unimaginative. He did a quick
outro, picked up the napkin, and stuffed it into his back
pocket. He never looked up once during the song. He still
didn't. The others in the room clapped politely. "That was
nice," he heard someone say. A girl. Mallory.

They didn't speak that night. Not for several days, until
he walked into Schoolkids. He had been coming to the record
store every afternoon, waiting for her to be behind the counter
again.

"Hey, there he is—Mr. Forlorn," she said. "I hope you're not still weeping."

He felt his face warm. "I know, it was a piece of shit, that song."

"Not a piece of shit. The lyrics could use a little variation, maybe. But I liked it. A lot. You have something."

"What do I have?" Yadin asked.

"I'm not going to tell you yet," Mallory said. "Maybe I never will. It'd give you a big head. Anyway, it's intangible and ineffable."

"Oh." He made a mental note to look up *ineffable* in the dictionary.

"Two-line chorus," she said. "Ever heard of Blaze Foley? 'Picture Cards Can't Picture You'?"

Blaze Foley—a good friend of Townes Van Zandt's—was one of the singer-songwriters he revered the most. Like Yadin's song, "Picture Cards" had a two-line chorus, but it was actually the same line, repeated.

"*I saw daylight in your eyes,*" Yadin sang quietly, and Mallory joined him for the second utterance, going high to his low. Without trying, they had melded in beautiful harmony.

"What're you doing later?" she asked. "Want to get a Big Mike at Sadlack's?"

He sat next door in Sadlack's until she got off her shift. They ordered cans of Miller High Life and two Big Mikes, pastrami sandwiches with sweet peppers and provolone, melted in the steamer—a heavenly, welcome departure from his tomato sandwiches.

Tentatively, they talked about where they grew up, their families. Her mother had been a waitress, her father a juvenile corrections officer who'd had a gambling problem. She was an only child, as Yadin was, or as he had ended up to be. She said she'd been introverted and unpopular in high school. No one had ever asked her out on a date, she told him, which he could not believe. She might have been a little overweight, without many curves or angles, but she was cute, and her shapelessness made her more appealing, less intimidating, to him. Indeed, he'd discover later that he wasn't the only one who thought this way: she'd had a handful of boyfriends since arriving at NC State, and was hardly inexperienced.

"I was always fat and really straight," she said. "A weirdo. Everyone in high school hated me because I won all the academic awards every year. All I did was study and take viola lessons and practice and do recitals. I tried a little theater, just to be social, but I wouldn't go out for any parts with dancing. Boys weren't interested in me at all. I was too intense. I thought for sure there was something wrong with me."

He told her about Ohio, his father abandoning them, Davey dying. He had never told anyone about Davey before.

"That's so sad," she said. "So that's where it comes from."

Thereafter, Yadin spent every available moment with her. He followed Mallory to her classes, saying he wanted to improve himself, that he was fascinated by, say, Integrative Physiology, and sat beside her in lecture halls, moonily watching her take notes.

In her off-campus apartment, which she shared with another girl, they listened to records and talked about music.

"Lucinda Williams?" Mallory asked.

"Goddess," Yadin said.

"Emmylou Harris?"

"Goddess."

"Leonard Cohen?"

"Supreme Being."

Once, they spent an entire afternoon trying to figure out the opening chord to "A Hard Day's Night" on the guitar. Was it an Fadd9? A G7sus4? A G11sus4, or maybe a G7add9sus4? Yadin hadn't known half the names to these chords until then; he'd learned everything by ear.

They sang together, just the two of them, in her bedroom, playing guitar and fiddle. They started with a trio of Blaze Foley songs: "If I Could Only Fly," "Cold, Cold World," and "Picture Cards Can't Picture You." They did traditional gospel songs like "In My Time of Dying" and ballads like "Come All You Tenderhearted," "Long Black Veil," and "He Stopped Loving Her Today." Straightaway they had a special vocal chemistry, her harmony sweetening the upper register. They never had to spell out the arrangements in advance. It was as if they were having a conversation—a conversation they'd had all their lives. They'd exchange a look or a nod, and they'd go up an octave, ascending together in perfect pitch.

She helped Yadin hone his songs, his lyrics. "You can be vague in a verse, but never in a chorus," she told him. And: "Audiences like to anticipate rhymes, trying to guess them.

There's comfort when they do, but they also like to be surprised once in a while." And: "It can't be buckets of tears, down by the muddy river all the time. You need to avoid those kinds of clichés like the plague." She laughed. "So to speak. Get it?" He didn't. "You need some originality, some complexity."

She taught him about music theory and song structure. She had him listen over and over to "Down by the River," "Cowgirl in the Sand," and "Cinnamon Girl," all three of which Neil Young wrote in a single day. "You hear that?" she said, as "Cinnamon Girl" spun on the turntable. "Alternating four-on-the-floor. How brilliant is that? Those riffs in double drop-D, the minor 7th harmony. And no chorus! Just a middle 8."

They began performing duets at the Siesta Club jam sessions. They'd stare into each other's eyes and sing, a blissful, swooning collusion. After one session, a guy named Ross said to Yadin, "Why don't you guys get a room already?"

"Huh?"

"The two of you are practically having sex up there, doing those songs."

Yadin was twenty-two, and a virgin. He'd only made out with a few girls. Once, he'd almost had intercourse, although he was fairly certain it had been an accident, that in the dark basement of a party, the girl who had thrown herself on him—plowed—had thought he was someone else.

Ross had access to a house on the Outer Banks. Owned by his parents' friends, it was in the town of Avon, on Hatteras

Island, a four-hour drive from Raleigh, and he invited whoever was able to come one October weekend. There ended up to be nine of them, piled into two cars: Yadin, Mallory, Ross, Thorton, Charlie, Alicia, Esmé, Paul, and Laura. The three-story soundfront house was built on stilts and nicely appointed, with a wraparound deck and a hot tub on the second floor. In all, there were four bedrooms and four bathrooms. Several sofas folded out. The couples—Charlie and Alicia, Paul and Laura—got their own rooms, and Mallory and Esmé took dibs on the master. Ross and Thorton agreed to share the room with two twin beds, which left Yadin to sleep on one of the sofa beds in the living room. He didn't complain. Agonizingly, he felt a cyst emerging underneath his right cheek—such rotten, predictable timing—and he would likely have to do a few surgical procedures during the middle of the night.

The days were still relatively warm, in the seventies, and most of the group went swimming on the ocean side of the barrier island. Yadin and Mallory were too bashful to expose themselves in bathing suits. They sat on chaise longues on the deck of the house, fully clothed, smoking cigarettes and talking, looking out at Pamlico Sound, enjoying the sun and water and sky and each other's company. He had never felt so relaxed.

Paul was a cook at the Rathskeller. He made chicken and sausage jambalaya and coleslaw for them the first night, a bouillabaisse with clams, mussels, shrimp, and striped bass the second night. He also baked fresh baguettes, and Yadin used piece after piece to sop up the broth.

Late into the night, they played music in various ensembles. For Yadin's work, one lineup was particularly sharp: Ross on an acoustic bass guitar (they were unplugged that weekend); Charlie on an improvised drum—a five-gallon plastic bucket flipped upside down; and Thorton on lead guitar, running off riffs and licks on his dobro, with Yadin playing rhythm. Combined with Mallory on the fiddle, they brought Yadin's songs to life.

Thankfully, he was able to ward off the cyst, applying ice cubes throughout the first night to his cheek. On the second night, he was dead asleep on the lumpy sofa bed when Mallory joined him under the covers.

"Wake up, Yadin. Wake up," she whispered. "You ever hear the story about how Gram Parsons stole David Crosby's fiancée? Her name was Nancy—a knockout, by all accounts. She was living with Crosby in L.A., engaged to be married to him in three weeks, but someone brought Gram over to Crosby's house for a drink. He was smitten with her. He knew Crosby was leaving that afternoon to go on tour with the Byrds, so he came back to the house that very same night, knocked on the door, and when Nancy answered, he told her, 'I've been looking for you my whole life, and I'm taking you with me.' Yadin, it's been months now. I've been waiting for you to take me. But I'm tired of waiting, so I am going to take you."

She didn't know then (and would never know) that she was taking his virginity, too.

When they returned to Raleigh, he moved in with Mallory, although they never really discussed it. He simply never left. After two weeks, she asked him, "Don't you need to go home and pick up some clothes or something?"

"What do you mean?" he said. Everything he owned was already in her bedroom: two guitars—one acoustic and one hollow-body electric—and a duffel bag of clothes. She didn't understand that he didn't have his own place at the time, that he'd been couch-surfing and squatting. She was the first and only woman he ever lived with.

They formed a band with Thorton, who was a psychology major at Duke; Ross, who was a biology student at NC State; and Charlie, who was unemployed and sometimes dealt coke. They batted around names for the band, which Yadin didn't think was necessary—this was just for fun, they didn't need a name, they were only playing for themselves and the Siesta Club. The others insisted. Ross suggested Willow Creek, the name of the cul-de-sac on Hatteras Island where they'd stayed, even though there hadn't been a single willow tree in sight. Everyone thought Willow Creek was too bland, too generic, too bourgeois; there were thousands of suburban housing developments, and probably that many bands, called Willow Creek. Mallory proposed a slight tweak, Whisper Creek, and the name, though not terribly more unique, stuck.

For the next few months, they practiced in whatever space they could find—music rooms in the Price Center on campus, the basement of Ross's fraternity, a machine shop owned by a friend of Charlie's—and played together at the Siesta Club sessions. Yadin was writing more and more songs, better songs, but he favored alternating the members' tunes and trading off the lead vocals as equal partners. He fell in love with the process of making music with this group, in large part because he was in love with Mallory.

Amazingly, she seemed to be in love with him, too. Whenever she saw him, she'd wrap her arms around his head, hang off his neck. She didn't care who witnessed them. In her apartment, he'd be lying on his back on her bed, and she'd walk in the room and see him, and her face would illumine. She'd sit on top of him and kiss him, and then, her legs still straddled over his hips, she'd rest her head on his shoulder and stay like that while they napped. And the sex. He had thought about sex since he was thirteen, speculating what it'd entail, wondering if he'd ever have it, but sex with Mallory was entirely different from what he had imagined. The act wasn't about sex at all. It was about sealing their intimacy, burrowing inside each other, trying to merge into one.

She went to her classes and studied, and he took on more demo and landscaping jobs so he could contribute to the rent (her roommate moved out after numerous tantrums about how noisy and messy the couple was). They made dinners together, although neither of them knew how to cook. They settled for canned spaghetti and ravioli, mac and cheese, and pork and beans, often in combination, mixed with slices of hot dog and ketchup and topped with sour cream and shredded cheddar. These meals were augmented with take-out pizzas and fast-food burgers and fries during binges—long, late nights of drinking and drugging. They were both getting fat, and neither cared. Mostly, the two of them played music in the now-empty second bedroom of her apartment and performed at the Siesta Club with the band, which was sounding tighter with every session. Yadin practiced every moment he could, and eventually surpassed Mallory's guitar skills. He had never been happier. He wished it could last forever.

It didn't, of course.

One afternoon, when they were jamming in a garage in Boylan Heights, Thorton said, "We ought to try playing some clubs."

"Yeah," Charlie said. "We could start with an open mic, work out the kinks, then move up from there."

"No way," Yadin said.

"Why not?" Ross asked.

"Why do we need to play in front of other people, in front of strangers?"

"That makes no sense," Thorton said. "We're a band. The point is to be heard."

"This is enough, what we've been doing," Yadin said. "Why can't we just enjoy it for what it is?"

"Mallory," Thorton said, "where are you on this?"

She deliberated, clamping her bottom lip over her upper lip, then said to Yadin, "We have something good. We could make something happen."

"What?" he asked.

"Who knows. Maybe something big. We need to get out there and find out."

Yadin was terrified by the idea. He had participated in

a lot of jams and practices by that point, yet had never performed on an actual stage with an audience. It was the last thing he wanted to do, but everyone else kept on him about it, and eventually he agreed to try it once, as long as he could just play rhythm and sing background.

They signed up for the open mic at the Aquarium Lounge, a subterranean rat hole downtown, beneath West Street. They were almost last on the list, and they waited for hours, Yadin getting drunker and more baked, slipping outside with Charlie to toke up and do a few lines. When it was finally close to their turn, one act to finish before them, he locked himself in the bathroom and threw up. He wouldn't come out. Mallory knocked on the bathroom door.

"You guys go on without me," Yadin said.

"Honey, it'll be all right," Mallory said. "There's nothing to be scared about. No one's left in the audience, just a few guys from the Siesta Club."

Onstage, he was certain he would faint. He sat down in a chair, and as the first song progressed, he kept shifting the chair clockwise, inch by inch, until he was facing Charlie's drum kit. He was barely able to make it through the three-song set.

"I am never doing that again," he told Mallory.

But Mallory and the others were enthralled, playing live on a stage. They wanted to do more open mics and try to get booked for some bona fide gigs. The problem was, Whisper Creek's best songs were undeniably Yadin's, and they didn't sound right unless he sang them himself. He had, by far, the best voice among them. They wanted him to be the frontman once in a while during the sets.

"Why can't we do your songs?" he asked the others. "Why do we have to do mine? Or one of you can sing them—I don't care. No one wants to see me sing. Look at me, man."

"You didn't think you'd survive the Aquarium," Mallory said, "but you got through it. I used to be petrified doing recitals, but trust me: the more you perform, the easier it gets."

"I don't understand you guys. You don't need me. You don't want me. You want someone with stage presence, a performer, a looker. That's not me by a long shot. By any shot."

"It's the music that counts," Ross said.

"You know that's bullshit," Yadin said.

"I'll take care of you, bud," Charlie said. "You won't feel a thing."

For their next open mic, Charlie gave him—in addition to pot and coke and several shots of Jack—a triple benzo cocktail of Klonopin, Ativan, and Valium. Yadin didn't feel a thing. Midway through a song, he lost his place on the guitar and, after a bar and a half, picked up with the chords to a different song, but overall he was able to deliver, to his surprise, a decent vocal performance. Better than that. He didn't quaver. He didn't bleat or croak. His voice was crystalline and resonant and emotive.

"You killed it," Mallory said. "I knew you would. Wasn't that such a *rush*?"

More than anyone else in the band, Mallory was thrilled to be performing live. She stepped to the front of the stage,

spunky and loose, and swayed and danced and gestured the-
atrically with her hands—corny little flutter birds she'd never
unleashed before. She was different up there, *into* it, and she
was becoming different off the stage as well, Yadin noticed.
Something was happening to her. She wore more revealing
clothes all of a sudden, shirts with deep V's and denim shorts
that were cut almost up to her butt cheeks. She talked louder
and laughed hyenically. She preened in the center of rooms,
inviting everyone's attention, particularly the attention of
men. The changes were disturbing to him. He realized that
Mallory had discovered something about herself. She had
discovered that she liked people looking at her.

"What's with you and Thorton?" he asked her one day.

"What are you talking about?"

Yadin had seen her huddling with Thorton on numerous
occasions, whispering to him. The previous night at a party,
they had stood in a corner, and she'd touched his arm repeatedly, and at one point she'd thrown her head back and guf-
fawed at something he'd said. Had it been about Yadin?

"You two have become very buddy-buddy," Yadin told
her. "You like him, don't you? You think he's pretty."

"You are a whack job," Mallory said.

Graduating from open mics, Whisper Creek began to
work small clubs—routinely for as little as twenty-five dollars a night and all the popcorn they could eat. The spotlights
onstage hurt Yadin's eyes, so he bought a pair of oversized
sunglasses with the darkest lenses he could find—made for
glaucoma patients. They allowed Yadin to fool himself a little

into thinking that he wasn't being observed. He still needed to pop the pharms, though, to get anywhere near a stage, and sometimes he accessorized the benzos with too much booze or weed or blow. Their sets, depending on what Yadin had ingested, vacillated from chaotic to hypnotic. People would sometimes say it was the worst show they'd ever seen, sometimes the best—and often it was the same show.

He'd be floating. Between songs, he'd light a cigarette, then would discover that there was already one smoldering between the strings and headstock of his guitar, which would make him giggle. He'd fuss with his microphone stand, unceasingly adjusting the angle and height of it. He'd sip from cups and bottles, smack his lips, clear his throat, cough, need another sip. He'd tune and retune. Through his black-out sunglasses, he could see only small prismatic starbursts of the stage lights—so pretty—the follow spots, pins, and fresnels. Such funny names. A lighting technician had once told him the terms (Yadin always talked to the lighting technicians at clubs before gigs, requesting they keep him largely in the dark, or at least not position lights at sharp angles to his face), and he would tee-hee, thinking about the names.

Since Whisper Creek was featuring mostly Yadin's songs now, the band would have to wait for him to quit stalling and fetishizing before they could proceed. Occasionally they'd just begin playing and hope Yadin would jump in at the appropriate moment. Yet in those instances they might be doing a ballad and he'd launch into a fast shuffle, or they'd be in one key in standard four-four time and he'd start singing in a different key in three-quarter time. Now and then, he'd change a song's arrangements onstage without warning, altering the tempo or adding a pre-chorus or a bridge that the band had never heard before, even rewriting lyrics on the fly.

The morning after another disastrous show, Yadin was making coffee in the kitchen, terribly hungover, when Mallory came out of the shower in her bathrobe and said, "You need to cut that crap out."

"Huh?" he asked, thinking she meant coffee.

"You need to get your shit together," she told him. "Do you realize what a gift your voice is? You have any idea how blessed you are, that you can dash off all these songs on napkins and paper bags? It's nothing to you, and they're beautiful. The rest of us, we have to work at it. We might have technique, we might have craft, but no one ever feels anything listening to our music—not like yours. Honestly, Yadin, what do you want to happen with your career?"

"I've never really thought about it," Yadin said.

"Yes, you have. Don't lie to me. I know underneath you're ambitious. I'm not ashamed to say I want to be famous. I want to be a star. What do you want? How do you want to be remembered? Tell me."

"I want to be remembered as one of the greatest songwriters who ever lived," he admitted.

"Well, it's there for the taking, lying right before you," she told him. "You got it, that intangible thing. If you wanted to, you could hold a room by yourself with just your voice and guitar and your songs. You're a terrible performer, abominable, but you've got an innate feel for where you're going musically, a vision, even though you don't know what the fuck you're doing half the time, writing these songs. It's ridiculous. You're junked out of your gourd, you can't even look at the audience, and people are mesmerized. It's so unfair. Could you at least show me and the rest of the band some respect and not get so fucked up all the time? Could you try not to be such a jackass?"

He tempered the amount and combinations of drugs he took, and he began paying more attention to the details, giving charts to the band and rehearsing new songs with them, putting some thought into organizing set lists and sticking to them, becoming meticulous at sound checks and trying to perfect the acoustics in various nightclubs with their PA systems. His stage fright didn't dissipate, but he took ownership of his songs. He was proud of them, and he wanted them to come out right.

As he cleaned up, however, Thorton, Ross, and Charlie started making a hash of things, getting heavier into partying. At rehearsals, they would be sauced, glazed. They never seemed able to work through an entire song anymore. They'd attempt parts, but were incapable of playing anything from beginning to end.

"Come on, guys, this is important," Yadin would say. "Can we run through this once?"

"Dude, don't be so tense," Ross said.

"It ain't that complicated, Yad," Charlie said. "We could play it blindfolded."

"Here's what I want to know," Thorton said. "What's with the band-aids on your face all the time? You cut yourself shaving that much?"

"You do when you use a pizza slicer," Charlie said.

Onstage, they were lit and fried, barely able to stand, much less play with any competence. Ross fingered his bass with geriatric sonority, dragging every song into a coma. Thorton rushed willy-nilly into guitar solos. Charlie, in particular, was pitiful on the drums.

"Hold the beat, man," Yadin yelled to him.

"Fuck you!" Charlie yelled back.

"No, fuck you!" Yadin shouted.

"You're all useless!" Mallory screamed.

"Fuck you!" Ross and Thorton and Charlie screamed back.

Thus began a period when the band would heckle themselves during every performance.

Driving home from a show one night, Mallory said to Yadin, "We need to get rid of those bozos. They're deadweight."

"You think I'm deadweight, too?" he asked.

"What? No, of course not."

"Feels like it sometimes."

Often now, she would extend what should have been a little fill on her fiddle into a long solo. She wasn't satisfied with just harmonizing background anymore, singing almost every verse with him, sometimes taking over, nudging him aside from the center mic. Between songs, she would banter freely with the audience, enjoying all the eyes on her.

"You're talking nonsense," Mallory said. "What is with you lately? If anyone should feel like deadweight, it's me. You never listen to any of my ideas anymore. You want everything your way or no way. It's like we're just a backing band to you. You might as well go solo."

"But that's the last thing I want," Yadin said. "I love you, Mallory. I want to play music with you forever."

"I do, too," she said. "You don't realize how much."

Their next gig turned out to be the end of Whisper Creek as a full band. Two songs in, they were screaming at each other, almost coming to blows. Thorton walked over to his amp and turned up his guitar and let it screech in feedback. It went on and on. People booed. They threw things. They left. Thorton turned it up louder, the amp in a continuous piercing squeal. Then he, Ross, and Charlie walked off the stage, leaving Yadin and Mallory alone up there with thirty minutes to fill, albeit there were only seven people remaining in the audience.

"What do you want to do?" he asked Mallory after shutting off Thorton's amp.

"Let's play on," she said.

Yadin grabbed his guitar, sat down in his chair, and he and Mallory did the rest of the set acoustic, slowing things way down, just the two of them. It was the best show Whisper Creek ever gave.

As they were packing up, an older man approached them. "Those your songs? You wrote them?" he asked Yadin. He handed him a business card. "You ever get to Nashville, give me a call. We could use staff writers like you."

The card read *Acuff-Rose Music.*

"What's Acuff-Rose?" Yadin asked Mallory.

"It's the biggest publishing house on Music Row. He just basically offered you a publishing deal."

Yadin flung the card to the floor.

"What are you doing? Don't throw that away," Mallory said, and lunged after the card, dropping to her knees, sweeping her hand under an amp until she was able to dig it out. "Don't be an idiot. This is a lottery ticket. Keep it. You could make some real money. I bet you could write a hit song in your sleep."

"Screw that," Yadin told her.

The Nashville formula was verse-chorus, verse-chorus, bridge, verse-chorus. Only, for a song to be commercially viable on the radio, it couldn't be longer than three minutes thirty, so you often had to throw out the bridge. You could forget making anything interesting. You had to keep it dumbed-down and cookie-cutter. There was no room for nuance. Everything had to be obvious and tawdry.

He was too high-minded to ever compose that kind of drivel, and he would never sell the rights to his own songs to a company like Acuff-Rose. God only knew what those industry assholes would do to them. The only way to preserve the integrity of his music, he realized, was to record it himself.

"We need to cut a demo," he told Mallory.

It took them a while—months, during which they continued playing acoustic sets as a duo—but eventually the two of them cobbled together enough money to go to Sonic Wave, a studio in Five Points, and record four songs. Then Yadin duplicated and mailed out cassettes to two dozen independent labels, concentrating on the handful in the area. He also sent packages to the Triangle's college radio stations: WKNC at NC State, WXDU at Duke, and WXYC at UNC. All three were known to include local music in their programming.

It was through the radio that they attracted the owner of Lost Saloon Records, a new label headquartered (in the guy's house) in Cary, just outside the Beltline from Raleigh. He drove into town for one of their shows at the Comet Lounge, and afterward, at the bar, he said, "Let's do this." Just like that.

On the eve of signing the record deal, Yadin and Mallory went to Sadlack's for dinner, ordering Big Mikes, just as they had on their first date.

"Can you believe it?" Mallory said. "We're going to have an album. We're going to be *recording artists*, Yadin!"

He had worked so hard for this moment, but now that it was upon him, he found himself strangely rent with terror, not excitement. What was he getting himself into? he thought. Was this what he really wanted?

He looked across the table at Mallory. She was very pretty in this light, freckled and roseate, unburdened by any hesitations. *Ineffable* meant indescribable, unutterable. She had an ineffable quality about her. She was at once approachable and elusive—a polarity that drew eyes to her. He could easily see her becoming famous someday.

She chomped into her Big Mike. Juices ran from the sandwich, and she wiped her chin with a clump of napkins, giggling. She was so happy. Yet Yadin wondered: How long would she remain happy?

How long would she stay with Yadin before something or someone else came along, before she awoke to the realization that she was with someone who would only hold her back, who would, by his mere presence by her side, preclude her from becoming a star? How long would it be before she cast Yadin aside, like so much deadweight?

It was his last night with Mallory. The next morning, while she attended a class, he moved out of her apartment, taking his two guitars and duffel bag with him, leaving the recording contract behind, unsigned.

At the housekeepers' forum in the basement on Tuesday morning, Mary Wilkerson had a speech prepared for them.

"I know most of you are aware of the hearings in Sacramento," she said in the hallway. "I'd like to discuss the Centurion Group's position on this."

"Finally," Anna said to Jeanette.

This week, a group of union housekeepers were testifying in front of the state senate, trying to persuade the labor committee to forward the bill requiring hotels to use only fitted elastic sheets.

"Corporate's foremost concern is worker safety," Mary said. "We want to do everything we can to prevent injuries.

We want all our employees to have long, healthy careers with the Centurion. But there's no evidence that making beds with fitted elastic sheets would put any less strain on our house-keepers than flat bottom sheets. You'd still have to lift the mattresses to tuck in fitted sheets."

"That is such bullshit," Anna whispered.

"The big difference would be with our folding and press-ing machines," Mary said. "They're not designed to accom-modate elasticized sheets, and modifying them would cost millions. Even when they're pressed and folded, fitted sheets are bulky. They'd take up much more space than flat sheets, and that would be an added expense because we'd have to create more storage."

"How inconvenient," Anna said.

"It'd also diminish our green initiatives," Mary said. "Fitted sheets would be much more demanding on our laun-dry services, producing more soap waste and using more water and electricity. All these additional costs might cut into staff wages and benefits, and no one would want that to happen. I hope you see the logic in this. All right, let's talk about what's going on today," she said, and began highlight-ing the new VINPs.

"We should unionize," Anna told Jeanette as the girls lined up for their room assignments. "We should get UNITE HERE to come in here."

UNITE HERE was the largest hospitality union in the country. "I heard that's been tried already," Jeanette said.

"And?"

"Not enough people were interested in signing up."

"I don't understand how people can just let themselves be exploited," Anna said. "It's a travesty. A disgrace. Why won't they stand up for themselves?"

"For God's sake," Jeanette said. "There are wars happening out there right now—atrocities and genocide. There's famine and mass poverty. There's real injustice and evil and heartache in the world. People are dying. People are suffering. People are being eaten away by cancer. And all you can talk about is sheets? You want to unionize over sheets? Who gives a fuck about sheets in the larger scheme of things?"

"Okay, okay," Anna said. "Jesus. What got up your craw this morning?"

It was the talk with Joe the night before. It had made Jeanette think about all the years she'd wasted, the missed opportunities and bad luck and grief and fear that had rendered her inert, immobilizing her in this humdrum town. She had tried to be a good person. Why hadn't good things happened to her?

She reached the head of the line in the hallway. After she collected her assignments, Mary took Jeanette aside and told her, "Clarisa has a family emergency, so I gave you one of her VINPs."

Jeanette looked down at the top assignment sheet. "I thought Mallory Wicks left yesterday," she said.

"She never checked out. She's staying two extra nights in the Miramar Suite. You'll give her room extra attention?"

"Of course," Jeanette said.

"Good. I know I can count on you," Mary said.

Jeanette attended to several standard rooms before going to the Miramar Suite a little after ten, when Ms. Wicks was scheduled to be on the golf course. Still, she was more assiduous than usual about announcing herself at the door. Satisfied that Ms. Wicks was out, Jeanette entered the suite and followed the cleaning sequence prescribed by the *Policies & Procedures* manual.

First she turned on all the lights (checking for burned-out bulbs), shut off the HVAC system, opened the drapes (checking for damaged cords and hooks), and cracked open the windows to ventilate the room with fresh air. Then she gathered a few used glasses and leftover room service items and placed them in the hallway and dialed *69 for pickup.

She made a quick scan of the suite as she walked through it. It was quite tidy. Mallory Wicks was no slob. She seemed considerate, even. There were no towels or trash on the floors. She hadn't tossed the pillows about. She'd pulled the sheets and duvet back over the bed. She'd left the tip envelope on the coffee table and written "Thanks!" on it in an emphatically cheerful looping script.

Jeanette collected the rubbish, took the trash to her cart, and replaced the wastebasket liners. The two glass ashtrays on the terrace had already been changed by the floor attendant, who was responsible for lighting, cleaning, and replenishing the logs for the fire pit. She stripped the bedding, making sure no linens touched the carpet to save on wear and tear, and went through the exacting task of making the bed.

When she was done, she debated what to do with the sweater that was on an upholstered chair: to fold it and tuck it into a dresser drawer, or hang it in the closet. Trying to discern Ms. Wicks's preferences, she opened the closet. There was another sweater inside, folded, on a shelf of the built-in red mahogany organizer. She glanced at the labels of the clothes.

There was so much a housekeeper could learn about guests without ever meeting them, just from how they left their rooms and their possessions. Very intimate pieces of information about their lives—their personal habits, health, attitudes about hygiene, hobbies, financial and marital issues. From books on the nightstand, Jeanette could tell when someone was going through a divorce or was looking to diversify a portfolio or travel to Sri Lanka or start a diet. From medications, she could see if someone had high blood pressure or cholesterol or needed painkillers. From boxes on the counter and wads in the trash bin, she could see if a woman was menstruating, and, from containers or tubes, what method of contraception she was using. From creams and solutions, she could infer a guest's skin or hair concerns. From clothes, she could glean tastes in fashion, weight problems, athletic inclinations, if people cared about the quality of their underwear and socks. It was an ethnographer's dream. Yet the novelty of making such deductions had worn off for Jeanette. She didn't have much curiosity about her guests anymore. This was different, though. She was interested to see how a celebrity lived, even a B-list one (or had Ms. Wicks been relegated to the C list?). There hadn't been many celebrities at the Centurion since Jeanette had begun working there—a few athletes, but no one from Hollywood.

Mallory Wicks's size was, depending on the garment, either a 0 or a 00. The items in the closet were casual, sporty. Ms. Wicks was clearly here to play golf, not make a scene. Still, everything was expensive. She had Coach luggage, a Kate Spade clutch, and one of those Hermès Birkin bags that were all the rage, costing between ten and forty thousand dollars. There were Emilio Pucci boots, Christian Louboutin flats, an Isabel Marant gabardine blazer, and Stella McCartney pants. She was trendy, but not a trendsetter. All the brands had been deemed hot in the celebrity and fashion magazines that Jeanette subscribed to.

The same could be said for the products and makeup on the vanity in the main bathroom. Her things were laid out neatly, but not obsessively in rows, not evenly spaced, not perfectly aligned, as Jeanette was wont to do. She had the famous La Mer moisturizing cream that went for two thousand dollars a jar. Moroccanoil Body Butter and a lot of the Japanese SK-II skin-care line. Edward Bess and Tom Ford lipsticks. Daylong sunscreen. Kérastase shampoo. Chanel Gardénia perfume. She had an exfoliant, a couple of collagen and whitening masks, a swath of makeup brushes. Condoms and a vaginal lubricant in a drawer (was she expecting a visitor, or were they for unforeseen contingencies, always prepared?). A prescription bottle of the antidepressant Zoloft. Nothing terribly exotic. Ms. Wicks didn't indulge in any of the zany beauty treatments that other celebrities had adopted, like mayonnaise in the hair or Preparation H under the eyes.

She had a tube of tretinoin cream, Retin-A, for wrinkles, which Jeanette had asked a dermatology in San Vicente to prescribe for her not too long ago, only to discover at the pharmacy that her insurance didn't cover it. They considered it a lifestyle drug, and it would have cost her $147 out-of-pocket for the generic version. She chose not to get it.

Jeanette looked at her face in the mirror. The lighting from the wall sconces was bright and warm yet unforgiving, displaying every imperfection. Her complexion was wan. She would turn forty in November, but appeared older. Her eyelids were papery. She had crow's-feet, and there were two furrows between her eyebrows, as well as horizontal creases on her forehead. She really needed to wear more makeup, she thought.

With rubber gloves on, she pulled hair from the drain traps and sprayed hot water on the shower tiles and let three inches of water collect at the bottom of the tub for a few minutes (ten degrees of heat doubled the effectiveness of cleansers). She scrubbed every inch of the bathtub and walls, shined the brass fixtures, and cleaned the toilet, inside and out, before moving on to the vanity and sink. The housekeepers had sponges and cleansers in different colors for the tub and sink (yellow), toilet (pink), surfaces (green), and mirrors (blue), with matching cotton cloths for wipe-downs and drying. She positioned the provided L'Occitane amenities, which were unused but had been knocked askew, in their proper order (conditioner on the back right, shampoo on the front right, shower gel on the front left, body lotion on the back left), folded the toilet paper and fanned the Kleenex, resupplied the towels, and washed the floor. She repeated the same procedures in the half bathroom.

Then she began dusting, working clockwise (and from top to bottom) around the suite so she won't miss anything. Starting with the door, she dusted and wiped the knob and frame, the credenza and dining table and chairs, the bedroom closet and shelves and hangers and rods, the picture frames and mirrors, the lamps and bulbs (turning the seams on the shades toward the walls), the nightstands, the TV, the dresser, the main room sofa and chairs and tables. On and on it went, including the HVAC vents and windowsills and the chaise longues and patio table on the terrace.

She straightened the furniture and refilled the stationery supplies. Then she swept and vacuumed, moving this time from the farthest corner of the bedroom to the door. After noting on a Charisma slip that Ms. Wicks liked her sweaters folded and stored in the organizer, Jeanette closed the windows and sheer curtains, drew the drapes halfway, switched on the HVAC, and turned off the lights. She checked for anything she might have missed, then pulled shut the door. In the hallway, as they were instructed, she closed her eyes for three full seconds, took a deep breath, and then reentered the suite, trying to see it as a guest would, and rechecked her work. At last, she closed the door and moved on to the next room, tucking into her apron the tip envelope, into which Mallory Wicks had inserted a fifty-dollar bill.

Holding a wedding at the Centurion Resort was exorbitant, but there was one more affordable option—the "Intimate Wedding" package. The site fee included a bluff-side ceremony with folding mahogany chairs and a complimentary hotel room on the night of the wedding, with a rose-petal turndown and champagne and chocolate-covered strawberries awaiting the bride and groom. Everything else was extra. The major caveat was that the wedding could only involve a total of ten to thirty participants and had to take place between Monday and Thursday, excluding holidays.

Unbeknownst to Jeanette, Franklin had come to the Centurion to officiate an intimate wedding—a last-minute replacement for a justice of the peace. Jeanette ran into him in the corridor outside the fitness center, where she had gone to grab a cool-down towel and a sports drink for a guest, and where he had gone to use the restroom after the ceremony. The coincidence brightened her mood, yet at the same time she was embarrassed to be seen by him in her burgundy and gold uniform, particularly since he was dressed quite elegantly.

"That's a nice suit," she told him.

"You think?" he said. "It's new. I don't think it fits me exactly right. I didn't want the slim cut, but the salesgirl—woman—talked me into it."

"You look very dashing."

"Now you're making me blush," he said, which made Jeanette blush, too.

They were flirting again, she thought. Was it so outlandish to presume that a man like Franklin might have a tiny bit of attraction for a woman like her?

They talked about the wedding. It had been held at noon—a funny time, but the couple had wanted to do it under the gazebo, and that was the only hour it had been available. Neither the couple nor their families were from Rosarita Bay, and they did not have a connection to the First Unitarian Universalist Church or any other UU congregation. They had found Franklin through online reviews and one of two little websites that his son Lane had built for him. The other website was for his services as a celebrant at funerals. It hadn't seemed appropriate to offer the two services on the same website.

The bride and groom had been high school sweethearts, Franklin told Jeanette, and worked together at a plant nursery in Menlo Park. "They seem like nice kids," he said.

"Is the reception going to be here?" she asked.

"No, at Clotilde's Bistro, later tonight. They asked me to come. They always ask me to come, and bring my partner. I don't know why some JPs and ministers do it, even if they're being paid. It feels fraudulent and invasive, crashing a party when I've known the bride and groom all of an hour, if that. So I usually decline, and when I do, the couples always ask me for any advice I might have for them."

"What do you tell them?" Jeanette asked.

"What can I tell them?" Franklin said. "Should I tell them how hard it's going to be? Should I say marriage is mostly about arguing over the quotidian, and that those things will wear away at your soul? Should I say I thought I'd do so much more with my life, but getting married and raising a family negates most possibilities and leaves you feeling like you're not a man? Should I tell them it's been almost three years since my wife has had sex with me? I figured out who Caroline's been fucking."

The word jarred Jeanette. There were guests walking by in the hallway within earshot, and one woman flinched and turned toward them.

"Who?" Jeanette whispered.

"Not Yadin," Franklin said. "Gerry Lowry."

The city manager? "But he's the one who wants to outsource the library," Jeanette said.

"Exactly."

"You saw them together?"

"No."

"Someone told you?" she asked. She was still registering the fact that he and Caroline had not had sex in three years.

"I downloaded our phone bills for the past year," Franklin said. "One number kept popping up. Lowry's. I tried to hack into her email but couldn't figure out the password.

"But it doesn't make sense," Jeanette said. "If they're having an affair, wouldn't he arrange it so she could stay in Rosarita Bay?"

"That's just it. I've never seen such enmity between two people, and I've never understood why. Now it jibes. It went bad, the affair. Either she broke it off and he's disconsolate, or he ended it and she's been harassing him, stalking him ever since, jeopardizing his marriage. Either way, he's found a solution, a way to get rid of her. He'll get them to privatize the library, she'll lose her job, she'll have to move. He'll never have to see her again."

The theory sounded implausible, if not preposterous, to Jeanette. "What's Caroline say?" she asked.

"Apparently we're no longer speaking. But I know what to do, I know how to make her talk."

"How?"

"I'm going to the city council meeting on Friday and corner them," he said to her. "I'm going to make them own up to the whole sordid mess."

Jeanette couldn't linger in the corridor anymore. She told Franklin she had to return to work. She picked up the sports drink and cool-down towel from the fitness center and placed them upstairs in No. 517, then rolled her cart to the next room on her assignment sheet.

Clearly Franklin had become unhinged. Gerry Lowry was tall and thin and slouchy, with a sour mien and awful dandruff. No one's idea of an attractive man. Jeanette couldn't envision any circumstance in which Caroline would take him on as a lover. Franklin's plan to accost Caroline and Lowry at the meeting was demented. He would humiliate himself. He would humiliate Caroline. His standing as their minister would be ruined.

Later in the afternoon, Jeanette went down to the lower service level to resupply her cart and, while there, dropped by the employee cafeteria to grab a cup of yogurt. Several girls at the buffet table were discussing a second assault on a hotel maid in New York City, this time at the Pierre by an Egyptian banker, who had groped and propositioned a housekeeper on Sunday night. But the banker hadn't been arrested right away. The maid had reported the assault immediately to the manager, but she had been told she would have to wait until the next morning, when her supervisor returned to the hotel, for anything to be done.

"That's a lawsuit waiting to happen," a girl said.

"Multiple lawsuits," another said.

"They'll get us those panic buttons for sure now," a third said.

Jeanette hadn't intended to sit down, but she saw Anna at a table by herself and joined her.

"I'm sorry I snapped at you earlier," she said to Anna. "I'm dealing with some stuff."

"That's all right," Anna said. "What kind of stuff?"

"Nothing, really. Nothing important."

"I heard you got promoted to team leader."

"Yeah."

"Aren't you happy?" Anna asked. "I thought you'd be ecstatic. When do you start?"

"Tomorrow."

"Well, congratulations."

"Thanks."

"I've been thinking about what you said," Anna told her.

"About what?" Jeanette asked. "The fitted sheets?"

"No, everything. Maybe I could use a little attitude adjustment. My QCs have been crap. I must have the lowest scores on Empower. Do you think you could watch me one of these days and give me some pointers?"

Despite her preoccupations, Jeanette felt pleased that Anna was seeking her help. "If you'll give me some makeup tips sometime," she said.

"Deal," Anna said.

"Do you think I ought to do something with my hair?"

"You could use some shaping. Maybe do something different with your eyebrows, too."

"I got assigned Mallory Wicks's suite," Jeanette said. "You should see all the beauty products in there, the clothes. It's like she walked out of a page of *InStyle*."

"I saw her in the lobby yesterday," Anna said. "I was showing a guest the way to the spa. She was kissing some dude."

"What dude?" Jeanette recalled the condoms and lubricant in the vanity drawer. Perhaps they weren't for chance hookups, after all. Perhaps Ms. Wicks had had an assignation in mind, and that was why she'd extended her stay in Rosarita Bay, to rendezvous with a lover.

"I don't know. Not anyone famous," Anna said. "Just some guy, like a contractor or foreman or something. He was in a hard hat and a tie. It was bizarre. She was going *at* it. She was all *over* him. Right in front of everybody in the lobby. I wish I had a camera or my phone on me. I could've sold the picture to a tabloid. Don't paparazzi make a lot of money for a single shot like that?"

"Only when it's an A-list celebrity."

"She had her tongue down his throat. It was something. It was just like in a movie."

When their shift ended, Anna gave Jeanette a makeover in the locker room. She had talent as a cosmetologist. The transformation was subtle, not lurid or overdone, but Jeanette appeared very different—younger, more sophisticated. She wore the makeup home, careful not to splash water on her face as she took a body shower.

After she got dressed, she saw that Yadin had left a voicemail on her cellphone. She listened to it, then put the phone in her purse. On her way to the church, she stopped by the service station on the corner of Highways 1 and 71 and washed off the makeup in the women's room. She had mused that the makeover might impress Yadin, but now that he wouldn't be at rehearsal, she felt too shy about unveiling her new look to the rest of the choir.

She was a few minutes late. She snagged a copy of *Singing the Living Tradition* from the stacks on the back table and hustled up to the group at the front of the sanctuary.

"Yadin coming?" Darnell asked.

"He can't make it tonight," she said.

Jeanette felt guilty now that she had not returned Yadin's messages yesterday. He was no doubt miffed that she had not bothered to pick up when he'd called and texted and that he had driven all the way to San Bruno for nothing. They appeared to be in a standoff now. She was certain he wasn't tired or ill. He was not coming to the church tonight to spite her, and she had to admit that he had reason to be annoyed with her.

They ran through two hymns for Sunday's service, No. 389, "Gathered Here," and No. 413, "Go Now in Peace," before taking a break.

Jeanette stood by the coffee urn and sipped a cup with Siobhan, who told her that the police officers' association—all eight members—had met and voted to recommend to the city council that they accept the proposal from the San Vicente County Sheriff's Office. It would allow them the most job transfers as full-time deputies, and since the sheriff's substation was nearby, no one would have to relocate.

"That's what the council's going to do, anyway," Siobhan said. "I don't know why they're holding a special session about it. So they can watch people bawl about a decision that's already been made?"

The county's proposal would save Rosarita Bay half a million dollars a year by eliminating not only the payroll but also redundancies in infrastructure. They would no longer need the police station or a 911 call center or have to pay for booking and crime lab services, and the sheriff's office would provide a detective for major crimes and a police dog, neither of which they had now. The proposal from the Pacifica Police Department would have cut a mere eighty thousand dollars from the annual budget and guaranteed just three jobs for the current officers.

Siobhan, however, would not be a sheriff's deputy. She would be offered a part-time position as a "community service officer," responsible for parking enforcement and traffic control. "It's better than nothing, I suppose," she said. "Mish and Greg have to take early retirement. But what the hell. It means I'm going to be a goddamn meter maid."

She began to cry a little, and Jeanette put her arm around her.

"I'm okay," Siobhan said. "I'll be okay. Don't tell anyone till it's official, okay? I wasn't supposed to say anything."

"I promise," Jeanette said, although she intended to notify her father that his contract would be voided. "You have any idea how the council's leaning with the library?"

"What do you mean? They stopped discussing that months ago," Siobhan said.

So she didn't know about LMS's revised submission, or Gerry Lowry's alleged machinations.

"Hey, I'm curious," Siobhan said, "where does Yadin know that actress from?"

"What?"

"You know, Marion Wicks."

"Mallory Wicks?" Jeanette asked.

"Yeah."

"What are you talking about? He doesn't know her."

"Is this about your confidentiality policy?" Siobhan asked. "Forget that. I saw him with her yesterday at the Centurion. Didn't he tell you? Security called us because they thought he might be a stalker or something, but it was pretty obvious to everyone in that lobby they used to be very good friends."

Yadin was the man Mallory Wicks had been making out with in the lobby yesterday? The dude in the hard hat? It wasn't possible.

"They have some sort of connection through country music?" Siobhan asked.

Jeanette nodded. "They know each other from Nashville," she said, as if privy to everything.

She wanted to flee. Yadin had lied to her, never revealing that he knew Mallory Wicks and that he intended to see her. He'd concocted the whole thing about his van. Yesterday, while she and Joe were at the cemetery, did Yadin take the hotel elevator upstairs and have sex with Mallory Wicks in her suite—the very suite Jeanette had cleaned this morning? Music was the only way they could be acquainted, but when, how? She didn't think Yadin had ever been to Nashville. Jeanette wondered what else he had been withholding from her. Was he an inveterate cheater? Had he indeed been sleeping with Caroline all along?

She was a fool. She had believed he'd be faithful to her, he'd never leave her, and here he was, fucking a Hollywood star.

But Jeanette stayed in the sanctuary until the end of rehearsal. She didn't want Siobhan or anyone else in the choir to catch on how oblivious she had been, how she had been so easily duped. Already Siobhan must have gossiped to someone in the church that Yadin had kissed Mallory Wicks.

When they finished the rehearsal, she sat in her car

and tried calling Yadin. He did not respond. She hung up without leaving a message. Was he at the Centurion with Mallory Wicks that very moment, naked on the Rivolta Carmignani sheets, rutting into her on the Sealy Posture-pedic Plush? She couldn't go to the hotel—she'd be fired for disturbing a guest—so she drove to his house, the only other alternative. She got lost, making a wrong turn, it had been so long since she had been to his decrepit shack, but she finally found Las Encinas Road and spotted his van there, parked in front of a Mercedes convertible, newly waxed and spit-shined.

She tried the door, which was locked. She knocked, then banged. Nothing. They were likely in his bedroom, too absorbed in their lovemaking to hear her. She had a key to his house—Yadin's backup in case he was ever locked out—and she fetched it from the glove compartment of her car and unlocked the door and hurtled inside to his bedroom. There was no one there, the pillow, blanket, and sheets on his tiny twin bed neatly made, but she heard music from his den and stepped across the hallway and shoved open the door. Yadin was sitting in a chair, strumming a guitar, and Mallory Wicks was standing beside him, playing a violin, microphones angled before them, a profusion of instruments and cables and equipment covering the floor and hanging on the walls and standing in every corner.

"What . . . ," she said. She was stupefied by the sight of them playing music together in the den—almost more so than if she had caught them in flagrante in bed.

Bewildered, she turned around and walked out toward her car, and Yadin followed her.

"Wait, Jeanette. Wait."

They stood on the crumbling sidewalk in front of his house. "What are you doing in there?" she asked. "When'd you get all that equipment?"

"Some of it's hers. We're re-recording a couple of songs for my album," he told her.

"What album? You're working on an album? You told me you quit."

He started mumbling—a barely intelligible ramble about wanting to self-release one final record and refinancing his house and reading Hopkins and going on a spiritual quest and moving from desolation to consolation.

Not much was coherent to Jeanette, except the depth of his deceptions. "How do you know her?" she asked.

"A long time ago, in Raleigh, we were in a band together," Yadin said.

"And you never thought to tell me this?"

"It was twenty-three years ago," he said. "It was a very short-lived thing, the band. We played a few gigs, but never recorded anything together. She was Mallory Wickenheiser then. They made her change her name when she got to Nashville."

"If it was so short-lived, why was it so important to see her?"

"I don't know," he said. "It was just a whim."

"A whim? You went to the Centurion on a whim?"

"Who told you?" Yadin asked. "Siobhan?"

Jeanette saw Mallory Wicks's silhouette appear in the living room window for a second, then retreat from view. "You were more than bandmates, weren't you?" she said to Yadin.

"It was so long ago," he said. "It wasn't a big deal."

"You went out with a country music star," she said, "and it was no big deal."

"She was nobody back then," he said. "We were just a pair of struggling musicians, living in a crappy apartment in the student ghetto."

"You lived together?"

Yadin winced. "Not even for a year."

"Were you in love with her?" Jeanette asked.

He looked up at a tree on the next lot. "Maybe a little."

The admission crippled her. Early in their relationship, Yadin had alluded to a first and only love, but had not volunteered any specifics, and she hadn't thought to ask for some—she didn't know why she hadn't been more curious. "She was in love with you, too?"

"She said she was, but she didn't mean it," Yadin told her. "She took off to Nashville and recorded one of my songs as her own. It was almost unrecognizable, after Acuff-Rose got its hands on it, but 'Beds & Beer,' her one big hit, that was mine. She stole it."

"You should hate her, then," Jeanette said.

"It was a throwaway. I didn't care about it. I was drunk one night and wrote it as a joke on a pizza box."

"You should despise her. If anything, you should have

gone to the hotel and given her a piece of your mind. But you didn't, did you?"

"No," Yadin said.

A dog barked somewhere in the distance. There weren't many houses on Yadin's street, which was an access road to a commercial construction and demolition landfill. Bits of broken wood and fluffs of insulation littered the asphalt. "Did you have sex with her yesterday?"

"What?" Yadin said. "Christ, no. That's ridiculous, Jeanette."

"Did you go up to her suite?"

"No. We had brunch and took a walk on the coastal trail and then I left for San Bruno. How come you never called me back?"

"That's all that happened?" she asked. "Nothing else? Nothing I should know about?"

"Nothing else happened," he said.

"You're lying," Jeanette said. "I know you kissed her in the lobby."

"It was the other way around—she kissed me."

"I heard it was steamy. I heard there was tongue."

"Who said that?" Yadin asked. "There was no tongue. It was just a goodbye kiss."

"And then she decided to stay."

"Purely for the music. She offered to add some harmony and fiddle to a few songs. It's just two recording sessions. She's leaving Thursday morning. One more night of recording, and then that'll be it, that'll be the end of it. It'll be years before I can afford to release this thing, but having her on it—the novelty of her name—might let me break even when I do."

"That won't be the end of it," she said. "You'll go on tour and things with her—appear on TV and radio, get interviewed for magazines."

"None of that's going to happen," he said. "I'm not going on tour. This'll be my last album, Jeanette. I'm just going to put it out there and retire. No one is ever going to hear another note from me. I'm going to stay here with you and Joe and move on with my life."

"I don't like this one bit," Jeanette said.

"You know I love you. There's no reason to be jealous."

"You think this is about being jealous? It's about trust. You lied to me about everything."

"I'm sorry, Jeanette," he said. "I'm sorry. I don't know why I hid all of this from you."

It shocked her now, how little they knew about each other, how little they shared. She had been withholding things from Yadin, too—all the facts about Étienne, for instance—and she didn't quite know why. How was it that, at this point in her life, she understood so little about herself?

"I cleaned her room this morning," she told Yadin.

"You did? I thought it got assigned to someone else."

"What if I say I don't want you to do it?" Jeanette said.

"Do what?"

"Record with her."

"That's kind of unreasonable, don't you think?" he said. "She's here. We're already halfway done."

"Unreasonable?" Jeanette said. "You were in love with her once."

"Years and years ago. There's nothing between us now. We're completely different people. She's famous. She's rich. She lives in a mansion. Our worlds couldn't be further apart."

"I don't care. I don't want you to do it," she said.

"You're really telling me I can't do it?" Yadin asked.

Jeanette noticed a dozen or so cigarette butts on the ground, all of them flattened within a square foot of each other, the ends smeared with lipstick. "I'm not telling you anything. It's up to you to decide. You can decide to tell her you've changed your mind and there's no point in her staying in town anymore, or you can go ahead with your recording. You know how I feel about this now, my position, and the possible consequences." She started walking toward her car.

"Which are?"

"Maybe we break up," Jeanette said.

"I don't want to break up."

"Then tell her to leave," she said, and drove away.

On Wednesday morning, her assignment sheet still had Mallory Wicks checking out on Thursday, not this afternoon. Jeanette probably shouldn't have expected Yadin to listen to her, after disregarding her for weeks, but she had hoped that he would. Now what? Did she have to dump Yadin, as she had threatened? It wasn't, Jeanette realized, despite being furious with him, what she wanted to do.

She considered asking Mary Wilkerson to assign the Miramar Suite to someone else, but then she would have to explain why. It wouldn't set a good precedent, bringing up a personal conflict and causing a last-minute scheduling change on her first day as a team leader.

"It's a big step, your promotion," Mary said. "Are you excited?"

"Yes," Jeanette said. "I am."

As she cleaned her first rooms of the morning, Jeanette thought about what she might do to Mallory Wicks's suite. Pop the sheets. Wipe the floor with a bath towel and hang it up as fresh. Swirl her toothbrush in the toilet bowl. By the time she knocked on the door to the Miramar Suite, however, Jeanette knew that she would do none of those things. She would clean it with her usual meticulousness. "Housekeeping," she called out.

She propped open the door and walked in. The suite was messier than yesterday. On the dining table were sheets of paper with handwritten notes, pens, a laptop, several bottles that had a vaguely medicinal air, and the suite's Bose Wave music system, which had been moved from the credenza on the other side of the room. Her violin was in a case on the sofa.

Jeanette began pulling out the bags from the trash cans and twisting their tops and placing them on the floor. As she headed toward the bedroom, she saw that the duvet was dangling rumpled off one edge of the bed. Then she noticed that the French doors were open, and she glimpsed Mallory Wicks on the terrace, wearing a bathrobe and smoking what looked to be a joint.

"I'm sorry, Ms. Wicks," Jeanette said, resentful she had to be polite. "I thought you were playing golf." The assignment sheet had specified a ten-forty tee time. "I'll come back later. I apologize for disturbing you, Ms. Wicks."

"Wait." She squashed the joint into the ashtray, and after poking her feet into a pair of Centurion slippers, she stood up, bunched together her bathrobe, and came inside. "We weren't properly introduced last night, Jeanette. Never mind this 'Ms. Wicks' business. Call me Mallory."

"I don't feel comfortable doing that in the hotel."

"I know you're also not comfortable I'm helping Yadin with his album. I want to assure you, this is strictly a musical collaboration, nothing more."

"I'll come back later to clean your room."

"Do you have a sister named Julie?" she asked. "Was she a golfer?"

"Yes," Jeanette said, perplexed.

"I remember watching her in the U.S. Women's Open in Newport, the last major Annika Sörenstam won. Your sister, she finished in the top twenty-five with another amateur, didn't she? Does she still play golf?"

"Only recreationally."

"I thought she had a good pro career ahead of her."

"She's a divorce attorney now," Jeanette said.

"That's a shame. I'm not very keen on divorce attorneys.

I've had to rassle with too many of them in my lifetime,"
Mallory said. "Could you sit with me a few minutes? I'd like
you to hear something." From her Birkin bag that was on a
chair, she pulled out a small black contraption with two silver
knobs on the top. "These tracks—well, you'll hear for yourself. Please. Sit down."

What if she refused? Jeanette asked herself. Out of spite,
would Mallory lodge a complaint against her? Likely not.
Jeanette had no reason to stay, yet there was a part of her
that wanted to see if she could understand the allure of this
collaboration, why it was so important to Yadin. "Hold on a
second," she said.

She shut the door to the suite and sat down on the far
side of the dining table. Mallory powered up the black
device, its display lighting up blue, and plugged it into a
cable that was connected to the Bose system. Music began
playing from the speakers—guitar and violin, then Yadin
and Mallory singing.

Everyone's gone now, the darkness rides
The house is empty, rooms still and wide
Gather the glasses, chairs up, move slow
Someone left a wallet, no one we know

Who were these ghosts in our house tonight
And is there a reason, true or tried
I saw you with him in a corner, making pleas
At the same moment my heart said I should flee

If you can convince me that they're lying
I won't need you to explain
If you can pretend my heart isn't breaking
I'll pretend to feel no pain

At the end of the song, Mallory said, "There's one more we finished."

"No, I have to go."

"The sound's not great with this portable recorder. We fed the mics to Yadin's old TASCAM for the actual tracks. This was just an indirect recording. But you can tell, can't you?"

"It's good," Jeanette said. Listening to the lyrics, she had experienced a wild moment of panic, thinking Yadin had been writing about her—her infatuation with Franklin—but she realized that couldn't be the case. It was just a generic love-done-me-wrong ballad, typical for the genre, not much of a departure from the songs on Yadin's previous albums—just slower, more stripped down. She had to admit, however, that Mallory's voice and violin accompaniment added a nice dimension to the song, made it brighter and fuller.

"It's more than good," Mallory said. "It's truly special. This is going to be a great album."

"Why are you doing this?" Jeanette asked her. "What's in it for you?"

"I just want to help Yadin," Mallory said.

"Even with you on it, this album will disappear the minute it gets out."

"It might not. Even so, he'll have accomplished something. These songs will last."

"It doesn't matter," Jeanette said. "Where has music ever gotten him? He's already gone bankrupt once."

"You ask what's in it for me," Mallory said. "It's the same thing that's in it for him. It's about producing something beautiful. You listen to a great song, it makes you feel something for once, it reminds you how to feel. For a few minutes, it eases your pain. Having a small part in that, that's what's in it for me."

"You're getting his hopes up for nothing," Jeanette said.

"Haven't you ever had a dream?" Mallory asked.

"What?"

"A dream. When you were growing up, wasn't there something you wanted to do or be?"

"No."

"I can't believe that. There must've been something."

Even without makeup, her hair bedraggled, dressed in a bathrobe, Mallory was still beautiful, but her age was evident. She had lines and wrinkles on her face and spots on the backs of her hands and freckles on her chest from sun damage. Two tendons on her neck were distending into ropy bands. Her skin was losing elasticity. Soon, she'd have a turkey neck, a droopy wattle, and would take to wearing scarves and turtlenecks year-round. She could keep coloring her hair, as Jeanette knew she did from the gray-tipped strands she'd cleared from the drain traps, she could keep getting lifts and tucks and Botox and Dysport injections, as Jeanette knew she did from the puffiness in her lips and cheeks and the stretch and swell around her eyes, she could keep buying every anti-aging cream that came on the market, but they would not stop the creeping inevitability of decline. She would turn old and be forgotten. She looked so small and thin, sitting in the chair, swaddled in her bathrobe, like an emaciated child. Jeanette almost felt sorry for her. There was probably nothing worse than reaching the height of your dreams and then seeing them recede from you.

"I had a scholarship to art school once," Jeanette told her.

"You did?"

"I wanted to be a photographer. Documentary photography."

"Like Cindy Sherman or Jeff Walls?"

Jeanette had never heard either name. "I have to go," she said. "I'm behind schedule. I'll come back and do your room in an hour and a half."

"Do you still take photographs?" Mallory asked.

"I sold all my camera equipment years ago."

"It's never too late."

Jeanette stood up from the dining chair. "We're just people, you know. We don't ask for much. Just a good job where we're treated decently and have some security. We're just trying to make a living, but it's hard, harder than you could ever imagine. None of us can afford to be romantics. It's something you would never understand. One of your handbags could equal someone's wages for an entire year. All the things you have in your closet and bathroom, staying a week at this hotel, it's pocket change to you. What could you possibly know about easing anyone's pain?"

Wednesday afternoon, Yadin and Joe ate quickly. They were carpeting Livingston's Insurance Services on Sutter Road in town, and they'd staggered their lunch breaks with Esteban and Rodrigo to save time. They sat in desk chairs—ergonomic and nicely padded, with casters and soft rubber arms—in the small parking lot out back, where they had cleared away the contents of the office. As a matter of respect, Joe usually prohibited the crew from lounging on a customer's furniture, but he had tweaked out his back this morning, and he was stiff and aching.

"I might take tomorrow off," Joe said.

"That bad?" Yadin asked. Joe had never missed a day since he'd begun working for him.

"Jeanette gave me a gift certificate to Coastside Shiatsu for Christmas. If I can get an appointment, I might go. We've just got that little boat job, which should take no time, and the estimate for Mortensen. You can handle that for me, can't you?"

"Sure," Yadin said. "That'd be a good contract."

"Maybe, maybe not. He's fussy. And cheap," Joe said. "I told you if the council votes to outsource, I'll need to lay someone off. I decided it'll be Rodrigo. We can make a go of it as a three-man crew. If we get bigger jobs, we can call him in as a temp or find someone else."

"Rodrigo has a family."

"So does Esteban."

"Adelina might be losing her job at New Harvest."

"It's fucked, having to let either of them go, but I don't have a choice."

Joe was eating from a bento box identical to Yadin's. Jeanette had given the boxes to both men as birthday presents, years apart. Today, Joe's was sectioned off with bite-sized pieces of boneless fried chicken, cucumber salad, radishes, and rice. No complaints or requests to trade so far this week. He had a stockpile of Jeanette's prepared meals remaining.

"Last time I pulled my back," Joe said to Yadin, "I got an MRI, and the doctor told me I've got a condition, a degenerative disc."

"When was this?" Yadin asked. "You didn't say anything."

"I haven't said anything to anyone, not even Jeanette. I was hoping it'd just go away."

"Can you do PT for it?"

"Eventually I'm going to have to stop working altogether," Joe said.

"What would you do then?" Yadin asked, feeling awful for Joe. At the same time, he tried to quell his own distress. He assumed Joe would shut down Wall to Wall, and he would lose his job. Then he would never have the money for his album, refi or no refi.

Joe told him about Julie being pregnant, moving to San Diego, building an addition for Julie and Andy, maybe getting a dog, and leaving Wall to Wall to Yadin if he and Jeanette were to get engaged.

"You're serious?" Yadin said.

"This is a year down the line I'm talking about, not right away. Don't put me in the grave yet."

"I don't know what to say, Joe. I'm honored."

"You've been first-rate on the job. You've done good. You turned your life around, got out of debt, paid me back. That took a lot of work, a lot of character."

"You talked to Jeanette about this?" Yadin asked.

"Couple of days ago."

"What'd she say?"

"I guess I caught her a little off-guard, but she came around to the idea."

"She did?" That was before, of course, Jeanette had learned about Mallory and the album and Yadin's other assorted dissemblances. He was relieved to have confessed everything to her, finally, but afterward he had not done what

DON LEE

she had demanded, and he didn't know if this meant now that he and Jeanette were no longer a couple.

"You've thought of it, haven't you?" Joe said. "Getting married to her?"

"To tell you the truth, Joe, I've never gotten the sense she wanted more—you know, with us. It's never felt like she's wanted to change the routine we have, or that she's capable of doing anything different. That's why I'm surprised to hear you say she came around."

"I know she comes off as cold," Joe said. "She had a lot of life in her, a fire under her, when she was a kid. I don't know where that went."

"Did you ever meet Étienne?" Yadin asked.

"Why would I have ever met him?"

"Not even after they got engaged?"

"What are you talking about?" Joe asked. "They were never engaged. It was a fling. He was some sort of Don Juan or something, a slick little douchebag, but she let herself get carried away and got knocked up by him. She told you they were engaged?"

Yadin was completely flummoxed. Why had Jeanette lied to him about this?

After work that evening, Yadin and Mallory reconvened at his house, and she asked him, "Have you talked to Jeanette? Are things okay between you two?"

"I haven't called her yet," he said. He had been hoping to avoid another confrontation. Now he was at sea. At least his lies had been lies of omission. Hers had been fabrications, intentionally meant to mislead him. But for what purpose? To make herself appear more sympathetic, more tragic?

"Don't you think you should talk to her?" Mallory asked. "I think you should."

"I will," Yadin said. "But first we've got work to do."

They had been making good progress yesterday until Jeanette appeared. Tonight, they would have to rush through the two remaining cuts. Mallory needed to return to L.A. tomorrow for the callback on a commercial she had postponed ("A pill for gas and bloating. Can you believe it's come to that?"), and they wouldn't have any more time.

During this session, Yadin was more receptive to Mallory's ideas: changing the key and tempo in "Step Away," taking out the bridge and repeating the chorus in "All the Way from There to Here." He let her use a tambourine and an egg shaker occasionally for a little percussion, and they juked through the songs, reacting to each other, playing off of each other. They worked swiftly and without respite, and before he knew it, they were done.

They listened to playbacks of all four songs, and then Yadin took off his headphones. "They're perfect," he said.

"They're really pretty good, aren't they?" Mallory said.

"It's the album we should have made in Raleigh," he told her. They nodded at each other, and her eyes welled.

At the Centurion two days ago, what he had been most afraid of was that she wouldn't remember him, that she would look at Yadin with only the vaguest of recognitions, thinking him somewhat familiar yet impalpable, speculating they might have gone to high school together. And even after he told her his name and invoked Raleigh, and Whisper Creek, and the Siesta Club, and the ten months that they had lived together and had been lovers, maybe she would still barely recall that time, just a bedimmed haze of youthful escapades, nothing momentous, certainly nothing warranting a place of prominence in the screed of her life. She would regard Yadin with curiosity and pity and even a little fear—sort of a weirdo, wasn't he, that he had hung on to something so fleeting and minuscule, when really it had just been a fling, she had forgotten, actually, that they had once almost signed a little record deal together, what sort of music had they played again?

But she had not forgotten. She did remember.

"Having you on these tracks," he said to her, "the changes you suggested, it's made such a difference, Mallory. I want you to have co-writer credit on them."

"No, you don't have to do that."

"I want to."

She drank her Pappy Van Winkle, then said, "Maybe you won't after you hear what I've done."

"What have you done?"

"The songs we cut yesterday, I emailed MP3s of them to Ronnie, my music manager. He thinks we could get a record deal."

Yadin parsed through this, hoping he had misheard her, though he was sure that he had not. "How many times do I have to say this? I'm not interested."

last recordings I'll ever make. I'm never laying down another track. I'm quitting music for good."

"Why?" Mallory asked. "Why would you quit when you're on the cusp of something great?"

"I'm going deaf," he told her.

"What?"

"I've already lost something like thirty percent in my right ear, and the left is catching up fast."

"Can't you just get hearing aids?" she asked.

He took out his hearing aid from his pocket and placed it on the worktable.

"But you've been hearing me fine without that thing," Mallory said.

"It comes and goes." He told her about Ménière's disease and described the various symptoms he had endured. "My hearing's only going to get worse."

"There must be something that can be done," she said. "We'll get you to better doctors, Ménière's specialists."

"I've tried everything."

"We'll take you to Stanford, the Mayo Clinic."

"You don't know what I've gone through. I spent years going to doctor after doctor."

"There's still time, though, right?" she asked. "You're saying three, five years, maybe more. You still have time to make more albums. We could get you custom in-ear monitors. And there might be new medical advances down the road. Even if there aren't, you could still write songs. Beethoven was deaf. He wrote the Ninth Symphony completely deaf.

How could you quit? You love music. It's your life. You're a lifer, like me."

"I want to stop struggling with this," Yadin said. "I'm so tired, Mallory. I just want to make peace with it. I want to stop being angry, stop feeling sorry for myself, and just accept it."

"You've struggled because you've had to do it alone," she said. "Maybe nothing will come out of this meeting. Maybe Mirrorwood will laugh us out of their offices. I'll admit, it's a long shot, anything happening. But why not talk to them? What have you got to lose?"

"I have everything to lose—Jeanette, Joe, my job, being part of their family. When I can't make music anymore, what will I have? Without them, I'll have nothing. I don't know what the hell I've been doing. I might have lost Jeanette already." He needed to make things up to her. He needed, somehow, to earn her trust again.

"Do you love her?" Mallory asked Yadin.

"She's good for me. We're good for each other."

"That's not much of an answer."

"It's enough of an answer for me."

"It's just one day in L.A.," she said. "You wouldn't be committing to anything. At the very least, you might walk out of there with a publishing contract for these other songs. The royalties alone for a couple of them, if they did well for someone, could give you some financial security. They offer you an advance, you could self-release your record. Isn't that possibility worth one day out of your life?"

He looked at his notebooks, the scraps of paper, the cassettes. "What time is this meeting?" he asked.

He didn't say yes, and he didn't say no. He told Mallory he would think about it, he'd let her know. It was, in terms of his schedule, doable. He wouldn't be working on Friday. A customer had postponed a job, and Joe didn't have anything lined up for them until Monday. Yadin could drive down to L.A., assuming his van could handle the trip, listen to what Mirrorwood had to say, and find out what they would demand of him.

Thursday morning, he went to the Ambrose Senior Residential Center for the estimate. The director, Everett Mortensen, followed Yadin as he took measurements, writing them down on his clipboard. Mortensen only wanted to redo the carpet in the group exercise room and the TV/computer room.

"You don't want the entire ground floor to match?" Yadin asked him.

"That's not necessary," Mortensen said. "A close approximation or coordination of colors and patterns would be adequate."

The existing carpets were worn, spotted with stains, and smelled of antiseptic. All of them needed to be replaced. Going through the center, Yadin saw residents with walkers, wheelchairs, and electric scooters. No wonder Joe wanted to retire in San Diego and live in a guesthouse on his daughter's property. Anything to avoid this destiny.

"I was thinking of a loop pattern," Mortensen said, flipping through a sample book. "But I don't know if that would be too distracting. What do you suggest?"

"Maybe pin dots," Yadin said. "Stainmaster and Mohawk both have nice pin dot patterns."

"Pin dots. Do you have samples for those?"

Yadin's cellphone rang. On the screen was a familiar number, the main line for the Community Credit and Housing Program in San Vicente. He excused himself and walked out into the hallway.

It was the counselor, Joel Hanrahan. "Today's my last day at CCHP," he said. "I'm moving back to Boston. But I wanted to let you know I went through your file. I'm afraid a refi's not remotely plausible for you, as I suspected. The situation's more untenable than that. The next counselor will explain it to you. I just wanted you to know I did my best to try to figure something out for you. I hope you'll find a way in the future to release your album."

"Hang on," Yadin said. "How long will you be there?"

He told Mortensen he would return to the center in an hour and a half. By the time he arrived at CCHP, Hanrahan had already finished packing up his office. He had shaved off his half goatee, and the patch of skin where it had been was raw and pallid.

They sat across Hanrahan's empty desk from each other. "I got a job offer at Fidelity in their assets management division," he said. "I guess if you're going to sell out, you might as well go whole hog."

"I can't qualify for refinancing?"

"Look, I'm going to be absolutely candid with you," Hanrahan said. "Forget a refi or HELOC. There's no point applying to lenders. You're much more underwater than I realized. You could ask for a short sale or a deed in lieu of foreclosure, but it would be a waste of time. You didn't hear this from me— all right, who gives a fuck, I'm out of here in ten minutes—my personal advice is to walk away."

"What do you mean, walk away?" Yadin asked.

"Just that. Stop making your mortgage payments and walk away from the house," he told him. "It'll eventually be foreclosed and auctioned, but it'll no longer be your problem. There's no sense working so hard to retain the house, making the monthlies, keeping up with the insurance, property taxes, and maintenance, when you'll never see any of it back. Ever. You're just throwing your money away, and it's money you need."

Yadin felt his cellphone vibrating in his pants pocket. "That house is my nest egg," he said. "It's going to be my retirement."

"That's a delusion—always has been. More than anything, it's been your albatross. What if you get laid off? What if you get sick again? You're one medical emergency away from having to go back on food stamps."

"It's the only thing I have," Yadin said. "It's the only property I've ever owned. It's the only thing I have left of my family."

"It's brutal, I know," Hanrahan said, "but you can't be

sentimental about this. Save up and try to start over again in a few years."

"I can't start over," Yadin said. "I barely made it the last time. I can't do it a second time."

"I'm sorry. You're going to have to."

It had been Joe on the phone, livid in the voicemail he left. Yadin drove back to Rosarita Bay, to the harbor. The two Wall to Wall vans were in the marina parking lot. They had a small job on a powerboat, replacing the carpet on the stair treads and in the salon belowdecks.

Joe was standing beside the boat on the dock. "I cannot fucking believe you bailed on Mortensen like that."

"I'll go back right now and talk to him. I'll fix it," Yadin said. Joe was wearing a new pair of mirrored sunglasses, and Yadin couldn't see Joe's eyes, only his own reflection.

"I already went," Joe told him. "I practically had to suck his fucking dick. He agreed on the Mohawk pin dot, no thanks to you. Meanwhile, Rodrigo and Esteban were here, waiting for you on the clock. I can't take a day off without everything going to hell? I was going to hand you the business. What am I to think now, huh? Maybe it's you I should let go, not Rodrigo."

"I'm sorry, Joe," Yadin said. "I fucked up. I've had a lot of things on my mind."

"Too bad your job hasn't been one of them," Joe said. "Get out of here. I don't want to see your fucking face again till Monday."

From the harbor, Yadin drove to Pismo Beach. Dispirited,

he sat on the sand and stared out at the overcast ocean. A handful of surfers in wet suits straddled longboards, loitering for waves, while two standup paddleboarders caught rides on ankle breakers.

In all probability, Mallory had been thinking from the start about using him, appropriating the project and songs for herself. Maybe not consciously, but embedded deep in the back of her head, there might have been little tip-taps of ambition pressing her to commandeer the album. That was why she had brought along a portable recorder—to capture digital files that she could email; not, as she had said, to listen to playbacks during the day to keep in the flow of the songs.

Once Mirrorwood understood that Yadin would not tour or do any promotion, the meeting—at least in regard to him—would be over. But he was amenable to the idea of letting Mallory record his songs for an album of her own. He wouldn't give her anything off *Lonesome Lies Before Us*, but he'd let her take her pick of the B-sides. It'd be a fitting conciliation for abandoning her in Raleigh, forsaking their contract with Lost Saloon Records. And maybe he'd get enough of an advance to hang on to his house for the time being, and have cash left over for the self-release. He'd eventually receive royalties, too. If her album did well, the payouts would be much bigger than anything he'd garnered over his entire career.

At the library, he borrowed a pair of earbuds from the front desk and plugged them into one of the computers. He looked up Mirrorwood's roster of artists, none of whom he recognized (all of them were so young), and listened to a few of their songs. It was decent stuff, nothing egregiously poppy, more rock than folk but falling within the genre of alt-country, although the promo copy used the terms "roots-infused" and "Americana-based."

Caroline was in her office, a tiny room in the back of the library, crowded with books in towering piles. Propped up next to her on a chair were graphs on poster boards of patron visits and usage, presumably for her final presentation to the city council tomorrow night that would determine the library's fate.

"I need some advice," he said, standing in the doorway.

"And why not come to me for it?" Caroline said, not looking up from the papers on her desk.

"I was a musician once."

"I know," she said. "I've listened to your albums."

"You have?"

She set down her pen. "I was curious, so I asked Lane. . . . Forgive me. He knows how to download music for free, and he got all four of your records for me. I listen to them in my car. They're quite good."

"I've been going through some things."

"So you've said."

"My interest in Hopkins was related to it."

"So I gathered."

"But maybe it wasn't so much about religion as it was about my music," Yadin said. "What you told me last month, that Hopkins thought he'd failed as a poet. Is there more to it?"

She swiveled her chair around to face him at the door. She was wearing black nylons and had a run on her left leg, just above the knee. "Hopkins's best friend, Robert Bridges, thought he'd thrown his life away, becoming a Jesuit and not pursuing his poetry, not seeking an audience—or facing critics. He may have been right. Maybe Hopkins's real sin was that he had a gift but didn't share it with the world because he was too afraid. Or arrogant. He was pretty full of himself. He made a big ceremony of burning his manuscripts in a bonfire. He called it the 'slaughter of the innocents.'"

"How do we have his poems, then, if he burned them?"

"Bridges kept the ones he mailed to him."

Yadin wondered if Caroline regretted not finishing her Ph.D., if she believed that being a scholar or professor had been her calling. "Do you think Hopkins would be happy, knowing he's so respected now, knowing his poems have lasted?"

"Of course. Don't you aspire to immortality?" Caroline asked. She raised both arms high into the air and shimmied her shoulders, a squirmy stretch that diverted and perturbed Yadin. "Don't you crave adoration? Who doesn't?"

"I don't care about that," he told her.

"No?" She lowered her arms. "Why do you make music, then?"

"I'm not sure," he said. "To figure things out for myself, I guess."

"Isn't it meaningless, though, if no one else hears it? Isn't the whole point to connect with someone?"

He remembered after a show once, a woman came up to thank him. She told Yadin that she hadn't spoken to her father in eight years, but after listening to "Hard to Say," a song on Yadin's second album about his own father, she decided to break the silence and call her father. It was the first time Yadin realized that what he did mattered to someone out there, that he could make a difference, even if it was with just one person, and he felt lucky—lucky he could do what he loved, lucky he could put out albums.

Ross, Whisper Creek's bass player, lived near Minneapolis, where he worked for a Swiss chemical company that specialized in pesticides and genetically modified seeds. Charlie, their drummer, had won a big online poker tournament once and belonged to an anarchist organization. Yadin had had difficulty tracking down Thorton, their lead guitarist, on the Internet, whenever he tried to check up on his old bandmates. It was because Thorton had become a woman. She was now Theresa, a gender therapist. None of them were playing music anymore.

"You're writing and singing for communication, aren't you?" Caroline said to Yadin. "I don't think it's meant to be a private activity."

He had always been awkward and clumsy. In everything, with everyone. Music was the only thing he'd ever been good at, the only thing that could fill the hole that was inside him.

"They can get a little corny and sentimental, your songs," Caroline told him, "but they give people a few minutes of propinquity." Before he could ask, she explained, "Closeness, solace. They've done that for me, more than once, when I've been crying in my car. There's a lot to be said for that. I used to struggle with the question of theodicy, how to justify God's goodness, or even His existence, in the face of all the tragedy that befalls us. But I came to believe that such horrible things can only happen if there *is* a God, if there *is* a plan for us, because the alternative would be too awful to bear. Otherwise we'd be utterly lost, to think that all of this is for nothing. I realize that could be specious reasoning, but it's my solace. Did you know that Franklin and I are probably getting divorced?"

"No, I didn't."

"I've been having an affair," she said. "I can understand Hopkins trying to hide from the world. I wish, more than anything, I could do the same."

They sat in the living room of her bungalow, Yadin on the red velvet couch, Jeanette opposite him in the orange butterfly chair. He told her about the meeting at Mirrorwood tomorrow.

"You'll never come back," she said.

"Of course I will. My entire life is here."

"There's nothing holding you in Rosarita Bay. You could pack up everything you own in your van and be gone in twenty minutes."

He shifted his weight on the velvet couch, inadvertently wobbling the adjacent piecrust table and the ornaments arrayed on top of it: an antique crystal match striker, candles, and a collection of white porcelain bird figurines. "I meant you," he said. "You're my life here. Along with Joe."

"The only reason you're with me at all is Wall to Wall."

"You know that's not true."

"Do I?" Jeanette asked.

"It's just one day."

"Are you planning to spend the night there?"

"I'll drive straight back tomorrow night," he said, although Mallory had offered to let him stay at her house in Thousand Oaks. "It's only one meeting."

"One and done, right?" Jeanette said. "A onetime thing. Just like you said on Tuesday—one more night, and that'll be it. Only it didn't turn out that way, did it? You'll want to keep doing this, make another album with her, just one more."

"No, that's not going to happen."

"She's doing all of this because she still has feelings for you."

"Come on, you don't really believe that," Yadin said to Jeanette, although deep down, prior to Mallory's disclosure about Mirrorwood, it was what he had been wondering all week.

"I asked you not to go through with the recording with her," Jeanette said to him, "but you did it anyway. You didn't listen to me, and now you're going to L.A. You've already made up your mind about this."

"I haven't yet," he told her. "I wanted to ask you about it first."

"You're not asking me," Jeanette said. "You're telling me. All those songs about getting your heart broken, missing someone, they've all been about Mallory, haven't they? You've been pining after her ever since she left for Nashville."

"They're about people in general. They're not about any one person."

"Tell the truth."

"Some of them have been about you," Yadin said, and this was the truth. Maybe he had been carrying a torch for Mallory for twenty-some years, maybe he had collected all those magazines and tabloids about her, maybe he had watched her awful TV shows and listened to her dreadful records, but these recent songs, these apostrophes, were addressed as much to Jeanette as they were to Mallory.

"You've never felt that way about me," she said.

"You've never let me," he said. "I've missed you, Jeanette. A lot of times, being in the same room with you, I miss you. You've always been so far away. Why did you say Étienne was your fiancé? Why did you say you had a miscarriage?"

"Dad told you."

"Can you talk about it?" Yadin asked. "I want to know who you are."

She sat in her orange butterfly chair, her shoulders and legs squashed inward by the wings, her eyes fixed on the leather pouf near her feet. "I don't want to be alone," she said.

"I don't, either."

"Do you want to get married?" she asked.

Startled, he asked, "Do you?"

"I've taken you for granted," Jeanette said. "I see that now. I don't want to lose you."

"You mean it?" he asked.

"I know it's not ideal, the two of us, but I think I could live with that," she said. "Could you?"

A few weeks ago, Yadin would have been overjoyed, feeling he had finally broken down the bulwark Jeanette had kept shored between them. Now he wasn't so sure. Had her affection for him changed fundamentally, or was this being prompted by pressure from Joe, coupled with Mallory's intrusion into their lives?

There was so much color in her home, so much light. There was frivolity. A wooden owl mirror, peacock feathers on the walls, sepia-toned postcards of flappers and silent movie stars with exaggerated facial contortions. Each piece in the bungalow felt as if it held a story, but he wasn't privileged to the narrative of any of them.

"You're not saying anything," Jeanette said.

"We don't have to decide today, do we?" Yadin asked.

"Get out."

eplied that it was urgent she see him. He simply accepted this, not probing further, saying he'd be there within an hour, which reassured her that she wasn't acting without a tendril of reciprocity. There was something between them. They were drawn to each other. They both felt it, and Jeanette thought it essential that they acknowledge it now.

She wasn't exactly sure what she was expecting to happen today. Would they have sex? Although she was willing to, she thought, actually, it'd be better if they didn't and chose to proceed slowly. Maybe they'd kiss a little on the bed, losing themselves in a surge of ardor, before they composed themselves and made plans. Mariposa was a hundred seventy-five miles away. It was perverse to think this, Jeanette knew, but the best thing that could happen would be for the city council to vote to privatize the library. Everything would be much cleaner, then, Caroline and the children gone. Franklin could continue his part-time ministry in Rosarita Bay, Jeanette could continue at the Centurion, becoming a floor supervisor. They could let their romance develop. They could get to know each other, have dinners in her bungalow, eventually spend nights together.

She was sweating lightly. She turned on the air conditioner. She dampened a hand cloth and wiped her armpits and applied antiperspirant. She did her makeup—including lipstick—the way Anna had shown her, and fixed her hair. She didn't own many clothes that were not plain. From her closet at home, she had pulled out the plum-colored wraparound jersey dress with a V-neckline that she had worn for

12. Lonesome Lies Before Us   4:42

The Holiday Breeze in Pacifica had changed management, but not much else. The furniture, the wallpaper, the fixtures, the bedspread—nothing in the rooms had been upgraded since Jeanette last worked there.

She had first gone to another motel down the street, the Sea Plaza, which used to offer hourly rates, but it had been turned into a Best Western. With little recourse, she had entered the office to the Holiday Breeze just after eleven a.m., anxious about seeing her old boss, who had preferred to man the desk himself. Yet he wasn't there. A sign announced NEW OWNERS, NEW BREEZY ATTITUDE! She asked the woman at the front desk for the half-day rate, and the woman did not balk or flinch. New attitude or not, the Holiday Breeze was still a no-tell motel.

It wasn't just fleabags that were renting out rooms for the day anymore. The Centurion would soon be doing it, offering a Daylight Rest and Restore package, ostensibly for tourists or golfers on day trips who might want to nap or take a bath. The package would come with access to the fitness center, but not the spa, which would require an additional fee. Jeanette had heard that other luxury hotels were allowing so-called mini-stays as well, supposedly to accommodate travelers with long layovers or businesspeople between meetings. These were euphemisms, of course. Everyone knew that guests who booked rooms for a few hours during the day were there for only one reason—illicit sex.

In the Holiday Breeze, whoever had cleaned No. 14—a room Jeanette knew well—had done an okay job. Nothing horrific, no hairs or major blunders, just a gum wrapper underneath the bed and a bottle cap behind the dresser. Nonetheless, Jeanette had higher standards. The first thing she did was strip off the bedspread and fold it and stow it in the closet. The bedspreads were laundered only every three months. She remade the bed, creating a foot pocket. Then she took out a packet of disinfectant wipes from her purse and rubbed them over the TV remote, the light and lamp switches, the alarm clock, the phone, the headboard, and the doorknobs—the spots most likely to be overlooked and collect germs. Afterward, she tackled the bathroom: faucets, sink, tub, toilet, flush handle. There were no water glasses, just disposable cups in sealed plastic bags, which she left untouched. She had brought her own wineglasses.

At seven-thirty this morning, she had called Ma[...]erson to tell her she wouldn't be going in to work to[...]

"Are you sick?" Mary had asked.

Jeanette had not slept all night, and her hands we[...]ing a little, as if she were strung out, the world feeling[...] and woolly. "No, I just need a personal day," she ha[...] She knew it would have reflected better on her to fa[...] illness or say that her father was laid up, yet she could n[...] to Mary.

"Is everything all right?" Mary asked.

"I need to take care of some things," Jeanette said. "[...] sorry I'm calling so last-minute."

"I wish you could have told me yesterday, at least."

"I know."

"This is really going to jam things up," Mary said. "I have[...] to say I'm disappointed, Jeanette. This is only your third day[...] as team leader. I was thinking you had a real future with the Centurion Group. If there's a problem, please tell me. We're family here, you know."

"I'm sorry, Mary," Jeanette had said, "I have to go," and hung up.

What could she have told Mary? That everything was falling apart, and she was on the verge of having another nervous breakdown? That she intended to seduce her minister?

After checking in, she had phoned Franklin, asking him to meet her at the Holiday Breeze and giving him the room number. He had asked what was wrong, and she'd only

Julie's wedding, along with the high heels, and she changed into them now, and then waited.

Franklin, as promised, knocked on the door in less than an hour—like her, always punctual. "Are you okay?" he asked.

"Come in," she said.

He took a step inside and looked around the room. "So this is it, the famous—or infamous—Holiday Breeze."

Jeanette closed the door behind Franklin and asked, "Do you want a glass of wine?"

"It's a little too early for me," he said. "You sure you're okay? What's going on? Why'd you want to meet here?"

"Let's sit down," she said.

He glanced from the bed to a stuffed chair—the only two choices. He took the chair.

Jeanette went to the bureau, on top of which was a boxy old TV, a two-cup coffeemaker, a plastic ice bucket on a tray, and a bottle of Merlot that she had opened and left to breathe. After pouring herself a glass, Jeanette walked around to the other side of the room, closer to Franklin, and settled down on the edge of the mattress. To her chagrin, she discovered that she was too short for the height of the bed. If she wanted to maintain this pose, she would have to lean back on it while keeping her legs straight, both feet flat on the carpeted floor. Yet it was too late to reposition herself. It'd look childish to scoot up onto the bed and have her feet dangling in the air.

"What's going on?" Franklin asked once more.

"I wanted to talk to you," Jeanette said. "Are you still planning to go to the council meeting tonight?"

"Yes."

"What are you going to do? What are you going to say?"

"I haven't decided yet," Franklin said. "Maybe I'll direct all my questions to Lowry first. I'll ask him why he made such a one-eighty on LMS, if a little payola had swayed him, and when he denies that, maybe I'll ask him if the privatization's motivated by anything else."

"Don't do it," Jeanette said. "Don't say anything. Don't even go."

"Why not?"

He was dressed in jeans and a T-shirt and hiking shoes, and she noticed mud caked on the outsoles. "What would be the point?" she asked. "It wouldn't accomplish anything. Don't you see? You'll just embarrass yourself. Let her go, Franklin. Just let her go."

"Without putting up a fight?" he asked. "Just let her go to Mariposa with my kids?"

"Do you really think your marriage can be saved? You said she hasn't had sex with you in three years. She's probably been having this affair, maybe with Gerry Lowry, for a long time."

"Not 'probably' or 'maybe.' Definitely," Franklin told her.

"With all that, is there really any hope?" Jeanette asked. "How would you overcome all that?"

"For the sake of the kids, I have to try."

"Be realistic about this," Jeanette said. "Is there really any way you could make the marriage work at this point?"

He swept his hair away from his face and scratched his

scalp. "You may be right," he said. "But what am I going to do? I'll have to give up the church and move up there."

Jeanette drank from her wineglass, then said, "You could stay here."

"How would I see my kids?"

"What's in Mariposa for you? You said not much. You love the ministry, don't you?"

"It's the only thing I've ever wanted to do," Franklin said.

"You could spend part of the time here, part of the time there."

"The logistics would be impossible," he said. "It's a three-hour drive. That's if there's no traffic. What about school? We couldn't have them attending different schools, splitting up their weeks like that."

Jeanette had not been thinking about joint custody, shuttling the kids back and forth between towns; she had imagined the kids living with Caroline, Franklin going to Mariposa every other weekend for visits. "You know what?" she said, another tack dawning on her. "You could stop Caroline from relocating. You could stop her from taking the job."

"How?" he asked.

"Isn't the priority always about keeping things stable for the kids? Minimizing changes to their routine? My sister's a family law attorney. She's told me about this stuff. She could file an injunction for you and make Caroline stay here. She could mediate a separation agreement for you."

"I hadn't thought of that," Franklin said. "I could do that. If I can prove adultery, I might even get primary custody."

"I don't know if that would work," Jeanette told him. "I'm pretty sure California's a no-fault state."

"I'd have to pay child support," Franklin said. "If she loses her job, the onus will be on me. I can't afford much as it is. She'd have to find a new job around here, and there's obviously nothing in libraries."

"Maybe she could teach or something?" Jeanette asked. "What about at SVCC? Doesn't she have a Ph.D.?"

"ABD."

"What's that?" Her legs were getting tired from propping herself against the edge of the bed. She wished she could somehow cross them.

"All But Dissertation," Franklin said. "I guess she could try to teach high school or adjunct at a college, but it's not that easy, finding a teaching job in this economy, especially in this area."

"Let her commute," Jeanette told him. "That's what you've had to do to Aptos." It wasn't optimal, Caroline and the children staying in Rosarita Bay, but they could make it work, Jeanette thought.

"One of us would have to find another house to rent that's big enough for the kids," he said. "You know how much we're paying now? The rents in this town are outrageous. She should have to move out, not me. She's the one who blew up the marriage, who cheated. You think your sister could orchestrate that in the injunction? Infidelity has to have *some* consequences. But courts always seem to favor the woman, don't they?"

Jeanette had difficulty breathing. Her chest squeezed. Her legs were cramping. She marveled at how much could happen in a matter of days, how much could change. She felt as if her entire life hinged on the next few moments. "If you need a place to stay temporarily," she said to Franklin, "you can always stay with me."

"You have a guestroom?" he asked.

She set her wineglass down on the nightstand and straightened out the front wrap of her dress below the tie belt. "I broke up with Yadin last night," she told Franklin.

"You did? Why? What happened?"

"A lot of things," Jeanette said. "But maybe it's for the best. It made me think about us."

"Us?" Franklin asked. "You mean the church?"

"No, you and me," she said. "You said you'd miss me. I would miss you, too, Franklin. I've been thinking, maybe we could see each other."

"Oh, God," Franklin said, fidgeting in his chair in what appeared to be alarm.

"It doesn't have to be right away. I know you'll need time."

"Oh, God," he said again. "I had an inkling, the motel, your dress, the makeup. This is completely my fault. I'm sorry, Jeanette, but I have to be forthright. I don't have those kinds of feelings for you."

"But you must," Jeanette said.

"I'm sorry. I don't," Franklin said. "At all."

She had made a colossal mistake. Mortified, she stood up and bounded to the other side of the bed. "I am so stupid," she said.

"It's my doing," Franklin said, standing, too, backing up

toward the door. "I somehow gave you the wrong impression. I'm sorry."

"I am such a fool," she said. "I'm pathetic."

"You wouldn't have thought it unless there was something I was doing or saying. It was inappropriate, confiding in you about my personal life. I crossed an ethical line. I've been terribly remiss. It's just that I had no one else to talk to. I'm so sorry."

How could she have been so delusional? How could she have misread his signals so profoundly?

Yesterday afternoon at the hotel, Mary had come up to her in the locker room with a green gift bag—striped, metallic. It had had tissue paper wadded and crumpled on the top, obscuring its contents. "This is from Mallory Wicks," Mary had whispered to her excitedly. Jeanette didn't look inside the bag until she got home. It was a Nikon D3100, a digital SLR with an 18–55 mm lens. Her tip. There was a card. "Never forget your dreams. All my best, Mallory Wicks," it said in her cheerful looping script.

After she had kicked Yadin out of her bungalow, Jeanette had opened her closet and tugged out a plastic bin, which was filled with Kodak 8" x 10" paper boxes. Inside were photos of Joe, Jo, Jeremy, and Julie, and black-and-white prints from Watsonville: portraits of the squatters in Callaghan Park, *piscadores* in the strawberry fields, and Yolanda and Lauro Aguilar and the other Green Giant workers at Local 912. Many were of Étienne—at the beach, at La Perla del Pacifico, at Elkhorn Slough, at the Starlight Drive-In in his red Alfa Romeo Spider. She sifted through the photographs—they were good, there was something there, she thought for a second—and then she tore them into pieces, one by one. She had been so naive to think that she could be a professional photographer, working for *Time* or *Newsweek*. She had never stood a chance. She had been a dilettante. Her portraits were lies—no better than staged tableaus. They caught a convenient moment, but didn't reveal the deceptions and depravity that people were capable of, nor all the bad decisions and regrets and guilt that could strangle a life.

"I just want to feel something," Jeanette said to Franklin. "Why can't I feel anything? All these years I've been going to church, I've felt nothing. I want to remember how to feel, but I'm dead inside. I just follow the steps in manuals. I've been stuck, and I can't seem to get unstuck."

"It's okay. I understand," Franklin said. "You're going through—"

"I know people don't like me. I'm not a lot of fun. I don't laugh. I seem unfriendly and negative. Stiff. I've always thought everyone's perception of me was so different than the truth. But I think maybe that's who I've become, who I am. An empty, unlikable person."

She had stubbornly hung on to the notion that she was special. What, though, had made her believe that? She wasn't special. She wasn't important. She had done nothing with her life. She wasn't anyone who mattered.

"People like you," Franklin said. "Everyone in the church likes you. They wouldn't have voted you president of the board otherwise."

"They voted for me because I'll do all the shit work no one else wants to do."

She remembered a sermon Franklin gave recently on grace—its myriad meanings, from being in someone's good graces to having a grace period on a credit card to the addition of grace notes in music. But in his view, Franklin had said, they encountered grace whenever they gathered in worship, in fellowship, and in kinship. Grace was about relationships in all forms, but most deeply in their connections to family, friends, and partners.

If Yadin and Joe abandoned her, what would she be left with? A church whose underlying function she could not access; a congregation that would fold, anyway, if Franklin moved to Mariposa. A job as a hotel housekeeper that was measured in QCs and DNDs and Charisma slips, striving for five. A coworker who only respected her for her tricks with tennis balls and Alberto VO5. A dying town she had never been able to escape. A bungalow that she would have to give up eventually, the elderly owners sure to put it on the market someday; the interior of which represented not who she was but who she had yearned to be—a person who was artistic, educated, cultured, worldly.

"I wish I meant something to someone," she said. "There's no one who'd miss me, who'd remember me."

"You mean something to a lot of people, Jeanette," Franklin told her. "Believe me, you do."

Yadin had put his life back together, and now he had a second chance. She would give anything for a second chance. Instead, she had come to the stage where there were no more possibilities for her. She could no longer hope to reinvent or resurrect herself. She could only mourn the life she had been unable to create.

"Forgive me," she said to Franklin.

"There's nothing to forgive," he told her. "You've done nothing wrong."

"I had too much pride. I shouldn't have aborted that baby."

"What?" he asked. "When did this happen?"

"If I'd had that child, at least I wouldn't be alone."

"Is that why you and Yadin broke up?" Franklin asked.

She dropped to her knees and pressed her forearms against the edge of the bed. She clasped her hands together and bowed her head and cried. "Please forgive me."

Yadin left for L.A. early in the morning, well before daybreak. He didn't want to travel on I-5, afraid of the straight-line monotony of the interstate through the San Joaquin Valley, all the trucks on that route, and the chance of his van breaking down on the Grapevine. A few days ago, he had asked Rodrigo to look at his van, and he'd located a gaping crack in Yadin's exhaust pipe near the catalytic converter. Rodrigo patched it with foil tape, steel wool, a snipped-up Coke can, and stainless-steel hose clamps, but had told Yadin the repair wouldn't last long. He also thought the problem was elsewhere—something more serious—since the van was still making noise and leaking fumes.

So Yadin took Highway 101 down, even though it added nearly an hour to the trip, passing through Salinas, San Luis

Obispo, and Santa Barbara. Once he reached Ventura, where the highway turned inland from the coast, he hit horrible traffic. He limped along for fifty miles, the van shaking and smoking, until he got to 405 South, then chugged up Sepulveda Pass from the Valley, staying in the right lane but still getting tailgated and honked at until he was able to exit onto Sunset Boulevard.

From there, he rode the curves and bends past UCLA, Bel Air, and Beverly Hills, surrounded by beautiful palm and shade trees, hedges, flowers, and multimillion-dollar homes, the grass and sidewalks as pristine as at the Golden Gate National Cemetery. It was clear and warm out, seventy-five degrees, another perfect day in Southern California.

After five miles, the road abruptly became less residential, and he entered the business district in West Hollywood. Right at the start of the Sunset Strip was where the meeting would take place. Yadin parked across the street and stared up at the building, which was called the Doheny Sunset, a ten-story white concrete and blue glass structure with a restaurant and a bank on the ground floor. Mirrorwood's suites were on the eighth floor, but he didn't know which way they faced. The head of A&R could have been gazing down at his van this very moment, curious about the vehicle's age and condition, which was older, more worse for wear, than any car Yadin had glimpsed since crossing the county line.

The meeting was scheduled for one o'clock. Yadin had given himself seven and a half hours for the drive and had hoped to arrive in town before eleven a.m., plenty of time to eat lunch and gather himself. But now, because of the traffic, he had less than an hour.

He needed a restroom. He hadn't gone since stopping for gas in Carpinteria. He resumed down Sunset Boulevard, past all the music landmarks: the Rainbow, the Roxy, Whisky a Go Go, the House of Blues. He had been to L.A. twice to play in small clubs, but never, of course, in any of these famous venues, which he had never seen before. It was his first time on the Strip.

Several blocks after the Chateau Marmont, the street turned seedier. Gone were the chic boutiques and restaurants, the billboards, and the pretty, wealthy people. Now there were fast-food joints, strip malls, gas stations, tattoo parlors, fences with barbed wire, and doors with iron bars. There was trash in the gutters, tattered stickers and flyers taped to light poles, graffiti on every surface. He wondered where he could use a bathroom. He stopped at a gas station, and the cashier said the toilet was broken, so he kept driving east. Then, after a block that seemed lined entirely with guitar stores, he spied a library, a small modern building with a pyramidal roof. He parked in the lot and walked to the entrance, and when the automatic doors slid apart, he was assailed with the smell of sweat and urine and cigarettes. Nearly every seat was occupied by a homeless person. The men's room was locked. He had to ask the clerk at the front desk to buzz him in, and as Yadin opened the door, he was met face-to-face by a man with dozens of pink and purple ribbons twisted into his hair, who shouted at him, "I am the cloud king!"

As quickly as he could, Yadin got out of there. He climbed into his van, and noticed the cargo door on the passenger side was ajar. He walked around the van. Someone had punched in the lock cylinder and taken almost everything that had been in the back. The glove compartment was open and empty as well. Thankfully the person had not touched his spiral-bound notebooks or the cassettes for *Lonesome Lies Before Us*. The tapes were copies, not the originals, which he had left in Rosarita Bay for safekeeping, but they wouldn't have been able to listen to the album or the B-sides at the meeting. He supposed no one—thieves, in particular—had cassette players anymore. He had almost brought his TASCAM along with him for the meeting, but Mallory had checked with her manager, and he had told her that the head of A&R at Mirrorwood was an audiophile and had a collection of vintage stereo equipment, including an old cassette deck, in his office.

There hadn't been much that was valuable inside the van: driving directions, sunglasses, his hard hat, safety vest, and clipboard, a flashlight, a tire-pressure gauge, his acoustic earmuffs and ventilator mask. Other than the sunglasses, why would anyone have stolen those items? What most disturbed him was the theft of his soft-sided cooler bag, which had contained his bento box with his lunch and his bottles of mineral water. He had to eat something. He headed back west on Sunset, passing fast-food franchises, which would not do. He saw a food truck, but after parking on a side street, he went up to the truck and discovered they were serving spicy fusion tacos. The sun was blinding. The light was so harsh and flat in this city. He was beginning to get a headache, agitated by the brightness, all the cars and people, the asphalt and concrete and stoplights and buildings and noise.

He bought a garden salad from a convenience store, making sure there was no dressing on it, and ate it in his van. As he was backing up in the little parking lot, he heard a loud thump against the rear door. A kid ran up to his window, holding a skateboard. "What the fuck you doing? What the fuck you doing, man?" he screamed. "You trying to kill me?" Then he raised his arm and pointed a flashlight at Yadin—his just-stolen flashlight?—and flicked the beam on and off repeatedly into his eyes. "Asshole!" the kid said, and skated off.

He needed somewhere quiet to sit for a minute. He needed to get off this street. He saw a church on the corner, flat-roofed, windowless, with stucco wall slabs painted beige and green. A cross was on one side, a mural on another of a choir in a circle, hands joined. He walked inside the empty sanctuary, which had pews made with Scandinavian blond wood, carpeted in a taupe-colored loop-pile Berber, maybe from Shaw or Beaulieu. Inside the foyer stood a security guard, a gun in a holster on his belt. The guard nodded to Yadin, bobbing his chin toward a steel donation box on a stand, which was secured with a lock and bolted to the floor. There wasn't a suggested amount. Yadin put two one-dollar bills through the slot, and the guard frowned, so Yadin shoved one more into the box, which seemed to satisfy him. From a brochure on a table, Yadin saw that this was a United Church of Christ. He wasn't familiar with the denomination. Oddly there was no cross behind the pulpit, just another large painting similar to the mural outside—same artist—that depicted caricatures of choir members holding candles in a lurid, goony palette.

He sat down in a pew and took out his rosary and made the Sign of the Cross. He skipped the Apostles' Creed because it was long and complicated and he had yet to memorize it all, moving ahead to Our Father, then whispered three Hail Marys:

> Hail Mary,
> Full of Grace,
> The Lord is with thee.
> Blessed art thou among women,
> and blessed is the fruit
> of thy womb, Jesus.
> Holy Mary,
> Mother of God,
> pray for us sinners,
> now, and at the hour of our death.
> Amen.

That was as far as he had gotten into the rosary sequence, so he simply continued to push the beads between his thumb and index finger, trying to calm himself, to let himself be subsumed and borne away. He prayed that he would be able to make things right with Jeanette and Joe, that the three of

them could carry on as before, as if nothing had happened. He prayed that no one at Mirrorwood would laugh at him, that the A&R people would be enticed by the idea of Mallory doing an album of his songs. He prayed that Caroline and Franklin would not get divorced, that the library and church would persevere. He prayed that he would be able to keep his house and self-release his album. He prayed that he would never have to leave the peace and quiet and sanctity of Rosarita Bay again.

But as he prayed, it occurred to him that it wouldn't be as easy as attending this one meeting, giving Mallory his B-sides for her own album, and then being done with it. First he'd have to hire a lawyer, maybe a manager, too, to negotiate his contract and make sure he wasn't getting screwed. Then surely he'd have to return to L.A., perhaps multiple times, to work with Charlie Peacock or whoever they chose as the producer, because he couldn't trust that his songs would not be dumbed down for pop radio and prettified with an orchestra or harp or some such nonsense, that they wouldn't be layered and gridded and click-tracked, that Mallory's vocals wouldn't be comped and Auto-Tuned and buried under some Wall of Sound bullshit. He'd want to be in the studio for all the recording sessions, then he'd want to stick around for the mixing and mastering. That was, if Mirrorwood and the producer would allow him that much participation and control, which was unlikely. Hell, he might have to insist on producing Mallory's album himself, withholding his songs unless they agreed. He might have to be in L.A. for months.

Something different occurred to him then—something he had not considered at all up to now, thinking it impossible. What if Mirrorwood surprised everyone and was willing to take on Yadin and *Lonesome Lies Before Us*, either as it was, from his cassettes, or re-recorded analog at Sound City Studios, tracked live, stripped down, exactly the way he wanted? What if they actually acceded to his demands that he and Mallory would not have to tour or do any promo?

They might make those promises, they might even put it in his contract, but then they'd ask him to do just one little thing. One little show, one little interview, one little photo shoot. Soon they'd want meet-and-greets, music videos, festival appearances, record-store signings. Mallory would wheedle and pester him until he consented, and from there it would never stop. He'd get sucked right back into everything. How would he be able to do any of that with his Ménière's and stage fright? Booze and drugs had never worked well for him, and he knew that he could not depend on them at all now. He would be defenseless. The fact was, he had never been cut out for this business. It had been ludicrous for him to enter it. He just didn't have the constitution for it.

He walked out of the church. In his van, he started driving west toward Mirrorwood's office, squinting into the glare of the sun. He was feeling dizzy and a bit nauseous, and then all of a sudden it began to swamp him, the familiar whoosh and roar in his right ear, his head squeezing, his vision narrowing, the horizon listing. What was triggering it? The stress of the meeting, the anxiety of being in the

city? Had there been something in the salad? Salt or MSG or chemical preservatives? Or maybe it had been that skater kid, flicking the flashlight in his eyes. He veered the van to the side of the road, cutting off another car, the driver honking and screaming and flipping him the finger. Sweating and hyperventilating, Yadin put the van's transmission into park, closed his eyes, and waited for the vertigo to overwhelm him.

Someone rapped on his window. It was a cop, LAPD. There was another cop, a woman, on the other side of the van. Yadin rolled down his window, was asked for his license, registration, and proof of insurance. In his side mirror, he saw their police car behind the van, lights on the roof flashing red, white, and blue. He flipped down the visor and tugged out his registration and insurance from the plastic pouch there. When the male cop took the documents and began walking back to his car, Yadin opened his door. "Steinie!" the female cop yelled. The male cop whirled around and pulled out his gun and pointed it at Yadin. "On the ground! On the ground!" he yelled. Yadin tumbled out of his van onto all fours and vomited.

He passed out—for how long, he did not know. Time wrinkled, his awareness of events buckled. He vaguely recalled being thrown against the hood of the police car, frisked, and cuffed. There might have been questions about drinking, being under the influence of drugs. "Nothing, nothing," he remembered mumbling. He might have been administered a Breathalyzer test. He heard the cops discussing a possible stroke, a heart attack. He lost consciousness again. When he came out of it, two EMTs were examining him. A group of passersby huddled around him on the sidewalk.

"Ménière's. I have Ménière's," Yadin said.

"What's he saying?" the male cop asked.

"I'm having a Ménière's attack," Yadin said. "Just let me sit."

They allowed him to ride through the episode, and gradually—was it ten minutes, or an hour?—he surfaced. "We'll take you to the hospital," one of the EMTs said.

"No," Yadin said. "I have a meeting. I have to go to a meeting."

"You're in no condition to drive," the female cop said.

"I'm okay," he said.

"Doubtful."

He stood up and, not knowing how else to demonstrate his lucidity, tightroped a straight line on the sidewalk, then retraced his steps. The male cop handed back his license, registration, and insurance, the female cop warned him to fix his exhaust system, and, unexpectedly, they let him go.

He was still shaky and weak. It was a miracle he had been able to put on that little show and walk with one foot in front of the other. He checked his watch: 1:22. He was late. There were several missed calls and voicemails indicated on his cellphone, all from Mallory. He pulled his van onto Sunset Boulevard, his head thudding, his shirt seeped in sweat. His right ear was blocked up, and he swallowed again and again to try to pop it.

He got caught at every stoplight, and then couldn't find a parking space in front of the Doheny Sunset building. Mallory had told him there was an indoor lot, but he missed the entrance. He made a U-turn, drove past the building on the other side of the street, made another U-turn, and then swung into a loading zone a block before the building. He looked up at it. The entire east side of the building was a mammoth billboard. Or not a billboard, but as if the ad had been painted directly on the façade and windows. Then he figured it out. Some sort of material, maybe vinyl, had been stretched and adhered into place. He hadn't noticed it the first time, coming from the west.

A woman had her hands pressed against a glass wall in front of her, as if trapped in an invisible box. She was young and blond, with a comely body, dressed only in a black bikini or underwear, but she had been distressed with kohl eyes and stringy hair, as if ragged out on heroin. The ad was for Calvin Klein, abbreviated CK. As Yadin stared longer at the image, he noticed a subliminal message, intended or not. The leg and frame of a table behind the model and the dipping contour of her bikini bottom, together with the logo, spelled out FUCK.

His phone rang. Mallory. "Where are you?" she asked. "I've been trying to reach you. Are you stuck somewhere?"

"I'm down the street," Yadin told her.

"How far away?"

"I'm parked on the next block."

"Then come up!"

"I'm in a loading zone," he said.

"So what? Just leave it there."

"Can you come outside?" he asked. "I need to talk to you."

"We can talk later," she said. "Everyone's waiting."

"I really need to talk to you first, Mallory."

He watched the front of the Doheny Sunset for her. Everyone going in and out of the building, everyone on the sidewalk, was so slickly dressed and good-looking. None of these people, Yadin thought, had ever had a pimple in their lives. BMWs, Porsches, Range Rovers, and Mercedes-Benzes drove past, as well as a Hummer, a Bentley, and a Tesla. His ear popped and released.

She came out of the building and glanced right, then left. She was dressed entirely in black: strappy sandals, skinny jeans that snugged her butt, and a tight, sleeveless turtleneck top that varnished her breasts. She had styled her hair differently, parted on the side, a decidedly younger look. Her skin was lucent, her lips gleamed. Yadin honked his horn, and she walked up to his van.

"What are you doing?" she asked.

"Can you hop in?"

"We need to be upstairs!"

"One minute. That's all I'm asking."

She opened the door and sat down in the passenger seat. "You look awful. Are you sick?"

"Yeah," he said. "But that's not the problem. I have something to tell you."

"What?"

There was a sudden ruckus. A white Cadillac Escalade

screeched to the front of the Doheny Sunset, and a young woman ran across the sidewalk toward the car, flanked by two bodyguards in suits. Immediately they were swarmed by a dozen paparazzi, snapping their cameras and shouting. Where had they come from? Had they been hiding near the entrance the entire time? The girl and her bodyguards jumped into the Cadillac and raced off, chased by a convoy of cars and motorcycles.

After a few moments, Mallory asked Yadin, "What do you have to tell me?"

"You won't like it."

She breathed out heavily. "You're not coming up, are you?" she said.

"No."

She turned away from him. "I knew this would happen. I knew you'd sabotage it somehow."

"I can't do it," he said. "I'm sorry."

"Nothing's changed. You haven't changed at all."

"I have, though. That's the thing," he told her.

"This is Raleigh all over again," she said. "Why did you run away? I was so angry with you. I wanted to hurt you, the way you'd hurt me. That's why I ripped off your song. I thought you'd at least call me—even if it was just to tell me I was a conniving bitch—and I could finally talk to you again, but you never did. Nothing. Just silence. Why did you leave me, Yadin? Everything would have been different."

"We were just kids," Yadin said. "It wasn't real. What we had wasn't real."

"How can you say that?"

"You would've left me eventually," he said.

"That's not true. I wouldn't have. I was in love with you. Why couldn't you believe that I could love you?" Mallory asked. "I'm still in love with you."

He didn't—couldn't—believe her. She was simply saying so to get him to attend the meeting.

"It's pitiful," she told him. "You broke my heart, and I'm still in love with you."

It was wrecking Yadin, listening to her. Couldn't she see what she was doing to him? So much of him ached to believe her, but he knew that what she was saying was a lie. She was acting. She was an actress. She was reciting lines from some old soap opera script.

"I always wondered how I'd feel if I ever saw you again," she said. "Now I know. I still love you."

For a moment, he allowed himself to become engulfed by everything he had yearned for, all these years. For so long, he had anguished that he had done it all wrong, that he should never have deserted Mallory. Everything would have been different. He had never stopped thinking about her. He had never stopped loving her. Yet he'd never let himself fully inhabit those feelings, those longings, because he had thought it impossible he would ever have the chance to be with her again.

Now, sitting with her in his van, he knew it was still impossible. The woman across from him was a stranger. She belonged to a world that was not only foreign to Yadin, but repellent. She was not in love with him. She was in love with the boy and the girl they had been in Raleigh. He had been in love with them, too. But those people were gone. They didn't exist anymore. What they had once had together could not be revived.

"We could be happy," she told him. "You don't have to keep hating yourself, Yadin. It's okay to allow yourself to be happy. Stay with me. Will you stay with me?"

He stared up at the ad on the side of the building again. The fatigue from the Ménière's attack began to pool into him. "I can't," he said.

"Why? Tell me why."

"I just can't do it," he told her. "I would die here."

"Because of those weasels up there?" she asked. "Fuck 'em. Fuck Mirrorwood. We don't need them. I won't ever make you go to another meeting again, all right?"

He lifted the notebooks and cassettes of his B-sides from the floor of the van. "Take these," he said. "It's everything that didn't make it onto the record. I want you to have them."

"No," she said. "I don't want them."

"They're not scraps. They're good songs. They'd be perfect for you on a solo album. It could be your comeback."

"I don't care."

"It's what would make me happy, Mallory," he said. "Nothing would make me happier than having you record these songs."

"You don't understand," she said. "I'm not interested in doing anything without you. That was the whole point—the only point. You assumed I had other motives, didn't you? You've never had any faith in me."

She got out of the van, shut the door, and began to walk away, then after several steps turned around and returned to the van, bending down to peer through the window.

"Will you mail *Lonesome* to me when it's done?" she asked. "Cassette, CD, I'll take whatever. Or are you going to make me wait to order it?"

"I'll send you the first copy," he said.

"Don't give me co-writing credit," Mallory said. "If you do, my lawyers will be all over you. It's your album. There's no need to add my baggage to something so good."

As Siobhan had predicted, the city council meeting at the Pereira Community Center was largely a formality. Many people gave heartfelt statements: the mayor, the city clerk, the head of the chamber of commerce, the police chief, the president of the police officers' association, various citizens supporting local law enforcement. But the decision had already been made. The San Vicente County sheriff was there to answer questions about the transition. It was a long, sad evening. At last, it was moved and seconded to have the city manager enter into negotiations with the sheriff to assume Rosarita Bay's police services, and the motion was carried by a unanimous vote.

The other item on the agenda, the possible privatization of the library, passed without incident. Caroline presented her argument with her poster boards of charts and graphs, after which Gerry Lowry, reversing his position on LMS, recommended that the city maintain the library's present organizational structure. This, too, was approved unanimously.

Yadin got back to town just as the meeting was ending. Joe came out of the community center first.

"I still have a job?" Yadin asked him in the parking lot.

"I don't know," he said. "Maybe if you stop being such a fuckwit."

Joe filled him in on what had happened at the meeting. Wall to Wall would be losing its contract to recarpet the police station this summer, but he said he wouldn't lay off Rodrigo just yet; he'd try to find a way to keep him. Then Joe went home. The Giants were playing the Rockies.

Jeanette walked out of the center with Siobhan. The two women hugged briefly before separating, and as Jeanette crossed the parking lot, fishing in her purse for her keys, she spotted Yadin leaning against the trunk of her Honda Civic.

"What happened in L.A.?" she asked him. "Did the meeting go the way you wanted?"

"Not exactly."

"Oh," she said. "I'm sorry. What will you do now? Can you still release the album somehow?"

Throughout the drive from L.A., Yadin had asked himself why—all his life—he had been so afraid, why he had been unwilling to take any risks. Had he just made a terrible mistake, saying no to Mallory—another misguided decision that he would forever regret? She had said they could be happy together. Yet Yadin had never been happy, and didn't know if he ever could be. The best he had ever managed was not to be miserable.

"I didn't give you an answer last night," Yadin said to Jeanette. "I think we should get married."

"You do?" she said, looking up at Yadin's face. He was so pale and tired.

"Yes."

She saw Franklin, Caroline, and their children exiting the community center, their daughter skipping ahead, giggling *heh-heh-heh*. As Jeanette watched them, the clouds overhead shifted with the breeze, revealing a waxing crescent moon, an arched sliver in the sky that illuminated the parking lot with a rolling wave of light for a moment before it was ebbed by another clump of clouds.

All afternoon after leaving the Holiday Breeze, Jeanette had been contemplating what she would do with herself in the coming years. There was nothing holding her in Rosarita Bay. She could eventually transfer to another Centurion. They had hotels in Moscow, Bangalore, Santiago, Vienna, Barcelona, London, Beijing, and Tokyo. Mary Wilkerson had risen from room attendant to director and had worked in various cities and countries. Why not Jeanette? In the meantime, she could sell the Nikon D3100 that Mallory had given to her, buy a cheaper brand, and put the extra money toward a little vacation somewhere, maybe in Europe.

"I don't think we should get married anymore," she told Yadin.

"No?" he asked.

They would be together out of convenience, not choice, certainly not out of desire. If she married Yadin, they'd be companions, nothing more. She wished that could be enough for her, but it wasn't. "Not wanting to be alone isn't enough of a reason," she said to him.

Somehow, Yadin had known this would be what she would tell him. She was right, but still, it made him so sad, hearing her say it. "I guess it's not," he said.

"See you Sunday at choir practice," Jeanette said. She got in her car, and as she clicked in her seat belt, she was shuddering. Turning down Yadin, she knew, was the bravest thing she had ever done.

He returned to his house. He took a shower, then switched on the game. As he made dinner, he wondered if he and Jeanette would still go to Costco together after church, as friends, or if they would travel separately from here on out.

He ate and washed the dishes and sat in his armchair in front of the TV, not bothering with the radio simulcast. He would have to figure out where to live. He supposed he shouldn't regret having to walk away from this house so much. It really was a crappy little place, save for the den.

It was so quiet tonight. He stared at the closed captioning on the bottom of the screen, the words appearing in a staccato rhythm. He shut off the TV and, in his studio, lifted the Martin D-21 Special off its wall pegs. He tuned the guitar and played some chords: C, F, C, F, then C, E7, Am, then Dm and G.

On his worktable was a spiral-bound notebook, the pages blank—the journal he had intended to keep as he tried to follow the movements of his soul, enter the mystery of silence, and instead had talked to Davey and imagined them as grown men, imagined Davey telling him, "I know if you could've, you would have saved me, Yadin."

He played a little more. The D-21 Special sounded different tonight. Was it the guitar, or his hearing? Getting better, or worse. The mid-tones were cleaner, crisper, while at the same time sweeter, with a warmer sustain. On the low end was a throaty resonance, on the high end a shimmer. He could hear the rosewood and spruce vibrating, the filaments of the bronze strings reverberating.

As he strummed the guitar, a new song revealed itself to Yadin—not just a melody or a riff, but the entirety. Humming, he scribbled in the notebook, transcribing lines in a flurry until he was able to get the whole thing down, then inserted a fresh cassette into his TASCAM and began singing the first verse.

Author's Note

I am deeply indebted to the musician Will Johnson, who took partial lyrics for the three original songs in this novel and gave them life.

For their editorial insights and support, I would like to thank Alane Salierno Mason, Jane Delury, Jennifer Egan, Rebecca Curtis, Don Rifkin, Daniel Torday, Jessi Phillips, and Maria Massie.

For background on the alt-country scene in Raleigh, North Carolina, I relied heavily on *Ryan Adams: Losering, a Story of Whiskeytown* by David Menconi. Two other important sources were the films *Heartworn Highways* on Townes Van Zandt and *Fallen Angel* on Gram Parsons.

I am also grateful to Ross Cashiola, Kurt Wildermuth, Betsy Martin, Rob Arnold, and Marsha Weldon for their assistance.

Many thanks, too, to Ashley Patrick, Will Scarlett, Dave Cole, and Marie Pantojan at W. W. Norton.